HELLO THERE

LINCOLNSHIRE MURDERS

HELLO THERE

A tale of Yellerbelly Murders

Cary Smith

HELLO THERE

ISBN: 978-1-916981-24-9

For more books in the series visit Amazon and search for Cary Smith

PublishNation, London
www.publishnation.co.uk

1

December

Harry Simm often wondered to himself, if anything really good was ever going to happen to him. Living a humdrum often soulless and depressing existence, was never to him a proper life. Certainly far removed from the lifestyle many people he knew thoroughly enjoy. Those who suggest life has a great deal to do with sheer luck were to his mind, absolutely spot on.

He'd read more than once how the successful and rich are not always the most brainy, talented or gifted. Just the lucky ones. They experience events and situations they can then exploit to increase wealth and happiness. Such events are entirely random. Had Tuesday been such an event?

Once upon a time, a busker in London spotted by sheer chance by a record producer, finished up with a chart hit. The Royal family are bestowed riches and all the pomp in their position by freaks of birth. Sandie Shaw went to an Adam Faith concert as a teenager and managed to get into the star's dressing room to sing to him. Few years later she won Eurovision. Just the sort of things Harry'd read or heard about over the years, but never known anybody who'd won on the Lottery unless they kept their gob shut. Proper win with odds of 1 in gotta be fifty million.

Harry'd realized ages ago if he'd put a couple of quid in a pot rather than nipping to the newsagent for a ticket, he'd have a darn sight more than the tenner he got years ago, that thirty lousy quid last year or a free Lucky Dip.

Was that what was happening to him? Thinking about it day and night had become an obsession he'd been embroiled in since that out of the blue Tuesday night episode in the pub. Bad weather had waterlogged the Mariner's pitch and by chance he spotted the fixture postponement on his tablet to save him trailing up on a fruitless mission. He was already mad about missing out on their FA Cup run at weekends.

The odds against it being anything but sheer luck were hundreds if not millions to one. Bit like that damn Lotto.

A good four years ago he'd jacked in the perpetual torment of a relationship with Gloria, packed his bags, moved lock, stock and barrel away from the Cornhill Market and Lincoln. Out to the coast to follow his dream of opening a shop of his own.

Thinking about it now, he had to admit the decision to move had been something good for once. Sheer hard graft and a whole bunch of worrying nights had got him through.

Had he remained with that bitch in Lincoln he'd have gone to the City match which that evening was still on. Rather than planning to head off up the coast to Blundell Park. Then at a loose end he'd decided once the shop was shut, he'd grab a bite to eat, wash, get changed before heading for the pub. Better having that easy stroll than heading off up to Grimsby in the cold.

Shaggy white haired, gnarled and whiskered Harry was sat in his regular corner spot, near the window supping his pint and chuntering to himself as he waited for old pal Malcy. Late as usual. Then right out of the blue, this talent scout for a photographer just wandered up to the table asking if he might be interested in doing catalogue modeling and internet video work.

His first reaction had been an astonished grimaced gasp 'Me?' and looked about to see who else it might be aimed at. 'You being serious?'

Malcy turning up ten minutes later was well pissed off to have missed it all.

This was it. Lady luck it had to be and excitedly he'd taken the business card offered, called the number and tonight's the night. Sunday night for a meet seemed a bit bloody odd to him, but this was a great opportunity not to be missed. Anyway he reckoned these arty types are never your nine to fivers.

Harry had literally in between customers, bit by bit all day, given his flat upstairs a good bottoming. Tidied, cleaned and polished just as his dear old mum would always do for visitors. Been a good day, business had been quite brisk in the afternoon at that time of year, and all his hard work was paying off. Now this cherry on top.

Being a worrier, the weather could be against him. Very cold and foggy told him there could well be a no show.

Few bunce made from this modeling business would give him a good start towards a fresh look. Had that old boy in the shop again on Friday offering hand carved Hindu Gods, but claimed that was all he made. Once more he'd come out with the same old guff about Rishi Sunak making them trendy.

Who in Mablethorpe would want one? The single one he'd taken on sale or return still sat on a shelf told its own story. The guy could certainly carve, but why stick with one subject more appropriate to markets in Delhi, if its still called that. Could be it was all to do with religion.

Harry knew kids stuff always sold well. Billy out at Burgh le Marsh made good unicorns and fairies. He'd bought a dolls house a bit back and wished he could get more. Having it snapped up within a day or two had been good business. Harry'd sold paperbacks when he was at Lincoln Market. Ones he picked up from car boots for 10p a throw and sold for 25 was a good mark up. Might be worth trying them again.

Sharp knock on the shop door exactly on time.

'Hi,' Harry greeted his visitor excitedly.

'Hello there,' was the return as they firmly shook hands. After the usual welcoming pleasantries about the cold weather, his guest insisted on a guided tour of his stock. The choc-a-bloc hoard of quaint and curious.

A couple of big metal round wall art sculptures seemed to take this Jules' eye. Butterflies of all shapes and sizes, an old wooden wheelbarrow appeared to prove interesting but the general stuff he'd got from house clearances was simply ignored.

'I live upstairs,' he explained and gestured away from the shop in a bid to get on with it, to discover the whys and wherefores. 'Coffee, Tea?'

'Be honest it'll be fine down here,' said his visitor and sauntered towards the little cubbyhole Harry used as an office come kitchen. 'Coffee'll be good.'

'You live around these parts?' nervous Harry asked to make conversation.

'Based in Nottingham, but the job as you can imagine takes me to a whole load of places. Last week I was in Wales. Bit wet I'm afraid but fortunately this job keeps me in the car or indoors for the most part.'

Harry was making two Nescafe coffees with water from the old tin kettle as they chatted.

'This what you do, just sort of approach people?' Harry asked waiting for it to boil.

'Yes, in a word. But I handle this side of things for a whole range of publications, internet and video organizations. In Wales last week as I said, on the lookout for somebody to fit a particular Rugby product image one of the other spotters told me about.'

'And me?' he asked and waited.

'General. Been on the look out for if you don't mind me saying, a person of interest. A character. Rather than a bland looking average ten-a-penny guy for some new product launch. Please, don't get any ideas about tidying yourself up. You're ideal. You in collar and tie, one of our client's damn smart suits. It'll be a picture.'

'Gotta say, this is all a bit of a shock. Not something I'm used to all this'

'Could easy arrange for some shots in the shop here,' this Jules said sat there gazing around. 'Be good for our online clothing retailer. Be different certainly, but that's up to the director and photographer.'

Pre-boiling the kettle upstairs had been a complete waste of time. Once the coffees were made the pair settled down on the two old garden chairs to discuss what he was desperate to hear about.

'Can we talk about availability first up?' Harry was asked as his visitor peered all about. 'Is your spare time limited with this place?'

'Not really. This is not Tesco with the opening times on the internet and plastered on the door. Need to take a bit of time off now and again with delivering some o'me bigger items anyway.'

'Useful.' Jules nodded. 'Tell me. Are weekends better than weekdays do you think?'

‘Weekdays,’ Harry replied and lifted his tin mug for an initial sip. ‘Allus close on a Monday but it’s weekends when tourists are about. Not so much this time o’year but you get a good few now and again. Time then can be a bit precious.’ He shrugged. ‘Not carved in stone though,’ he said thinking of the extra cash.

‘D’you have sugar by any chance?’ was so frustrating.

‘Yeh. Upstairs,’ Harry said, hiding a sigh.

‘To be honest sweetener would be batter? Diabetes,’ was grimaced up as Harry got to his feet.

Harry scanned the cupboard top quickly. ‘Think there’s some upstairs,’ he suggested.

Back down he handed over a pink sweetener packet. ‘That do?’

‘Yeh fine. Thank you.’

Disappointingly so far there’d been no talk of actual money or what likely amounts, but the good news was the suggestion of a photo session actually in the shop for online clothing would prove ideal. Was this more from that lady luck? He’d get his good stuff in the background, and move all the tatt out the way.

From their chat about the arrangements they moved back to a question and answer session about the variety of goods he had on offer. Not antiques by a long chalk, but certainly a good amount of rubbish alongside a number of unusual pieces. Jules had already stopped to look interestingly at what the label said were Vintage Chinese Porcelain figures, Harry knew were not vintage, not Chinese that was for sure and never likely to be Porcelain

‘You okay?’ Harry felt a bit odd, sweaty and had to sit down. Be all the excitement he told himself. ‘Can I get you anything? Aspirin, paracetamol? Where are they, upstairs?’

‘Sorry about this,’ Harry said and blew out a breath. ‘Be alright in a bit.’ What an absolute bugger. Lady Luck turns up and...

‘Do you have to take anything?’ Jules his visitor asked. ‘Maybe you forgot with all this going on. Any pills at all I can get for you?

‘God I feel shit!’

2

The road from Lincoln out to the coast was never a quick swish along a motorway so many enjoy. In summer it would be almost permanently clogged A roads with traffic and hoards of caravans, especially weekends. Saturday change-over day could be an absolute nightmare.

On this freezing cold foggy December early morning, the issue was not the traffic, simply the conditions. Weather guy on *Look North* had forecast a cold night, but Jake Goodwin was convinced he'd never said it was so cold he'd need to nip home for a thicker coat before setting off for Mablethorpe. Being dressed for the comforts of Lincoln Central was one thing, hanging about in this weather was quite another.

Dispatch had told him DC Sandy MacLachlan had headed off straight from home and Jake was following on behind. Through experience he knew his Scottish colleague would have it all under control by the time he got there. It was a role he had been born for. Seriously a round peg for a round hole. He'd almost made coordinating his specialist subject for Mastermind.

Uniting a complex range of specialisms such as the Crime Scene Investigators, Underwater Search Units from time to time and even the likes of Shoe Print Capture specialists. All this as well as organizing other loosely coupled organizations such as ambulance and the fire service along with the local coppers, more often than not, first on the scene.

Not forgetting the Major Investigation Team (MIT) back at base. Plus nowadays of course, the computer analysis geeks running the Tech Crime Team. A suspicious death is never easy, yet he knew Sandy would just cope with it all calmly and conscientiously.

Talk of the devil the hands free beeped.

'Sarge?' was the Scot.

'Sandy.'

'Word of warning...boss is here.'

'What?' Jake gasped.

'Here before I was.'

'What the hell's cracking off?'

'Dinna know anything about a holiday cottage.' Sandy tossed his way.

'Thought this was a shop.'

'Yes. But the boss got here sharpish. Poking about when I turned up.'

'What's a holiday cottage got to do with anything?' Jake posed.

'Och aye. Got a holiday cottage up Sandilands way apparently? Spent the weekend he reckons putting on the heating, giving it a good clean up he said. Ready for Spring.'

'In this weather? In December? That's weeks away.'

'So he says.'

'Hang on, hang on. He lives near bloody Grantham…why is that guy all secrets?'

'Same with wine. We all thought he'd been to Tesco if you remember, truth was his ol' woman owns a bloody vineyard.'

'What d'you know about him apart from that?'

'As my old granny used to say. Blethers say nowt. Folk who say too much say nothing.'

'That's the problem, he does say nothing. Then turns up out the blue.' Jake sighed with frustration. 'Anything else I need to know?'

'Odd one. Cadaver's naked. Well almost. I'll explain when you get here.'

'Really?' Jake grimaced and sighed to himself. 'Fifteen minutes or so.'

Detective Sergeant Jacques Goodwin known to all except his mother Celeste as Jake, had to park on double yellows way past the shop beyond the ambulance, liveried police vehicles, CSI team cars and Forensic van. Further back he'd noticed Sandy's car and DI Oliver Bristow's Renault Clio hybrid parked up outside the business next door.

Frost covered the ground still, and he had first heard and then seen some poor soul scraping ice off their windscreen back home when he left.

'Excuse me. What's going on?' This old fella in nothing more than Union Jack braces over a green check shirt, no coat and no teeth in, asked the moment he'd alighted from his Volvo. Ahead of him, the crime scene with the blue and white tape already in place and this garrulous old 'un, just the sort always on the lookout for someone to listen.

'No idea yet,' was to some extent true 'We'll probably want to talk to you in a bit, so please stay put.'

At the front of the property, white suited and pale blue booted Jake gave his name to the uniform on the door and spied a cluster of six or seven nosey-parkers congregating further down the street. Phones at the ready, one using a can of de-icer.

'You didn't need to come all the way across here boss,' DS Goodwin greeted his Detective Inspector with.

'Only down the road. Code red on my mobile,' he said without any further explanation. 'Need to be round the back,' stopped Jake entering the premises. Dressed in a navy blue jacket under his rustling +white suit, oddly with scarf in his neck and the standard pale blue gloves, Oliver Bristow gave a shiver as they turned left and then took the first right. 'Feel I just need to slip back in the saddle. Bit of fresh air I thought, but chose a damn cold one that's for sure,' he grinned. 'Trust some silly bugger to pick a day like this.' Down a passage at the side of the shop and through a gate the pair trundled.

'Hi Sarge,' Sandy greeted the DS as they entered what amounted to a bit of a yard with an extension attached to the property. 'Doctor's in with him,' Sandy gave a gesture towards the CSI tent erected right outside the open door. 'He's from Skeg,' he advises quietly.

'Doc or the body?'

'Doc,' the Scot said as he handed Jake a business card in an evidence bag. 'That's who we're talking about.'

'Harry Simm,' Jake read from the grey card held in his pale blue nitrile gloved hand. 'Curious Odds and Sods. What's that all about?' he asked.

‘You’ll see once you get in the shop. Sorta mixed bag,’ said Bristow. ‘Odds n’Sods is about right.’ The DI grimaced. ‘P’raps it’s me but think it should read curios.’

Bodies of murder victims Jake knew from years of experience, were seldom discovered in ideal, spacious, dry locations. The pathologist’s name was new to him and guessed he’d want to spend a minimal amount of time inside the tent out in the freezing cold. Be heading back to the environment he was used to at the mortuary. A place Jake’d not give you tuppence for except on a morning like that.

Not managing to see the body and do the initial walk through to prioritize initial actions was in need of a rethink. Jake produced his phone. ‘Team know about all this?’ to him was a priority.

‘Waiting for you,’ Jake saw as an excuse. Without further ado he sent texts back to Lincoln Central with all the info from the card for searches to begin.

‘Alisha can start her social media search from that, see what the early chatter is.’ Jake looked at his DC. ‘Somebody say he’s naked?’ Sandy nodded and grinned. ‘Outdoors!’

‘Just his black pants to nae shock the neighbours,’ Sandy remarked alongside a chuckle.

Jake knew cases such as this are never only about getting to the truth. The difficult bit is knowing what to do when it appears. For the most part as he waited he spent his time on his phone. Search to organize, Ambulance liaison, leaving Sandy to co-ordinate with CSI’s Shona. Deal with her needs and wants and her team’s requirements.

‘Rufus’s in charge back home. I’ll call him,’ he did so by setting actions by phone and once completed returned to Sandy. ‘Froze to death I should imagine, if he felt anything like I do now.’

‘Seems that way,’ said the enigma that was DI Bristow. ‘Just slumped back against the wall, out of sight. Possible drunken stupor but doc can’t smell anything. Thinking so far he’s heading down the hypothermia road. I’m bloody freezing me, thought of it makes me shiver.’

Jake so wanted to query why he'd not got a coat but thought better of it. Maybe it was too big to get the coverall on top.

'Shona reckons its still well below zero,' Sandy added.

'Just imagine that.' Jake watched as two of the CSI white suited team walked past. 'But why? Not like a summer's evening and he just stepped out for as bit of air or a fag.'

'Given what we know so far to Rufus, he'll start all the searches.'

'Two local plods are doing door to door,' said the DI. 'But some places aren't open yet.'

'Not like a housing estate with nosey neighbours who are usually a pain,' is Jake's suggestion. 'If he's just been plonked out here, how d'we find out how or why?'

'Dead guy's sort of friend's still here,' said Sandy. 'A nurse, Kelsey Pinhero. This way,' he ushered Jake back out of the alleyway. Pointed towards the police car fifty yards back up the road, and checked his incident clipboard. 'Called getting on for an hour or more. According to her the old boy sells stuff her husband makes.'

'What sort of stuff?'

'Nicky's working on it. Anyway, door was open she reckons, walked in and Simm the owner didn't appear. Went on through the place, upstairs to his flat still no sign. Opened the back door to check if he was out at the sheds and there he was slumped up agin the wall. Dialled 999, young Tim and Alex first here,' Sandy explained pointing towards another copper leant against his car. 'Answered the call, looked natural causes, ushered the local doc and he became suspicious.'

'CSI, forensics…?'

'Shona's been here twenty minutes or so just got the tent up when you arrived. Connor's busy wi' cameras and video. Pathologist en route. Just Bill Ribbans the local duty GP still inside waiting on the pathologist. That's your lot. Except,' he sucked in his breath noisily. 'The shop's a bit odd ball,' was comprehensive Sandy MacLachlan as ever.

'I've just spoken with the young DC Thwaites from the local cop shop. Sent him off to search out somewhere for an Incident Room for a day or two,' Bristow announced. 'According to him there's a hall close by,' they all knew such a facility is the engine room of every major inquiry. He looked left and right along the road. 'By the way, it looks to me as if this Simm had a visitor apart from that woman.'

'Show me,' said Jake and leaving Sandy, he and his boss walked back round to the shop, grateful to be able to head indoors.

'Tim is it?' Bristow asked the tall thin Response Officer who nodded. 'If you've disturbed the crime scene now's the time to speak.' Jake thought was quite unnecessary.

'No sir. Alex went in first, both of us walked through and out the back as that woman told us, saw the body and he checked for vital signs that's all and I phoned it in. Since then been stood out here and Alex's with the woman. Didn't even go back in when the doc got here.'

'Fair enough, but you better not have.'

Jake often felt the boss was sometimes too hard on young bobbies probably because it was a role he'd never had to fill. How often he wondered had the poor sod encountered such a scenario he had faced earlier. To be able to follow each and every fastidious aspect of a major crime scene was in need of previous experience.

Jake gave the lad a comforting tap on his shoulder as they walked in. The inside of the shop appeared dark probably due to the dank weather.

A whole galaxy of strange and to a degree interesting objects. Plenty of textiles, throws, tablecloths, unusual stuffed animals, big paintings, refurbished furniture pieces, very odd ornaments and bric-a-brac. 'Curiouser and curiouser,' said Jake.

'Some of this stuff is more than a bit strange,' Bristow suggested looking all around. 'Artisanal they'll tell you, which translated means expensive. People really buy stuff like this d'you think?' was a statement and question rolled into one offering.

'Allegedly.'

A teapot with a crooked spout Jake knew had to be a second. Silver plated cheese knife with an engraved motto. What was described on the label as a Vintage Champagne Spoon, a rusty bar sign and a bizarre mosaic 'Tumbledown' house sign was more than enough for the DS.

From there the pair walked carefully through a small clean and tidy but scruffy office come domestic area.

As experienced as he was Jake Goodwin knew he will never get used to it. There were some officers he knew who claim they have become indifferent to the sight of a dead body, in such circumstances.

Strangely that morning he was pleased this Simm was at his own property. The discovery of mutilated bodies in fields and ditches, in disused buildings and strewn along alleyways to him had always added to the scenario of grimness. Without thinking about the cold. All resulting in a tightening of his stomach. Adding to a degree of anger at the utter waste.

'Boss,' said Sandy as he appeared behind the pair trying hard to take it all in. 'Nicky's here and so's pathologist. Andrew Farrar. Thought it best wi' the witness being female, to call her o'er. You know what some are like these days. Told him nae signs of assault, nae blood, nothing obvious. Just froze to bloody death by the look on it.'

'He really sell enough of this stuff d'you think?' Bristow queried as Sandy disappears back out. 'Debts maybe.'

'What you thinking?' Jake asked of his DI. 'Can't pay his bills so tops himself?' he shook his head. 'Got really pissed off. Strips down to his shreddies then sits out in the freezing bloody cold when he could easy stay in the warm, swallow a box of Nurofen, down a whisky or two.'

'Postmen wearing shorts in winter is one thing,' said Bristow. 'But this is ridiculous.'

'See some places have stopped it,' Jake suggested,

'Stopped what?'

'Postmen wearing shorts.'

'Why?'

' Health and safety, what else? Health hazard.'

'Read how one place they were bullied into wearing them on days like this.'

'Can't imagine by the look of him this Simm being bullied into this. But you never know.'

Jake knew the chances were his team and Shona's would initially work long unsociable hours in poor conditions, grabbing basic food stuff and suffering broken sleep. Only then for lawyers to make a much better living trying every trick in the legal or otherwise book, to obtain the release of the killer.

The wait for the pathologist and access to some areas of the building had been frustrating. Why was Bristow there if he was only going to talk about postmen in shorts?

More to the point. Why be so secretive? The team knew very little about him. Lived near Grantham and his mother owned a vineyard in France. No mention of a partner, wife or husband. What about kids?

Light relief came from the two PCSO's been sent off to carry out an initial check door-to-door close to the shop.

On their return they told DI Jake Goodwin what little they'd discovered from places if not actually open to the public, at least now occupied by owners or staff. Not good news. First any of them had heard about it was on arrival to discover the road congested.

As per normal there was a self-important moaner suggesting he had a business to run and leaving his car in the Co-op car park was not a suitable compromise. At one point in what had at times become quite heated according to the young PCSO, this dick had suggested he be allowed to park as normal, and vehicles such as the CSI van be moved to the Co-op.

Jake wondered if this was to be the form. Too many of the shops had been closed overnight with proprietors living elsewhere. Hardly a nosy neighbourly environment they were used to.

3

An antique standard lamp Jake spotted had its frilly shade replaced with something akin to a plastic bucket. On a shelf was a pale blue metal colander he guessed could be used for the same purpose. It was obvious by what he saw there was a degree of creative talent of a kind enjoyed no doubt, by those desperate to be on-trend among friends.

To be fair, the shop contained a whole host of unusual and to a degree exciting pieces of work. It also in the DS's considered opinion, was home to a whole host of strange crap. A saddleback armchair seemed so out of place. Possibly not for sale, just somewhere to sit. Something in his opinion more shops could do with.

By the time the pair were back out acknowledging they were getting in the way of the CSI team, more of the mandatory gawpers had begun to gather. Oliver Bristow was hoping there'd soon be signs of the local PCSOs they had become used to relying upon.

'Time for Nicky to have a word with the witness woman me thinks,' Bristow said.

'I'll sort it,' Jake suggested and walked off as the DI wandered across to speak to Dr Bill Ribbans the local GP sat in his car with the door shut firm, engine running, writing, waiting. Once he'd briefed him along the same lines as Sandy, he went along to his own car for a warm.

Foreign looking Kelsey Pinhero looked upset obviously but composed as one would expect from somebody more used to trauma than the average. DS Nicky Scoley introduced herself as she slid onto the rear seat beside the upset woman. 'Sorry about the delay,' Scoley said and introduced herself. 'Can we start with why before what, please Kelsey?' appeared to confuse the woman. 'Why were you here, then move onto what actually happened.'

‘Do it now and again,’ she said quietly, looking pale with more than hint of dark shadows under her eyes. ‘Pop into see him. Chatting a few weeks back realized we’d both got a day off in the week which itself is unusual for me with the way things are.’

‘What d’you mean got a day off? Who runs the business if he’s off out for the day?’ the blonde questioned.

‘Shop’s pretty much a token gesture really during the week, especially on Mondays. Does most of his business on line and weekends are much busier here, more tourists passing by o’course, specially in summer. Gives Harry more time to be creative...sorry I meant gave Harry more time. Most Mondays he’d be in his workshop making and mending. Ring the big bell on the counter if you need him. Reason I went out there lookin’ for him. Rang and rang but no reply, seemed a bit strange. Popped in as I said I would, then planned to head off for a decent coffee, bit of shopping, all done. Gets a bit manic in my job at this time of year,’ She smirked and shook her head. ‘Used to be rammed in Winter, but it’s any time of year these days to be honest. Didn’t expect to finish up here like this.’

‘Didn’t the weather put you off?’

‘Did a bit, but couldn’t just not turn up.’

Why Scoley wondered had she not phoned him? ‘You live where?’

‘Here. Mabo. Back out towards Trusthorpe,’ she gestured over her shoulder.

‘And you drove straight here I take it?’

‘Yes. Just walked in the shop like I’ve done a good few times.’

‘This you do frequently?’ The woman was asked by Scoley.

‘Not that often,’ was no reply. ‘Like I told that policeman, just pushed down the handle and the door opened…’ She gathered herself. ‘Did what I could,’ shook her head. ‘Sort of known each other quite a while,’ she sighed. Is that for effect Scoley wondered. ‘Look I know it was your crime scene I’ve probably messed up, but I didn’t stop to think when the procedure, the routine just took over, tried everything. Could have done with the crash trolley though.’ An amusing remark in a different environment. After a moment or two she went on. 'Death is something I've got used to dealing with, but...this was different. Wrong place if you like…' She stopped and took a few breaths.

'That's fine. Tell me,' the DS said. 'If the shop wasn't opening would he normally leave the front door unlocked?'

'Pretty much because he knew when I was due I guess,' was a clear reply.

'You buy stuff from him on a regular basis I take it.'

'Not at all. Hardly ever in fact.' Frowning Scoley waited. 'Look,' this Kelsey shrugged, sighed and appeared a little awkward. 'It's my husband's hobby. Makes creatures out of wire. Sells a few on line and through Harry's shop and a little place down in Skeg.'

'So, you know him well then?' Scoley queried.

'Not really,' Pinhero admitted. 'Maybe once a month, pop in check what he's sold and pop back when I can with fresh ones if we've done well.'

'And you work where?' the DS asked.

'Skegness and District.'

'Thank you for the time being.' Scoley opened the door, then turned back. 'Think you could do with that coffee you planned. How about you nip off, but I want you to come back. I need to get our CSI team to take a DNA swab, they may have questions and then you can be on your way. May need to talk to you another day though.'

'Jake,' Nicky said to him in the back yard after organizing the Buccal Swab, and ignoring Oliver Bristow. 'According to Mrs Pinhero who found him, its somewhere she pops into once a month at most.'

'Hmm.'

'Not adding up?' Bristow asked.

'Wondering,' she whispered to the pair. 'Affair?'

'Aah,' was the DI, as Jake sucked in a breath noisily.

'Might have a girl to girl word.'

'Already know there's no woman,' said Jake. 'According to Shona's lads, not one living here at least. No clothes, no shoes and its all man stuff in the bathroom.'

‘Bloody frustrating stood out here with coffee makings in the kitchen,’ Shona Tate the Duty Digital Forensics Officer moaned as she appeared behind Nicky. ‘Takeaways down the main street they tell me.’

‘Anything significant?’ Bristow posed immediately as Nicky wondered if that was a hint.

Shona held up an evidence bag. ‘Two mugs and two spoons washed up on the draining board.’

‘Would you sit down for a comforting mug of tea and a cosy chat with the guy you plan to kill?’

‘Read a while back about this woman getting out of bed and joining her boyfriend for a drive in his car in her pyjamas and dressing gown.’

‘Why?’

‘That’s the unanswered question. Found her dead down a lane.’

‘Plate of Digestives too,’ Shona chuckled going back to the here and now. ‘All of which may have been there a good while and not involved,’ Shona added. ‘Anyway,’ she sighed. ‘Good news possibly. Found this under the coffee table. Sugar sachet,’ she explained as the two detectives peered at another evidence bag. ‘Lot to go through, but this is a start.’

‘But not if it’s his,’ Bristow suggested pointing at the tent

‘Two mugs, two spoons, two people’s a lot better than we get some places.’ Shona looked around. ‘No Darke boss?’

‘On a Criminology Course on taking ownership.’

‘What’s the betting he didn’t volunteer,’ Jake adds.

‘No surprise really, never see top dogs this far from their kennel,’ caught Jake’s attention.

‘Two mugs,’ said Nicky thoughtfully. ‘Was the Pinhero nurse here last evening? She stay overnight you reckon? What’s her husband do? How about kids? Interesting.’

‘Think you’ve got a job on your hands,’ a grinning Bristow told Nicky.

‘This Simm it appears lived alone,’ Shona went on. ‘But unusually for a bloke, no porn videos or anything dodgy unless they’re in the loft. Got his phone and laptop being punted off to the Digital Forensics lads. Apart from the clean mugs, spoons and sachet it's pretty much just the usual detritus. Got the rubbish bin to go through back at base though.'

'Why do you have all the fun?'

'Aye up,' Shona grunted and wheeled away as the Home Office Pathologist all dressed in pale blue emerged from the incitent. 'See you in a bit.'

'Morning Doctor Farrar,' Oliver Bristow greeted the pathologist and guessed he'd be Andy to his friends. 'Nice morning for it.'

'Not so nice for him. At least we've got clothes on.'

'Thank goodness.'

'How are you?'

'Fine, thank you,' Bristow spoke brightly.

'Little more than guessing at this stage…er,'

'Inspector.'

'Right, yes. Died anywhere between say six and midnight, too cold to be more accurate at this stage. Hypothermia until we get him on the table and get all the tox and tests done. No visible marks of force used to him or by him. Bit of broken and grazed skin tends towards him being dragged out. Overweight, in his middle to late fifties at earliest I should imagine. Need more, you know where I am,' he grinned at the two coppers. 'Hot strong tea with a decent breakfast beckons.'

'Enjoy,' Bristow decided was best rather than hint at jealousy.

'PM tomorrow but I'll text you,' Farrar called back over his shoulder.

No he'd not. Be one of his assistants, thought Jake from previous experience as he watched Farrar disappear out onto Victoria Road and the traffic chaos caused by all their vehicles.

'Shop's in his name along with a 15 reg Ford van in dark blue. We've nae spotted,' Sandy offered as he turned back.

'Send that to Rufus for DVLA check,' said Bristow. 'Get him to do ANPR as well. Time for a look see,' he suggested and gestured for Jake to lead them into the incitent and the frozen stiff cadaver. Grey going on white long shaggy uncombed hair and matching out of control straggly beard. Bit chubby with a beer paunch and thick legs.

Once the pair were au fait with the circumstances for themselves it was time to move on.

The two PCSO's spoken to by Jake earlier were back out on the streets but two more were being questioned by the DI.

'If you don't mind, need an extra question answering,' and without a word he moved aside, rubbing his gloved hands. 'Know some of your mates have already started visiting shops close by, but something's cropped up I need to know about,' he told a male and female stood before him. 'Where did this guy Simm,' he pointed in the general direction of the yard and the intertent. 'Park his car? All we know so far is a blue Ford van. 15 reg is as close as we've got.'

Jake thought the pair had come back too soon until they were able to fill him in with vital information.

'Sarge,' said a slightly blushing PCSO lad. 'During the night he tends to tuck it into the alley here, or so a woman two shops down, reckons. Wasn't supposed to, as its a pedestrian cut-through. It's a Ford Transit, navy blue,' said they were talking about the same.

4

The open plan scruffy lounge/diner/kitchen furniture upstairs Nicky guessed, had to be from a charity shop or some sort of house clearance. Nothing matched and was seriously out of date, but there was a huge flat-screen television on the wall opposite a tired two-seater sofa with wooden arms. Having seen the cadaver with all that unkempt long hair and scruffy un-trimmed beard along with some of the utter garbage in the shop the Detective Sergeant was not at all surprised by what she discovered upstairs.

If anything the décor for what it was, reeked of being manly and functional and if she had not already been aware Nicky knew by instinct there was no woman of the house. Not on a permanent basis anyway. No ornaments and just a single crooked landscape picture on one wall.

The kitchen was based around fake wood units, an old fridge, no freezer, well worn Formica work surfaces and grubby grey mottled floor tiles.

There was a smell about the room. Nothing in particular she could put her nose to, just the aroma of a tired old kitchen in need of a damn good clean.

She and her DI Oliver Bristow back downstairs stood discussing what was in front of them. ‘One good thing,’ Nicky said. ‘No blood,’ as Connor the Crime Scene Photographer and Nicky’s partner appeared through the shop. He then freely gave both Bristow and Nicky access to the scene shots he’s taken so far to save them having to enter the tent again and disturb the forensic women and man.

Connor excused himself and headed off upstairs after somebody called his name. Nicky followed the boss over to the kitchen area complete with three numbered yellow markers on the draining board against where two cups and two spoons had been. Another had been placed strategically and obviously on the top of the rubbish bin and another alongside the pale blue old kettle.

'No puncture wounds I could see or from the photos,' offered Oliver Bristow. 'So it'll have to be another case of waiting for tox as the doc reckoned. Just our luck he didn't cut himself on anything he wasn't aware of. '

'Why would you visit the home of a guy who runs a place like this?' Nicky mused. 'Unless of course he had something to sell.'

'Few quid, but no load of cash, no cheque book or card so far.'

'Unless after the deed our crim took a wad away with him.'

A big mahogany hat-stand Nicky guessed would be difficult to get rid of these days, but what looked to her like an old ship's bell on a shelf beside it might stand a better chance. Chest expanders were as out of place as anything she'd spotted so far among a tedious amount of junk. 'Drink his tea or coffee then...I was going to say kill him, but we don't know that for sure,' was the blonde Detective Sergeant almost thinking out loud. 'Drugs? Any mention?'

'Not so far, but could easy be. No way CSI can check inside and out of every bit of this. Be a job for the drugs dog.'

'Shot a line got in a confused state, took his clothes off and went out for a smoke.' Nicky realized was not likely if he was a regular user, being aware the pathologist would have seen needle marks or scars.

'No mention as yet, least of all from that Farrar. With Simm being naked gotta be easy to spot. Unless he enjoys coming up with, aren't I a clever boy surprise, at post mortem. Plus nobody, least of all Shona's, mentioned a spliff or fag end so far.'

'Why would you kill somebody like him?' was Nicky's turn. 'Charged too much. Done a crap shoddy job. Customer changed their mind.'

'Knew he'd be here alone.'

'With the door unlocked who else knew?'

'What's not our bad luck, is to be stuck with sourcing DNA from the toilet seat and his underpants,' said the DI as his phone rumbled. 'Thanks for that. Well done,' he told the caller. He looked at Nicky waiting. 'Peugeot van belongs to a Harry George Simm, all taxed and insured at this address according to Rufus.'

'Except we've not seen one.'

'Garaged some place?'

'Message from Alisha,' Oliver Bristow advises. 'Simm's death's appeared on the net. So far it's only a Police incident with some scum bag from this street sending a photo of all our vehicles to WhatsApp.'

'Brilliant'

'They don't waste any time.'

'Excuse me boss,' made the pair spin round. 'Door to door?'

'How many?' Bristow asked a uniformed officer sharply.

'Five.'

'Thanks. Organize it with Sergeant Goodwin out in the alleyway will you?' He suggested to the uniformed copper.

'Nothing appears to have been specifically cleaned,' said Shona stopping as she passed on her way upstairs. 'Bathroom clean but not sparkling. Bathroom cabinet held no clues; hand held tooth brush and tube of Colgate. Aftershave, packet of plasters, electric razor. Ibuprofen, pair of tweezers and fresh unwrapped bar of soap. Think that's your lot,' she read from her notes.

'Laptop, phone?' Oliver queried.

'Spare bedroom used more as an office,' their lead Forensics Officer advised. 'Laptop and Kindle on a desk, no burner phones anywhere so far, but a mobile was under the table there,' and she pointed back towards the kitchenette affair and the markers. 'Connor got…'

'Sorry,' Oliver Bristow jumped in. 'D'you say his mobile was under that little table?

'That and the sweetener sachet. Not necessarily his, that'll be down to the bright eyed in tech.'

'How'd they get there is a question for us.'

'As I was saying,' was a tad sarcastic even for a busy woman. 'Connor got shots of everything in situ upstairs before we sifted through the paperwork including a few paid and unpaid invoices, but not reams of them to be fair,' She turned to go back upstairs. 'Oh,' Shona said over her shoulder. 'Empty mug.'

'Where?'

'Bedroom office.'

'DNA?'

'Good chance,' she said but only took a pace or two before she turned. 'Only one though.'

It was a good cold twenty minutes before big burly DC Alexander 'Sandy' MacLachlan hurried back down the street. 'Looks promising,' he said to Jake. 'Spoke to one guy with a shop up the top, said he'd need tae speak to his boss before he'd hand anything over. One with a camera out the front, got no reply but got one disk even though the set-up's on the side of the premises, but we'll see when we get it back. Now gaunie try the garage up on Seacroft Road.'

'We'll do that for you,' his DS told him. 'Except like you we've no idea what we're looking for. Walker, runner, car, van and it was foggy. But where is it now? We're off for a coffee, want one?'

'Yeh' he replied. 'You seen the boss?

'Inside with Nicky,' he glanced left. 'How many more selfies do some of these bastards need?'

'Pain in the neck' said Sandy looking fifty yards down the street at the corralled crowd. 'Couple doon the passage towards the next road and houses we need to check too, when we get maer bodies.'

'Shona's got a phone and laptop,' Jake advised the big Scotsman. 'Door to-door has started both sides,' he added and pointed up and down Victoria Road. 'Need to get the next street down the alleyway, which looks the most likely way in. These CCTV folk you spoke to. They say anything?'

'One said he dinnae know him to talk to, just knew he was called Simm. Young lad though, don't think the grot in there's quite his cuppa tea. Another one said Simm always looked odd and could be a bit moody.'

‘Sorry, but yeah he does look odd. Even in this day and age.’

‘A sort of olde worlde bearded hippy. Usually found living in a caravan with pet rats, banning the bomb and smoking weed.’

‘But not causing any trouble to anyone, unlike today’s shower of shit.’

‘Guys with hair in a bun and pony tails are a bit odd too, but wi’ Simm he’s once seen not forgotten, when we ask about.’

‘We can only hope with a bit of luck door-to-door get more,’ said Jake Goodwin. ‘Any sightings with the way he looks have to be positive. Hardly a neighbourhood favourite going by the reactions so far. Only be a matter of time I reckon,’ he grimaced.

‘Bit like Weegies wi’a mass o’tattoos cannae understand how they get spotted so quick.’

‘How many of them have we got pictured or described on PNC? Right,’ Jake sighed. ‘We’ll get off. Americano?’

‘Yeh, anything hot. Where is it you’re going?’

‘Machine in Tesco’s.’

‘Double shot. Ta.’

‘From a machine?’

5

'Here we are then,' said bearded Detective Inspector Oliver Bristow the next morning sat at one of the small tables the Hall Manager had kindly organized. With take-away coffees to hand this was not Lincoln Central. They'd done well getting use of The Parlour in St Mary's Church Hall for an Incident Room not much more than a stone's throw from the crime scene. Warmer than Monday but unlikely to get much above zero.

Mobiles ringing, room buzzing after early chatter about another rail strike and more to come, told him motivation was high. 'On television a few days ago there was some dozy woman telling us all to relax,' he said. 'Just take a step back and decide who we are,' he smiled when he'd gained their attention. 'I'm a copper with an old dead guy frozen to death. That's who I am. No blood, no weapon, no drugs, blue washed up mug. Stupid *May The 4th Be With You* empty mug, food in the fridge, bottle of wine and two beers. Workshops out the back with loadsa tools bit like something out of Repair Shop. I know who I am have no fear of that, but the thing I don't have, no matter how far I step back, is any bloody idea.'

'You're not on your own boss,' Jake Goodwin chirped in with. He assumed the boss had spent the night in his holiday place up the coast, but as per normal he remained silent on all personal matters.

'Operation Galloway so we're told,' the DI went on. 'Breeds of cattle apparently,' he slipped in for those who want to know just out of interest, and one or two he was sure keep a note of what the system churns out. 'We have a frozen to death whiskered guy in his odds and sods bric-a-brac sort of antiques shop, for want of a better description.' He pointed at Connor Mitchell's photographs of the inside of the premises. 'Shop owner Simm according to a witness had a stall on Lincoln market a good few years back. Long before they kicked folk out and modernized it.' Oliver put down his mug on the edge of Jake Goodwin's table and moved to stand in front of a makeshift murder board with a whole host of photographs the Crime Scene Photographer, Nicky's partner had taken. 'Scene shots from Connor cover pretty much the whole place. You can see what I mean by odds and sods. Shona's team are still down there getting on with forensic harvesting amongst all that junk. Three nines call yesterday morning 08.36 from a woman. Nicky,' he gestures to. 'Tell us all about the woman caller,' and he sat down.

'Kelsey Pinhero from Mablethorpe. Nurse at Skegness General. Married with two kids. Claims her husband makes creatures out of wire he sells on line. Things like squirrels, dogs, cats and some birds. She knows Simm,' said Nicky. 'Because Simm stocks a few of these wire figures. Now and again Pinhero claims she pops in to see if he's sold any so she can replace them.

'There were three in the shop,' said Jake. 'A hedgehog I think it was, a dog but could be a wolf and probably an eagle on the wall. Well made I've gotta say.'

'Here's the odd bit,' Nicky said before taking a sip of Latte. 'Admits she doesn't really know him that well yet when she called him last week, Simm for some reason mentioned he'd be off on Monday. Day he doesn't bother to open and she told him it was her day off too.' Nicky sighed.'

'Calls round as arranged and eventually finds him sat outside frozen to death,' DI Bristow concluded for her. 'That it?'

'Reckons she planned to get a coffee next and do a bit of shopping.'

'There were two coffee cups on the side,' Bristow reminded everybody. 'Not for Simm and Pinhero in the morning as he'd been dead a good while. But what if she was there all night?'

'Just a thought,' came from Michelle brought across by Nicky from Lincoln. 'How about in her defence she's keeping in with Simm to get him to stock more of the figures?'

'And he thinks he's in with a shout.'

‘Thanks for now Nicky,’ said Bristow as he got to his feet and ignored Michelle’s idea. ‘Shona Tate reports there were no signs of areas having been specifically cleaned. Front door open according to...Pinhero, and the bathroom was fairly clean,’ he pointed at the board. ‘But not spectacularly so. The spare bedroom in essence is an office,’ he tapped the photos. ‘Visited by the CSI boys and girls. Laptop and Kindle on a small desk are being forensically examined as we speak back at base. Now they’ve done DNA swabs. His phone was discovered downstairs under the small table in a little kitchenette place with an opened sweetener sachet.’

The team all sat there listening as DI Bristow repeated what Shona Tate had explained to him.

‘Let’s think about actions,’ he suggested at the end.

‘Sorry boss,’ said Nicky suddenly back with more. ‘Forgot. Mobile’s across with Tech Crime Team’s Hari Mistry. They’re answering when it rings explaining Simm’s otherwise engaged,’ produced a chuckle or two. ‘Asking callers for their details.’

‘Jamie, can you look at the business side, while you’re here.’ said Bristow after the interruption. ‘ Bit of a rag bag of a shop as you’ve seen and I doubt whether the likes of him’d get involved in some of the silliness like customer churn they go on about. Shona has the paperwork and invoices. Can you go back down to the shop, take a note of the people he was dealing with, and start checking his bank account. Or phone Rufus for that. Guessing details have gotta be amongst his paperwork,’ he looked back to the team. ‘No cannabis smell, no drugs found at all. Like I say, we have next to nothing so think we can rule out turf war. Just by the look of the place, chances are he wasn’t married. Diversity also tells us there was no live-in partner, male or female.’ He looks across at Nicky, ‘Unless you know different,’ was sarcastic.

It all appeared to be woke free but she’d not say that to him.

When he first arrived from Grantham on promotion she’d guessed dry-voiced southerner Bristow had military experience by his bearing. Turned out not.

‘No boss,’ she reacted. ‘Spoke earlier with Alisha and she agreed. Simm’s very short on social media and in fact even though his death’s appeared it’s all about when and where so far. Facebook page apparently is all about his business. Not much more than basic photos of all the stuff, with a few good comments and none really bad. Generally the theme is about what folk perceive as a ragamuffin, a hippy to quite a few and even gypsy’s been bounded about.’

‘As per usual,’ said Jake. ‘Chances are these damn trolls have never met the poor sod. Being desperate to keep onside with any spurious trend, they’re never adept at ignoring complete twaddle.’

‘Think it might wake up when callers to his phone start querying what we’re telling them.’

‘Be some half baked celeb taking all the likes. With everything else going on we’ll be lucky if any’ll be bothered to respond to dull news like an unexplained death.’

‘Thank Alisha will you,’ Bristow told Nicky. ‘Ask her to carry on delving and see if she can find any mention of next of kin. Sending birthday wishes to his brother or whatever. Need them and any kids from any previous. His name’ll come alive soon enough. Michelle,’ Oliver switched across to. ‘Can you get hold of his phone records or ask Rufus to. Digital Forensic guys up in the Tech Crime Team have his mobile, clean of known DNA and prints. They also have his laptop Jake took back last night and with any luck the team’ll be going through them as we speak. Personal and business. So far all we have to go on are business cards in his wallet.’

‘To some extent we are where we are,’ Jake Goodwin added. ‘Waiting. Sandy’s still at the scene or in the area organizing and spreading door-to-door or should I say, shop to shop so that might give us something. Could east get bits from the PM tomorrow with any luck.’

‘CCTV boss,’ Bristow was reminded.

‘Prisoner Handling Unit have given the boring task to two newbies. Got their work cut out seeing as we don’t know what we’re looking for in the dark and in crap weather.’

'Make sure they're all told to keep all tapes for the past ten days and not to bloody over write what they've got.'

'Be better when door-to-door's done,' Jamie suggested. 'Least then we might with any luck know what car if any, or if it's our lucky day, site of a stranger.'

Nicky chuckled under her breath. The thankless task of checking hours and hours of CCTV, often from cheapjack systems some go for, was always a job for rookies. Having no spares in the Major Incident Team with five of them in the church hall. Bristow had obviously spoken to DCI Luke Stevens and the job had gone downstairs across at Central.

Sat there Nicky guessed it'd be the sort of work Rufus Barrie would have got lumbered with before moving up to MIT. Nicky wondered how he was coping back at base. When she spoke to him earlier he sounded cheerful enough. He was another one who could handle himself. Taller and leaner than both Sandy and Jamie, he'd not be a pushover in times of trouble.

'Question is,' the DI said. 'Did our man Simms know his attacker? Had they had a nice cup of tea together or was it as Shona reminded me, the two washed up mugs could have nothing at all to do with it.'

'Could have been there all week.'

'All a bit of a faff don't you think for a murderer?'

'How then?' Jamie queried. 'Did the mobile and sugar packet get under the piddly little table with no indication of a ruction?'

'Possible the phone will tell us. At least who he called in the time zone.'

'Guv. We thinking this was all a planned operation? Could easy be the dumping him outside business could've been a spur of the moment thing?'

'Does naked mean sex?' made two suck in their breath.

'You can't plan that far in advance to guarantee sub zero temperatures. With global warming anything can happen.'

'Talk about freeze your nuts off.'

'Had snow in April few years back. Think we're looking at him being drugged to be honest,' Oliver Bristow admitted. 'By himself or by others.'

'What's the naked business about? If you drug someone they don't need to be naked.'

'To guarantee death as far as is possible. DNA on or in his body if you follow my meaning could point us in the right direction. As ever we wait for the PM, wait for forensics, wait for toxicology, wait for…' Nicky shook her blonde head.

'Am I allowed to ask a stupid question?'

'Why not? You usually do!'

Michelle ploughed on. 'If this is all about an overdose, ripping his clothes off and sitting out in the yard. What would the offence be apart from utter stupidity? If somebody incapacitated him and sat him outdoors. What's the offence? Drug administered, drink spiking or whatever'll get him a fine maybe, or a slap on the wrist.'

'Manslaughter,' said Jake before Oliver could get it out.

Michelle hadn't finished. 'Be a good one for the lawyers, they'll love to fight that one out. How d'you prove Man A spiked Simms' drink?' Michelle shrugged. 'Just saying.'

'Is his business in a poor way and he overdosed? Maybe on some psychological drug causing hallucinations and in that stupor decided to go sunbathing.'

'Spice makes 'em do daftest things.'

'We discounting robbery boss?'

'Sixty odd quid and cards in his wallet says not. Laptop and Kindle upstairs. Till empty though, but that'd be normal practice surely.'

'Killer could have nicked a load of crap out the shop.'

'To do what with? Give it to your mum for her birthday? Or nice thoughtful gift for your missus on your anniversary?'

'Better than forgetting,' Jake offered.

'But only just.'

'One good thing,' Nicky chirped in with rather than making a response. 'Shona's not had to deal with blood. guts and blood splatter, we usually get down dark alleys.'

'Not exactly a dark alley but there is a walk way through.'

'And in this weather too.'

'Shit!' Oliver Bristow exclaimed loudly. 'His clothes. In god's name what happened to them?' he asked skimming a look around the room.

'In the wardrobe possibly,' Nicky suggested as Bristow opened his phone.

'Sandy. Hi. What about the clothes Simm was wearing?' he asked of his coordinator still on site down the street. 'If he stripped off or somebody did it for him where are they? Get Shona to check please. We need DNA. How many more door-to-door to go? Oh great. Thanks.' Phone closed he scanned the room. 'That'll do for now. Back to it.'

'Now we're getting somewhere,' was Jake phone in hand, with a hint of enthusiasm. Was Oliver suddenly more positive, more like a DI? 'Locals have found a blue Ford Transit Courier on the seafront. Bad news. It's locked.'

'I'll buzz Shona.'

Nicky Scoley felt their hands were tied out there on the coast. Passing every query, every thought through Lincoln Central meant they spent a great deal of time waiting.

Not as easy as nipping onto PNC [Police National Computer], a quick hop and skip up to the Tech Crime Team, sat beside Hari or Dexter Hopwood allowing them do all the work.

Trotting off to the Co-op for a coffee fill-up was becoming a proper drag. At one point she'd even considered coughing up to buy a kettle from somewhere, but then what would she do with it after?

When Connor phoned her from the Simm crime scene saying he had to head back to base to look at another unexplained stabbing, she was all for hitching a lift.

Family, friends and workmates are always top of the list for a quick chat and interview if matters come to light. With this Simm they'd spoken to neighbours who knew of him, basically by the way he looked more than actually knew him.

Fortunately the geeks up in the Tech Crime Team back in Lincoln had the good sense to visit the inside of his laptop. That told them about his business of buying and selling.

Peering inside some scrote's computer or phone was akin to poking your nose into their private life. Hari Minstry had not dared keep count of how many minds he'd poked his snout into. Now he had a Mac laptop to deal with.

One thing he hated about dealing with MIT investigation work was how Nicky Scoley had become a permanent link between departments.

In the sixth form he had decided he must be gay, but also worryingly being too involved in what was back then a hobby and now his job, to imagine how anyone would ever be able to put up with a relationship with him. Male, female or in between.

Nicky Scoley had changed his mind. No stupid high heels, no mini skirt or open necked blouse, she was all too frequently a target he absolutely dare not approach. Anyway Connor Mitchell was bigger than him. The look of her. Charm, wit, her personal interest in his work and the smell of her was always such a delight.

Hari had not as yet come across a computer he could not recover almost every bit of data, deleted or not from. He was fortunate to be one who found it easy to drag out every single digital footprint, no matter how complex.

Such talent he knew would keep Nicky coming back for more. Just the sight and sound of her would have to do. At least for now, unless she had a sister.

No friends. This was never a chatty email type laptop, this was business. Hari had carefully extracted all his sales and purchases for a month back and produced a list. He'd used their special memory stick to disseminate passwords and put it all back to the start. Created a new password and off he went.

'One bright spot,' said Michelle. 'One customer we've spoken with he made a bespoke sundial for,' she checked her iPad. 'A Lizzie Main reckoned she'd been told he had a partner. Not a wife so we can check of course. Apparently they split up few years back and he moved to Mablethorpe. Called Gloria was all she knows.'

6

Hello there. Allow me to state first and foremost; I'm not Linkisheer born and bred. Not far away though, but at least I'm not from some foreign land as so many are these days. I'm from the world of *"Yew two tergither gow", "I dussn't dew that"* and *"coupla three"* county. Flit from Suffolk in my early teens when me dear old dad got promoted and moved to a new food processing plant deep in yellerbelly flat lands.

I've not entirely abandoned my place of birth as my wife and I often spend weekends down there. House in the Clouds a sight we've seen many a time at Thorpness. Lovely Aldeburgh of course with the Moot Hall and home to Benjamin Britten and his Snape Maltings. Plus the 'Scallops' sculpture created on the shingle beach in his memory. On the way home we always stop off in Cromer for delicious crab. Bit of a long way round but always worth it.

Went well I thought across in Mablethorpe. That's the first box ticked despite all the energy sapping business with paunchy Simm in need of a good shave and haircut. Another in serious need of Weight Watchers but seems the way of the world these days. All the planning I did, trolling through the internet, plus all that time spent bored to tears watching him do next to nothing, but stupidly I didn't take one thing into account. If that was my only mistake, so be it.

It wasn't just the physical exertion involved, it was the nerves tiring me out at the time. Dragging that dead weight out that grubby kitchenette place, was a real struggle for starters. The nerves and sweat will dissipate over time they say, according to the books about serial murderers. I now know from here on, I seriously have to make it easier on myself. Having to go all the way out to Mablethorpe a good few times, was more than a tad annoying. Doing the deed wasn't so bad in the end, but all the tedious evenings and weekends spent doing on-site research had become a bit much for me.

Lots of the *is this really worth it* thoughts until my mind took me back to the great days I'd shared with Miriam. To the life she had left she wasn't allowed to enjoy.

Checking where he went and who Simm met had been an absolute pain. Stood in his road just waiting around for sight and sound of callers. Hoping to provide me with the knowledge of his level of business and participation in society had been a real drag at times. Never going to be hopelessly easy as pie enough to be able to relax, but my future efforts just have to be less fraught and tiring, than it turned out to be with that scruffy fat git.

Fortunately it wasn't that far off the major drag down to the sea, so a coffee and snack was not something I'd had to search too hard for.

And that stuff in his shop. Dear me. Do people seriously fill their homes with garbage like that? Must admit though, I spied a piece or two I'd considered nicking on the way out. A case of standing there thinking how good is that piece and next to it utter disbelief in anybody daring to put such obviously damaged junk on sale.

Nerves were the worst part, I have to admit. Stood there outside his bloody door in freezing fog pretending to window shop for ages plucking up the courage to take the plunge. Big deep breath, nervous as hell, but in the end went pretty much like clockwork. Always had the planned fallback in my armoury. Practice makes perfect and that's one down.

The fallback had the sugar trick not worked, I'd chosen to leave to on site decisions. Fortunately as it turned out, had thankfully not been required. As with the whole process there was always the no action option. Receive a pretend phone call and I'd be out of there. A call yourself system discovered on the internet I set up before I got there.

Divesting that nasty smelly bastard of his clothes when he was unconscious was much harder than I'd ever imagined. Never stripped a man before.

Would have been easier in the summer in t-shirt and shorts, but as you can imagine those stupid tight jeans were an absolute nightmare. Especially with somebody that dead weight so overweight and with him offering no help of course. Dragging him out the back door in the dark, to prop him up in the back yard in the cold had not been the best idea ever under the circumstances. Got him all rumbled up with a mat just inside the door I should have got rid of first. Turned out to be a real pain. Lesson learnt, but choosing by chance the coldest freezing night was a proper bonus ball.

When I first spotted him, I thought the dope was wearing a wig like me, just a lot longer obviously and a lot more unkempt. At least I've never gone in for a daft straggly beard like that. Has to be laziness or having no pride in himself.

Wig off, bagged up all his clothes along with my coat and hat, grabbed his car keys, then drove his van off as quietly as I could. Dumped it on the seafront tossed the keys in the sea. In no time a now freezing cold me reached my clapped out old motor in the Boulevard. In no time I'm off heading for Skeggy, Sutton-on-Sea, Alford, Louth with heating full on all the way home.

As a dear friend of mine says frequently. Job's a good'un. Certainly was when after dark next evening, another freezing one I stuffed it all in my incinerator. The one I use to rid myself of odds and sods in the garden. I could easily have found a home in there for a good amount of crap Simm was trying to sell.

I've decided it most seriously has to be a change of plan for the next one on my list. Change of location for the next two would certainly help a great deal, and better weather. Needing to ensure Simm would die, it had been necessary to put him out in the cold or ensure he'd swallow another potion to guarantee demise. Time to go back and see what Google has to say about ways to get rid of folk. Probably go back to that Ten Best Ways To Kill website or hunt down another. YouTube has proved useful with videos as a sort of do it yourself instruction.

In fact I'm sure the Home Office and the Police must absolutely hate people like Google and YouTube. Using them

I've learned for example, if I shake hands, then touch a door handle in a shop, the next customer who then touches it collects what they call my touch DNA. He then leaves my DNA on the handle of the knife he stabs his wife with.

As an added precaution with Simm I wore a pale blue Covid mask, explained how I have a weak immune system and suggested as a result I'm among the vulnerable to all sorts.

Being no CCTV for quite a few doors close by made everything a lot easier, meaning I had no real need to dodge cameras. The three research visits in the middle of the night had provided the easy escape route. The disguise save for the wig, just in case of the totally unexpected had not been needed to nip down the twitten. But it's always better to be safe than sorry. Attacking when the News was on and the nearby restaurant busy had to be a good pre-occupying decision. That was especially true for any witnesses hanging about as well as it being dark and cold, all adding to the plus points.

Not having the stomach for a decent meal prior to the event, at one time I'd thought of stopping off somewhere to eat after. The thought of being witnessed anything other than twenty miles from Mablethorpe put a stop to that idea. Think that was a case of making good decisions, when on one of my research trips I realized the journey was not exactly packed with an array of convenient drive-thrus and all-night McDonalds.

When I arrived back home I felt weary not just physically but emotionally, not a trait I'm at all used to. But to cheer me, as good as their word Deliveroo came up with supper for the pair of us right on schedule.

Using that sterilized hand sanitizer before nervously knocking on Simm's shop door had to have been a really good move. One I'll repeat in future. Kills 99% of all germs they claim including DNA was the theory. Washing the two mugs in the sink thoroughly with his cheap own label washing up liquid along with the sink, would have had the poor cops salivating over what their forensics people had discovered.

First rehearsal deed done for big sis, then another before the prize who of course remains my main target. I realize Miriam may not totally approve of what I'm doing, but she'd know why and the simple alternative was to allow all the bastards to live. A free and easy life and more than likely striking again, means I'm doing this for the innocent as well as my own flesh and blood.

Not taking all this on when mum and dad were still alive was of course a given. Life has been fortunate to some extent with that caring loving couple not being forced to endure the shame and ignominy of one dead daughter by her own hand, to be quite possibly followed by the lengthy incarceration of sibling two.

That Brendon Quinton is next up. No way now the whole half dozen I've considered could be done, but as many as possible would be a source of great satisfaction. Andy Ross of course will move up the charts after a bit more practice. Then if there's enough time left, get rid of that nasty cunning sod Donny Milosavic who made Suzanne's life a complete and absolute misery. At least I know how much that would please dad. Knowing how he absolutely hated that evil bastard's guts.

I'd chosen Mabo, simply because unfortunately that's where Simm lives now. Or lived should I say. Meant I was somewhere I'd visited a few times so I knew my way about but still easy to be able to remain unknown.

I'd not just picked him at random of course and what he suffered he'd brought entirely upon himself.

Early scouting trips and late night location visits had produced nothing untoward. This one had been a particularly nasty boy, but bright enough not to be taken for granted. The Simm treatment was not for the next nasty shit. Far too risky with Quinton, far too bright eyed and inquisitive from what I've gathered so far.

No way I could do with Quinton what I'd at one time considered for Simm, by coming up with some ridiculous scheme to offer him objet das to display in his ramshackle grimy shop. Too good looking was a thought about Quinton which often comes to mind. Back on almost home turf is much preferable, now the first one, the awkwardly placed one is all done and dusted. With a hoard of coppers working night and day, it'll be overtime I guess, so its not all bad.

I bought that old car a few months back specifically for the purpose, conveniently listed as a cash sale on Autotrader. You know the sort of thing all pockmarked around the wheel arches. Bought it in Miriam's name and her address, or rather the place she'd lodged at for a while. This old boy up in Retford had been advised by his doctor to stop driving before DVLA took away his licence. Hired a lock-up garage locally pretending to be Miriam from an address I know no longer exists. Notice that did you? Gave Miriam's address down south for the car purchase and some place fairly local for the garage. House in a street they demolished for the building of even more student luxury flats and paid six months in advance by cash of course.

Tick box list on my tablet seems to get longer by the day. With one down, the inherent experience gained in Mabo had added a good few items and thoughts to the list. That business of dragging Simm out into his yard was not something I'd considered in detail. Looking down my list at least the rest are not as bulky as he had been. I also have no plans to be dragging them about if everything goes to plan. If for some reason I need in an emergency to switch to Plan B, then I'll just have to play it by ear.

After that extraordinary episode – not quite what most people get to experience, now I have a bit of time to return the remainder of my life back close to normal. Always remembering there is that deadline. Luckily I kept this morning free of all appointments so I'm taking a rest with Sunday having been so utterly stressful.

Could have done with today being at a better time of year. Trip down to Dry Doddington for example to have a chat with their so gentle Alpacas would have been a real tonic with a decent coffee thrown in. Open the clinic tomorrow, keep my clients happy and walking well, all as if nothing happened if I can manage it.

Back concentrating on providing a good service is like stepping back into another world. The stuff some women want to talk about fascinates me and I often wonder if they'd ever say the same things in mixed company.

Take Yasmin Dean. Last time she had an appointment she was telling me how she was struggling to find a new property to move into now her marriage was over. Says she has a desperate need to move out of the city and to discover the right energy for a calm room. For her, or so she says, each viewing has to be a rather lengthy process, in order to be able to meditate. Then back home, if she is to be believed, she takes time reflecting to allow her mind to be taken back to the property to see if the vibes remain.

I can see why her husband walked out, can't you? As she says she has a profound desire to being able to create a calming atmosphere to dispense with her feeling of being overwhelmed. I cannot imagine what she'll come out with next.

Having said that when she has moved I think I'll invite myself for a grand tour to get some idea what this nonsense is all about.

I know a bit about this cognition business. Regularly evaluating feelings, thoughts and behaviour provides better memory in the old. Also so they say, aids concentration and problem solving. Useful for completing crosswords. Maybe that was what Yasmin meant by meditating.

Another post-Covid surprise was clients being pleased with how to some extent the world has changed. That Greta Thunberg was one. Having gone from being sort of world famous, to the universe moving on seemingly without her. I was not surprised at her withdrawal from the front pages with Covid, the cost of living and energy crisis. Then we had Boris Johnson being kicked out, followed by the drawn out Tory leadership battle to bore the pants off one and all. Then when it appeared calm had returned, we endured all that mind boggling mess from that Truss woman.

With all that going on what chance was there of the media bothering with Thunberg? I was I have to admit, even more surprised to discover so many women unlike their children, admitting to not being followers.

Morning after the night before means different things at varying phases in their life to a whole bunch of divergent people.

Drunk too much and it'll never happen again. Until the next time. *Did bad last night. Oh in God's name why did I do that? Need to seriously make amends I'll have to sort when I get rid of this bloody headache. Hope she forgives me. Why in God's name did I choose that Naked Burrito other than to show off when I've got a jippy tummy?*

Nothing like that, and I'm as sober as a judge this morning after the Simm event thank goodness. Good job I've kept my morning free of appointments, because as I said to myself. You just never know. There's no chance of me working from inside a prison cell.

Breakfast as per normal during the week was Granola for me, I do swap flavours week and week about. I washed down with a cappuccino.

Ruthie stuck to her Special K and Latte and we chatted as we tend to at the start and end of every day.

My client list for this afternoon doesn't appear too difficult to handle. None of those listed are likely to chatter continuously and with any luck unlikely to mention the guy frozen to death out at the coast.

Next up each morning for me after Ruthie has left for work, is to do that little bit of washing up, a wipe down and tidy up. I've checked my emails, listened to the BBC Radio Lincolnshire news and popped into Facebook. Nothing about Simm as yet is good news and now when I've finished this it'll be time for a decent Americano from my Tassimo.

7

The Nurse Practitioner had been given a couple of days off work under the circumstances and was on her own when butterscotch blonde DS Nicky Scoley called.

Apart from work based issues, Nicky'd not been out to the coast since she and Connor ventured to the Boatshed in the Coastal Country Park a summer or so back.

What she discovered on arrival was a very agreeable mid-90s built three-bedroom detached house, and the dining room she was shown into was all oak furniture. As Nicky took her place at the sturdy dining table she wondered how much use it got day to day.

She and Connor normally ate on the round table in the kitchen and never with food on trays on their knees in front of the gogglebox. However she knew they were unusual in their determination not to give in to what both their mothers would class as downright slovenly behaviour.

Kelsey Pinhero offered and Nicky Scoley accepted the offer of a cup of tea. Made in a pot no less, and nothing untoward or fancy such as Herbal and Lime she'd had to suffer once.

'While I remember,' Scoley said. 'Have you got Simm's phone number?' Aware only a mobile had been found at the shop despite the efforts of CSI to seek out another or a burner.

Kelsey produced her phone and spun down to *'Simm'* on the list for Scoley to make a note. She'd check it against the one they'd found later.

'Tell me about yourself,' Scoley said then took her first sip of tea, aware she dare not mention the nurses' strikes or she'd be there all day.

'Kelsey Pinhero. Nurse Practitioner at Skegness as you know,' she said. Scoley sat there listening asking herself again having Simms number meant this nurse could easy have phoned to ask if he needed more stock. 'Married to Goncalo, he's

Spanish,' she had no need to add even though Scoley'd no idea of her nationality. 'Lays floors and we have two kids. Rio nine and Kiki six.'

'Happy?'

'Yeh, why?'

'Just wondered,' Kelsey looked at the DS with a degree of concern and wondered if she should say anything. 'Tell me about your relationship with Harry Simm.'

'Please no,' she insisted. 'Don't get any stupid ideas. We're happily married. Yeh, we both work bloomin' hard especially with what I do. With that bloody pandemic business Gon,' she pronounced as John, 'couldn't lay floors so he ran this place. Did the lot. Washing, ironing, shopping, fed the kids allowing me to relax when I wasn't dressed to the nines in PPE,' she grinned.

The DS knew attacks on Police particularly in London rose sharply during the pandemic. Some were Covid-related assaults and incidents when officers were spat on or coughed at. Putting stop to illegal parties were regular events when such attacks took place.

'Yeh, get your point,' said Scoley. 'This wire model business, tell me about that.' She'd seen examples in the shop of course. A wire fish and a copper wire tree to hang on the wall.

'Always been good with his hands, just needed something to do. Sort of hobby stuck here at home. Used to play five-a-side but bit old for that now. Wanted something as far away from laying floor after floor as is possible. Saw one in a shop on holiday he found fascinating. Bought it, brought it home and it all started from there, and when Covid appeared it was a God send.'

'Now he sells them on line,' blonde Scoley suggested.

'And fills my lunchtime standing in a queue at the Post Office.'

'How did Simm come into the equation?' Scoley wanted to know.

'Friend told me about his shop, plucked up courage and walked in with two of Dave's dogs and a whale. Sale or return and that was that.' She stopped to drink tea. 'Look I can't imagine he's everybody's cup of tea. Bit of a curmudgeon with a temper some say. But what you see is what you get. Always been alright with me.'

Because you're female was a thought Scoley kept to herself.

'Called him to check if Gon's stuff'd sold and during general chit-chat mentioned I'd be in town on Monday. He suggested I pop in anyway. What could I say? If I made a silly excuse would he refuse to stock the animals?' she shrugged. 'Couldn't say d'you want any stock or not? That's it, that's all there was to it.'

Next on the list of people to interview which Oliver Bristow had pushed in Nicky's direction was a joiner in Skegness who had undertaken a number of initial salvaging roles for Simm according to notes on his laptop.

Mitch Cummins explained when Nicky visited his workshop, how he does normal joinery work day to day to make a living but as a sideline rejuvenates and reconstructs furniture, and with Harry Simm this often amounted to particularly tatty specimens.

Said how he found working on Simm's projects very liberating compared with the frustration of working for bored housewives who can never make up their mind about how they want their kitchen.

Mitch explained to Scoley as he worked, how between them they transformed the items Simm has saved from landfill with revitalized and usually self-designed modern materials.

'Really cannot imagine why somebody would do him in,' Cummins admitted. 'Never been close friends to be fair, just enthusiasts with a love for the unusual. Never know do we, what's going on in other people's private lives? Talking to him a couple of weeks back I think it was, you'd just never guess.' He stopped what he is doing to look up at Nicky Scoley. 'I take it this was nothing more that just a one-off spur of the moment attack by some complete bozo.'

'We don't imagine so,' she replied.

He was enthusiastic about his restoration work away from the humdrum business of putting in a new newel post or re-hanging doors and took the opportunity to show Scoley photographs. Basically items which had been transformed through his workmanship and Simm's design ideas.

The rest of the team in addition to Scoley dealing with people like this Cummins from Simm's address book on his laptop had until that point not known of their existence. Artists, blacksmiths, weavers a whole host of people with particular craft skills Jamie Hedley and Michelle Cooper sought out. It was obvious to Nicky how in the end everything going into the shop, no matter who had had a hand in the early stage changes, ended up with a particular look to emphasize Simm's style. Perhaps the place was not as ramshackle as it appeared.

One metalworker DC Jamie Hedley had spoken to explained how he understood Harry Simm was completely self-taught

'He can turn an old dilapidated chair he found at a car boot for a couple of quid, into something'd finish up with a damn hefty mark-up.'

Nicky Scoley learnt how Simm was magnanimous in his attitude to those who had assisted in creating the final product for him. He had always been thoroughly willing to bring in other experts when the basic construction facing him was way out of his comfort zone. Experts were entrusted with work on salvaged metal objects, car parts and lumps of seemingly useless, valueless and badly engineered items.

His 'Contacts' file on his laptop was full of people who when interviewed turned out to be like-minded enthusiasts with particular and often unique skills. Trouble was it appeared he used their skills very infrequently.

Jonny Vernon was such a craftsman, who Michelle Cooper had got to interview. The DC with her tidy bobbed dark hair, scrubbed face and happy demeanour knew little or nothing about wood turning or what somebody like this Jonny could produce.

Fascinated initially when he gave her a quick tour of his small workshop and display of his handiwork, but his hand turned wooden bowls all had a hefty price tag out of the reach of an everyday copper.

Seemed too pricey for Simm's place. Vernon had, possibly because she was Police and good looking, confessed unashamedly it was a way to rid himself of cast offs he'd normally chuck in the bin.

A fleshy surly man with pockmarked face, to indicate to Michelle he'd cultivated zits at one time and then picked at them when young. All down to not munching even one a day she decided, as he gabbled on.

Simm according to Jonny, always created his own style by coating the bowls with milk paint. Then became bemused when he went onto explain in detail how he'd then cut them back with sand paper.

His opinion of Harry Simm was his shop was not one thing or the other. Complete junk mixed in with an amount of good crafted bits and pieces.

Michelle knew to remind herself back in MIT to have a close look at Connor Mitchell's scene shots. See if any of Jonny's bowls had been captured.

8

Suppose I should say that awful "Hi" but that's not me. Hello again. When I first got into all this seriously, miles and miles on from the *"I really need to do something"* stage, I'd been amazed at what abused women were willing to confess to me.

Choosing number one as my initial attempt had to some extent been easy enough. So much of course had been based on what Gloria told me on the quiet during treatment. About what life had been like living with this objectionable Harry Simm. Think early on Gloria was one of those women who found me to be a totally independent listener in whom she was able to confide.

She like many others knew whatever they were wanting to admit to me would never leave the confines of the treatment room. No matter what. To be honest, only in exceptional circumstances would I even discuss the matter with Ruthie.

We have always tended to keep our work and marriage quite separate. I realize not everybody is of that nature but that's how we are.

Maybe this was me suffering from first night nerves but Simm's age had come into it. Along with her suggesting he over time had become violent when he couldn't get his own way.

In Gloria's case it was mental torture she'd suffered in addition initially.

'During the pandemic," she told me one day. 'We'd gone in for that food delivery business from the supermarket like everybody else. Harry's buggered with being unable to work his stall in the market for a good while. First couple of deliveries were absolutely fine and then next time there was an item missing and yogurts were the wrong ones.' She shrugged overtly. 'Hey ho. Read about all that on line. So what?'

Gloria stopped, pushed out a breath and grimaced. 'Problem?' I'd asked gently.

‘Times were really tough back then and I still feel really stupid even now at how I’d put us in real danger of going under. Called Customer Services and gave this woman a gobfull, when she insisted my order had been delivered exactly right.’

‘This on line or in person?’

‘Their Head office s’pose. Probably Mogadishu or some place,’ I was pleased to hear. ‘Life to be honest was not at all good with Harry unable to work. Perpetually in a sulky mood as if Covid was my bloody fault and when idiot Boris shut the pubs…’ She blew out a breath. ‘Crissakes! It became a real bloody nightmare. Bought him cans o’beer but soon got told in no uncertain terms how they’re not a proper pint. Into real ale and all that business, said cans are fizzy pop. ‘ Gloria pulled a sad face. ‘Sex was allus for him and not for me but it’d got worse. Particularly when in an attempt to prove Tesco wrong I managed to dig out me order on their website with help from a pal much more savvy about IT than me.’ She shook her head. ‘Felt such a pillock when I read in black and white I’d only gone an’ ordered bread but no rolls. Yogurts I’d gone for were those odd-ball Prune and Date ones they’d delivered.’

‘IT can be confusing if you’re not used to it,’ I’d offered to her as a reason. ‘Created by bits of techy kids is my excuse,’ was my theory.

‘Next time I’m so damn careful and twice they delivered just what I’d ordered. Almost got paranoid about such a simple every day task some women have coped with for years. Then it happened again. Luckily I’d been keeping a note of what I’d put on the system. Except…’ It was time for a big sigh and I stood back to allow Gloria to regain her composure. ‘Couldn’t find the bloody list!’

I guessed she’d suffered twice over. She’d somehow mislaid her note but then had to defend herself against the hostility dished out by stuck at home Harry Simm.

‘Next time the driver turned up he told me there were no changes and a quick check told me all was fine. Stupidly convinced myself it had all been a case of being a bit dipsy.’ Gloria scoffed. ‘Week later no potatoes, no miniature Pork Pie and I was in trouble, serious trouble.’

Half of me wanted to suggest it was all down to the lockdown affecting so many people, but if that had been the case I'd never have met her.

'Can't ever be sure of course, but me bestie reckons Harry'd been going into the website and changing the orders. Then somebody sent nasty messages to my friends in the middle of the night in my name I had to cope with. Unsuccessfully in one case. But a pal I'd known for ages's not spoken to me since, like.'

The other half of me proved to be right. This was mental trauma, cruelty, causing her through his controlling untold confusion over simple parts of her life.

Then she said something as if it was on a loop. 'Began to wonder if it was all my fault. Was I stupid, was I difficult to live with?' The look of concern was clearly printed on her face. How many times had I heard that from abused women?

Think she was right when he grabbed her face one night in a fit of anger and frustration she accused him of messaging her best pal, did she finally see the light.

Gloria's face so she was telling me one time, had been gripped so hard, she reckoned the two sides of her mouth almost met and banging her head against the bedroom wall told her their days were numbered.

Her mother's warning about one strike and you're out of there shone brightly but for so long, too long, she'd done nothing about it. Suffering in silence is never good.

When I'd first come across sad and damaged Gloria during the course of my time helping women, the damage was done, mental scars would remain, but she was at last physically free of the torment.

Talking of physical damage she'd never been badly hurt by him during his perpetual anger over Covid restrictions. Instead he'd even phoned her work to explain how she'd proved Positive which meant she had to stay at home.

I did my best to help but one thing I'd never to this day been able to persuade her to do, is go to the Police. At least not that I'm aware of.

Threats from angry Harry and one of his mates had always remained in her mind enough for her to be running scared, but not willing to do anything about it.

At least after her visits I knew I'd played a part, she was evidently more relaxed, free from the mental torture to a great extent and her feet looked good.

Since freezing Harry Simm to death, I've not made any particular or unusual efforts to see Gloria for fear of one wrong word slipping out. To be honest I've done my level best to avoid her. That in itself has had an effect upon me. At times I've felt a desperate need to go and see her, offer my services once more and try hard to discover how much she knows of what happened to him plus what her reaction is. If anything.

Has her cloistered community I wonder saved her from both the bad news of her past and the good news about her future?

Do wish there was interest from schools about discussing real life. Do we really need some of the flimflam they dose kids with? Why not offer advice to girls about the dangers of playful force during sex? Is the guy you've just linked up with, jealous you have a better job than him? Does that make him feel inferior? Warn them about friends he's lying about and as a result your social life is not what it should be. Verbal or physical abuse has to be the last straw. Message to young women at school above all else has to be, if you've not gone already, then go.

Forever on their phones I know, but never in a million years are they likely to flick to something serious. Even in my early teens I watched the BBC News on television, but they'll not do that today. Nobody has ever been able to explain to me why they have such a short attention span.

I've been told by more than one, how their children are in effect living in a different world. Jumping from one bizarre latest fad to another. Obsessed with all this peer pressure business they go on about these days, my generation never encountered. Rather than reading about signs of bullying or the latest terrible real life stabbing. Once Simm was done for, although my planning for number two was well advanced I took my foot off the gas. Every copper for miles around would I guess be on the lookout for anything odd. Or out of place.

9

First job in Mablethorpe for Sandy MacLachlan after morning briefing was the knitting machine shop close by the crime scene. It was never likely to be a positive reaction from the notes the MIT team had made from the cursory door-to-door. Whereas some of the neighbours had been out and about watching the goings on, the Oldales had it would appear, stayed put. Pretending not to be interested.

Initially Dudley Oldale said he was a retired civil servant which could mean anything. He was now helping out his wife with running their shop. Not just knitting machines but an array of materials and wool in particular. Jake and Jamie started off chatting generally with Dudley.

'What the Hildreds said was right,' Dudley told his wife. 'Mr Simm was murdered,' made his grey haired buxom wife clutch her hand to her mouth.

'In this street?' she gasped between her fingers. 'You mean he actually died here?' she pointed right with her hand extended and then looked mystified.

'We obviously can't go into too much detail while the case is ongoing,' said the DS. 'But he was discovered outside in his yard.'

'Attacked?' Dudley Oldale asked. 'Some of his stuff is quite nice, but not wishing to speak ill of the dead there's plenty'd be at home in a Jumble Sale.' The old boy sniggered. 'Why would you attack anybody for some tatty stuff.'

'On trend dear,' said Connie. 'All in fashion they say,' left her husband shaking his head.

'That's what we're trying to fathom,' MacLachlan admitted. 'We know our door-to-door team spoke with you on Monday but we're now calling to ask if since then, has anything come to mind? Is there something you've now recalled which might prove relevant?'

'Such as?' Dudley asked.

'Strangers hanging around,' the big DC suggested.

'Simm was strange enough on his own.'

'Vehicles,' said MaLachlan. 'Have there been any strange vehicles in the area? Parked up on the yellow lines, one you've perhaps seen hanging about,' he tried. 'Have the other shop owners said anything maybe?'

'If we saw a car young man in a busy road like this. How would we know it's out of place?' Oldale asked and he was right.

'On the subject of cars. Did Harry Simm have a car?' If he did where was that?

'Yeh, a …' he pulled in his mouth as he thought. 'Blue van. A transit something. Needed a van to move some o'his stuff about. Tucks it down the alley,' they already knew. 'Sorry son, not a...petrol head, don't know the brake horse power or how fast they can reach sixty. Some modern ones I don't know what make they are. Just foreign muck like you used to get on that awful *Top Gear* nonsense.'

'You may not have known at the time but now maybe something jolts the memory,' DC MacLachlan suggested. 'Thoughts perhaps have come to mind about an old Renault or something hanging about for an hour or two.' Whoever it was they assumed had moved Simm's van, would have been in need of transport to get there or got a lift.

'Sorry,' said quiet Connie. 'We tend to keep ourselves to ourselves, lad. Not very good neighbours I'm afraid, in that we're not as upwardly mobile as they say, like some o'others round here. Certainly not at this time of year. Remember not all the shop owners have to live upstairs like we do. Got posh houses along the coast quite a few of them,' she offered with a twinge of jealousy.

'And our caravan,' Dudley added to improve their image. 'Could be these delivery people we see running back and forth all the time. How do we tell them from a....somebody who would attack Harry?' he asked Sandy. 'That'd be good cover,' was an interesting idea.

'How well did you know Mr Simm?' the DS posed to change tack but his mind was on that delivery driver suggestion..

'Well enough to say hello to,' Dudley admitted. 'Well enough for the delivery people they have these days, sometimes drop off his parcels with us. Bit of a football fan. Not my cup of tea with all those hooligans and the cheating. Cricket's more my game,' he added.

'This very often?' MacLachlan had to ask.

'Not really. Once in a blue moon,' was another dead end. 'Being neighbourly that's all.' He sucked in a breath. 'Bit cantankerous at times.'

'Are you on the internet?' MacLachlan asks realizing these two'd not be poking their noses into anything. Probably understandable at their age at night. Mixing with all sorts, with the majority very much younger was probably not them.

'Yes,' said white haired tubby Oldale as if to say what do you take us for. 'But none of that social media business. Use it to check out bank, send emails to friends all that sort of business.'

At least the couple had been pleasant to deal with and co-operative, even if short on facts. Compared to the sort detectives personally doorstepped over the years with an immediate anti-copper stance.

By the time he'd visited two more shops, it was obvious to Sandy how it was the situation working against them. When and how Simm died, not a reluctance by his neighbours to co-operate he'd come across in a good few places.

At the other premises he paid a visit to they were in the main co-operative but not able to provide information. Except one man suggested there were one or two vans trying to back down the alley at Simm's place most weeks, rather than getting a ticket for being on the road.

Theory was, even those who for whatever reason had taken a step back from Simm's death, would now hopefully talk to family or friends to give the inquiry the kick start the DC was after.

Oliver Bristow went home for the night, all the way to Grantham. Leaving Jake at the church hall in Mablethorpe to brief Detective Chief Superintendent Craig Darke back at Lincoln on the day's events. What was there to tell over and above what Shona would have already punted across already. They knew the name of the victim but little else of real interest, plus he had to admit no inkling of a suspect. Not only no prime suspect, just no suspect.

Jake knew from gossip at training courses how some forces in their position would put an innocent into custody for no better reason that to show the naive public how well they were doing. Maybe Bristow would turn out to be the sort to do that, with his future career at the forefront of his thinking.

10

The little nudge the inquiry was in desperate need of, arrived in the form of social media messages punted across by Alisha O'Neill from Lincoln Central. People on Facebook initially asking if anybody had been able to make contact with Simm. Followed by somebody who had obviously tried to call on him, only to discover the path to his front door was blocked. Meant talk of 'cops' and 'rotten rozzers' got aired.

Being a tubby bloke of his age, looking the way he did meant there was never going to be many. Replace male with female and there'd be a torrent. Odd thing this equality business. Young women get attacked at night and there's absolute uproar. Young man gets knifed in the day in broad daylight'd be lucky to be on the news tomorrow.

Assistance from Facebook is always welcomed. As it turned out it was one such message saw Michelle Cooper being given a walk along to the main street in Mablethorpe to talk to a Dean Adams who managed a Betting Shop.

They sat together in a very cramped office come store room in the middle of town. This Adams' story was he and his brother had paid for his parents to have a big metal spinning sunflower made for their back garden as an anniversary present. Somebody he knew had recommended Harry Simm.

Job well done and a few weeks later he was in the Book In Hand pub with a pal of his when in walked Simm. They got chatting over a pint or two.

'It was obvious to me the guy was lonely,' Adams told the DC. 'Some'at I've heard before about self employed folk. Not got a base of regulars to interact with. No work colleagues, not working as part of a team like most of us do. We do and I'm sure you lot are the same. Go from one set of strangers to another. People they're unlikely ever to see again, particularly tourists. I obviously have customers I see on a very regular basis, but not old Harry.'

‘Did he appear to have issues on his mind at all?’ Cooper asked. ‘Talk of bad customers or even threats maybe?’ she added.

‘To be honest didn’t know him well enough to voice an opinion. Me mum dealt with him when he was checking location and size and she were there of course when it was installed,’ Adams told her. ‘Couldn’t talk better of him. Unkempt scruff bag to be fair, but polite and hard working, She was saying when I told her what’d happened, how she never got feedback from him about his life. Almost as if he was a closed book,’ Dean shrugged slightly. ‘I don’t know much more about him now than when we first met.’

‘Any mention of women?’ she asked.

Dean pouted and shook his head. ‘Met a time or two, not regularly as I said but it was just all the usual stuff and a bit of banter. Talked about football. Mainly Cod Head stuff. No politics, nah,’ he sniggered. ‘Nothing intense and profound of course just natter about the crap government. He’d tell us stories about pillocks he’d had to work with. Both me and JJ’re happily married so women was hardly a topic of conversation. But then, if something special walked in…’ he pulled a face to end with. ‘Bit old fashioned sexist business I reckon. Almost as if not having a woman meant he’d not moved on. Not had anybody to put him straight.’

‘JJ?’ she posed.

‘John James Nicholson. Called him JJ since we was at school. Better’n Nick.’

‘Did Simm ever visit you at home?’ Cooper asked then added: ‘Except at your parents’ of course.’

‘No,’ he said with a shake of his head.

‘Christmas say?’ Cooper dropped in. ‘Did he ever say what he was doing?’

‘Not specifically, just assumed he’d see his family.’

‘But you have no information on them.’

‘No. Nothing...sorry.’ He grimaced slightly. ‘Not sure he’s from round here.’

‘Any idea where?’

‘Just bits and pieces he’s said, but remember we’re not best pals and that.’

From there it was a chemist where she discovered he wasn't on their customer list. Newsagent said they knew him as a customer once Michelle described him but nothing more.

At the end of chats all over the place, Michelle and the others realized they were really no further forward, but hoped any info gained would maybe trigger something with one of them. Just might get them to talk to others about the mysterious Mr Simm.

Who was this Simm, apart from being an odd ball shop owner of +a place most folk had never entered? One of the local papers referred to him as a 'character'. What about family? Why was nobody asking where he was? Why had nothing much come out on social media? Even the usual bunch of trolls were almost absent? The three who knew a bit had appeared in the *Lincoln Leader*, but with it all cracking off out at the coast the media moved on quickly to some Z list celebrity appearing in pantomine.

The DI was becoming keen to play some positive part in inquiries rather than just sitting back. As a result arrangements were made for Michelle and the boss to visit a Molly Cramp who had been on Facebook praising the standard of Simm's handiwork.

Almost before the pair had set off to meet the woman, their social media monitor Alisha was on the phone. Her father was white and her mother black. Creating an attractive daughter with naturally curly brown hair and with no need for a spray tan.

'Boss,' she said. 'Got some Simm action at last. People asking if anybody's seen him. Then one said he's not answering his phone. Why's the shop shut? He on holiday?'

'Any details apart from their names?'

'Not so far, but I'll check them all out. See if any are messaging each other. Got one having a bitch and a moan about wanting to pick up something she's ordered.'

'Keep on top of it,' he told her. 'Somebody close has to be asking questions surely. Need a partner, parents, close friends anything. Leave it with you, we're off.' Michelle Cooper and the DI were soon heading for that Cramp woman at Sutton on Sea.

Before they'd gone off Nicky was called by the Tech Crime Team back at base to advise they had come across calls on Simm's phone to unknown numbers. Chances are, cheap jack phones off the market or burners. Bristow couldn't imagine he'd be the sort to have a prepaid SIM, but then he knew so little about him. Just the one phone contract when he would have expected Simm to at least have one for personal use and another for the business. But then just the sight of him made that suggestion unlikely.

One of the local coppers had described him as a Wursel Gummidge, Jed Clampett sort of figure, some would have to Google. Then almost on cue Alisha was alive with gathering social media interest with somebody very kindly having placed an old photo on Twitter of Simm with two others at some charity event in the town a good few years previous. Slim, tidy in jeans and sweatshirt, with the absence of long untidy hair and scruffy beard.

At St Mary's and the temporary Incident Room, it was good to see things had moved on to some extent with help from the Tech Crime Team.

First up for Jamie and Jake was the DNA news from Shona to study in detail.

Jamie had ANPR data to check and view. Blue Ford Transit Courier backing out of the alleyway by the shop at 20.42, made everybody who watched it sag. It backed out towards the camera and drove off. They already knew it was found abandoned on the seafront. Check of the registration number confirmed it was his.

CSI delving had produced absolutely nothing untoward apart from the DNA from three, one of which was Simm. Other two annoyingly not on the database.

'Listen up everybody,' silenced his team as senior DS Jake motioned for quiet. 'Forensics at CSI Leicester have a match. Put the name on PNC and from what I can gather. Back in 2016 down south of the river, as they say in London,' he started with smiling. 'A woman committed suicide. That was linked to a domestic incident where this…' He stopped to check. 'Lewis female pulled out a pepper spray, illegal of course. Then bloody shot some bloke with it she's arguing with in the street. Witness phoned the Met, Lewis got herself arrested, being the reason for us having her DNA. Charged obviously, finished up in court with a hefty fine.' Goodwin stopped as he read to himself again and peered up.

'Three weeks later she jumped in front of an Underground train at Blackfriars in the city.'

Jamie grimaced. 'Sad I know, but true to form. Time I've spent in Mablethorpe and typically so far the only clue we've got's a dead violent woman in London a good few years back.'

'Decision time,' said Jake as he stood up. 'If this has all moved to London d'we really need to be sat out here? Messaging base by semaphore. I'll call the boss, but start getting prepared to pack up and get back to Lincoln.'

'Sandy,' said DS Goodwin to his big Scot. 'You finished in Victoria Road?'

'Yes Sarge.'

'Like you to take this on in the morning back at base. What's with this attack and subsequent suicide? How's it connected to us if it is? Give the Met a call will you please. You may have to go through the Darke boss. Reckon the boss and Stevens'll give you pointers, as they worked down there at one time.

'Will do.'

'Simm's place all shut up?'

'Shona's lad's are doing it, and letting the cop shop up by Tesco know.'

'Jake,' Nicky Scoley called across the hall, phone still in hand. 'Just been told there's a guy says he knows Simm. Been onto Central.'

'Somebody at last. Thank god for that!'

'See if he'll see me tonight, what d'ya reckon?'

'He from around here?'

'Yeh sort of west of the town.'

'Better than trooping all the way across here,' Jake suggested. 'If you're stopping on make sure you eat eh?'

'Yes Jake.' At times he was worse than her mum, but his intentions were in the right place.

11

Deciding not to refresh themselves before they set off, turned out to be the right decision for Michelle Cooper seated beside boss Bristow in his Hybrid. Improvement in the weather was indeed a help.

There was nothing special about this middle-aged Molly Cramp at the door of her detached big bungalow, at Sutton on Sea.

The woman was of medium height with dark hair pulled back to form a pony tail, enjoyed a slim build along with a hint of blusher. Pale yellow jumper and blue jeans with fluffy slippers were not out of place.

Shown into a tidy lounge the detectives were ushered to sit either end of a three-seater sofa with Cramp flopping down in a matching armchair. No sign of tea or coffee but from the get go wanted to know the whys and wherefores of the case and hinted at wishing to be privy to more graphic details than the pair were willing to divulge.

Bristow was concerned realizing there was no heating on. Would this Cramp woman have sat with a blanket over her knees had they not turned up, with energy costs being what they are?

Cramp appeared somewhat concerned in the knowledge Simm had been murdered and then almost as an after thought she offered tea and coffee. Murder would certainly be better gossip with her pals than natural causes. All three chose the tea Cramp served in matching blue mugs. No biscuits Cooper noticed to remind her the old boss Inga Larsson always regarded something to nibble as a perk of the job.

'How did you come into contact with Harry Simm initially?' she started with.

'Told about him, somebody suggested him…'

'How was he as a person,' Michelle slid in. 'As somebody you had to deal with?'

'He was fine to be honest,' was her retort with glotta fry to her voice. 'Not like some we've had over the years. Had one doing an annual service of our alarm system at one time thought he was God's gift to women and another gave me the creeps when he came to change a radiator.'

'Had you known him before you commissioned the gate?' Which neither detective had so far been able to view.

'No. Sort of heard of him. As I said, friend told me about him,' she disclosed. 'Then picked up a review on social media when we were looking for something different. A talking point. Timmy gave him a call and he came round to have a look.'

'Timmy?' Cooper had to slip in.

'My husband.'

'Was there only him?' the quiet Detective Inspector asked.

'Plus when they started, some guy digging the hole and sorting concrete.'

'Anything odd you noticed, maybe somewhat pre-occupied as if he had something on his mind?'

'Not that I noticed, just looked a bit unusual if you get my meaning. Please bear in mind I left him to it most of the time. Filled my time popping to the shops and that.'

'Did your husband get to know him at all?'

'Bit like ships passing in the dark. First day he did, when they were digging holes, putting in the posts and concrete, I seem to remember. Think he stayed to see it all dry. Something tells me, second day Timmy got home I seem to remember around the time he was leaving.'

'Did you meet socially,' was a Michelle Cooper probing whilst meeting her gaze,

'How d'you mean?' was abrupt.

'Meet him for a coffee, for a drink as people do. Maybe.'

This Cramp hurried out a breath. 'Why d'you say that sort of thing? This person doesn't,' was firm and blonde Cooper almost sighed. 'All this silliness such as everybody watches Netflix, when I don't know a single person who does. Everybody this, everybody that. With the same everybody drinking gin, flying abroad they say time and again on the news when the sensible have more sense.'

'Anything else you can think of?' the chestnut haired detective asked in an attempt to move on. 'We're trying to paint a picture of him and his life.' This chat just the same as the whole case was going nowhere at a good rate of knots. To some extent Cooper felt this was how it would be trying to understand the life style of a hermit and write a biography.

'Remember, one evening he's working late, so we offered to order more take-away to include him. Told him I think I'm right in saying it would be Indonesian, one of our favourites at the time. Said it was not his sort of food as if there was a nasty smell about it. Seemed a bit odd turning down the offer of a free meal. Nothing out of the ordinary, just Nasi Goreng and Gada-gade. So we took it he was a picky eater and probably heading straight for McDonalds when he left us.'

'Or had a partner to go home to with food waiting. Had you thought of that?'

'Never mentioned one.' Cramp picked up her blue mug and drank, then sat there with it in both hands at her lap.

'Any chance you smelt alcohol on his breath?'

Momentarily she just peered at Cooper as if trying to comprehend. 'Thinking about it,' she mused after a few moments contemplation. 'Realized he'd been smoking cannabis. Couple of times when he was here working I went out and could smell it when I got back.' She put a hand up to stop the queries. 'Our daughter at one time knew a lad who used cannabis. Thankfully she saw sense, but did go through a bad phase with her around that time accusing us among other things of being old fashioned and out of touch. Trying to tell us cannabis was part and parcel of everyday life.' Cramp was quickly back to her tea and Cooper took the opportunity to do the same. 'Don't think Timmy's record collection of country rock albums he played to annoy her helped at the time, ' she admitted. 'But, hey. She got over it and to be fair he still plays the Eagles. Creedence Clearwater and all that.'

'You say he didn't mention he had a meal waiting for him at home, but did he ever mention a woman in his life, former partner maybe? Talk about kids?' boss Oliver Bristow asked as Cooper took the opportunity to sit back trying to fathom how the Eagles had got into the conversation and what sort of milk was in the tea. 'Male or female,' had Cramp shaking her head immediately and eyes widen. Molly sat back in her comfy armchair, mug of tea in hands as she pondered, but that suggestion brought her to life.

'Difficult to remember, but could easy have mentioned somebody but I don't think he did. While ago now of course,' she suggested. 'Maybe...when...could be when the other guy was here first day, they were laughing about some woman. Could have been his woman I s'pose, but how was I to know?' she shrugged at. 'Didn't spend much time with him when he was out there working. Chatted mostly when I made a coffee for his break and his snack lunch.'

'Would you say he appeared pre-occupied, nervous maybe?' Bristow asked.

She pursed her slim pink lips. 'I've no idea. Remember I didn't know him until he started the work. Timmy dealt with him when he came round to have a look initially.' She sighed again to show she'd lost interest.. 'Sorry I'm not being much help. I know the local butcher better than him.'

'What about phone calls? Did he have many when he was working?' Cooper knew the phone data would be with them any day, but knowing how frequently he used his phone could be aligned to the provider's info. Might also hint at another phone.

'One or two calls I think. Those I heard seemed to be with the other people who helped him, or made stuff for him. Didn't go out the back much so I couldn't hear or do anything sly like that.' Tall Bristow was about to speak, but. 'Got to say as far as I can remember none of the calls as far as I could recall, sounded like they were with a woman,' Cramp added.'Nothing like thanks pet, bye duck or anything like that you get round here. Sort of thing you get with other tradesmen. Some are never off them.'

'Thank you, Molly. Think that's about it for now. Mind if we have your phone number?' Cooper asked.'Our tech analysts will be checking his phone and it makes life easier if they know in advance who some of the people are and their connection.'

Drinks partly drunk, questions answered, info exchanged including Cooper handing over her card and the woman showed them out.

'Look,' said this Cramp woman at the door. She looked left and right down the road for no reason. 'Please don't tell anyone, but...he squeezed my breast when he left the last time. Sort of cupped it, smiled at me, then walked off to his van.'

'Mrs Cramp…'

'Nothing more,' she said flapping her hand in front of her face as some tend towards. 'Understand? My Timmy gets wind o'this be hell to pay. Get accused of egging him on and all sorts.' She pointed her finger at the Detective Inspector. 'You tell a soul and I'll deny it, I'll tell the bloody world its something else the bloody Police ballsed up,' and closed the door.

Oliver Bristow and Cooper just looked at each other.

'What was that all about?' Michelle queried in the car before Bristow pulled away. 'Why d'we get all that business right at the end there?'

'Quite agreeable, not much help and then that nasty spat.'

'Tell us earlier and with a bit of probing, maybe we'd…'

'Psychiatrist'll tell you she's been desperate to brag to someone.'

'Chances are, bit of a cheap thrill in her boring little world.'

'Another enigma,' Michelle sighed. 'You into Indonesian food?' she asked her boss as they headed away from Cramp.

'If I go foreign tend to stick with Thai and Chinese but only occasionally,' Oliver remarked. 'Trouble with Korean or Indonesian is, I'd not know what to order. Finish up with their version of fish and chips with a coating of jelly and cold custard as a side dish,' made Michelle chuckle.

'And how on earth did we get round to the Eagles?'

'When I left home this morning I never imagined I'd be trying to fathom a connection between somebody's stupid daughter's angst, pride in a sexual assault and Simm's hypothermia.'

‘With Hotel California thrown in.’

‘Think we could do with a decent coffee,’ was almost an instruction as he pulled off right and headed back towards Mablethorpe and a decent coffee.

Michelle had never heard of the DI suggesting coffee with anyone. Knew DS Goodwin had issues over the boss’s behaviour at times and she’d check with him when they get back.

The pair chatted about bits of pieces of news before Michelle moved inevitably back to subject.

‘So, what d’you reckon? Any further forward?’

‘People do the strangest of things,’ Oliver suggested after sipping. ‘What we’ve just encountered was a prime example.’

‘If you’re scared stiff your old man’ll find out, then why say anything at all?’

‘Added nothing to our inquiry. Sorry but we’re not looking for a sexual offender. He’s the one attacked.’

‘Or are we?’ brought their conversation to a halt temporarily.

‘Sorry?’

‘That why he was killed?’ was a suggestion from Michelle out of nowhere. ‘This somebody’s partner getting his own back?’ Bristow was sat there slightly opened mouthed before he took a good drink.

‘He pulled that stroke on somebody else,’ was a slow bland reaction. ‘She like Cramp had to tell somebody or told her partner and wham bam it’s lights out.’

‘Husband walked in and caught them. She told a friend who blabbed.’ Oliver saw her big smile. ‘What now?’

‘Sorry, but you’re suggesting he could only have assaulted a female. In this day and…’

‘Sorry,’ was fast. ‘Yeh, yeh whichever way.’ Oliver sat sipping and peering at Michelle over his big cup. ‘Say he assaulted the husband. Are you saying the killer was female? That’s why there’s no gun, no knife no fisticuffs CSI can fathom. Something was plopped in his drink, dragged outside.’

‘Not necessarily assaulting a woman, but even if it is,’ she put up a hand. ‘Hear me out. He assaults a customer in the same way he did Cramp but maybe a few stages further on, and its her partner who deals with him,' she said and hesitated. 'Why there's no sign of a fight or anything.'

'And at times like these we wonder why we have trouble fathoming what's going on. Now to add to it struggling to find out anything about Simm and what he's been up to. A house near us has been sold but remained empty for a few months. Then suddenly so my friends were telling me last week, a hire van turned up for three days and unloaded furniture and all sorts expecting them to move in. Now they're back with a different hire van removing all the stuff again.' He just smiled and shook his head slightly. 'Nowt as strange as folk, as they say.'

'Any idea why?' DC Michelle Cooper queried before returning to her Blueberry muffin.

'Not as yet,' he responded. 'That's where this job tends to get in the way. People I know close to me are just curious and nosy because its very odd. Not me. I've been asking for descriptions of what they're removing. When it came to a load of big boxes apparently they needed the tail lift to get them in the van. I'm all ears. This could be where they store stuff,' he stopped and smiled cheekily. 'Somewhere less conspicuous, just an average property in an average area. Could easily be stuff for a cannabis farm?' He shrugged as he tended to. 'Well, it was just one idea a brain like mine has come up with and to make matters worse nobody has moved in. That idea, stolen property and boxes full of heroin is best I've come up with. Things out of the ordinary stand out in somewhere such as where I live.'

'This is not getting the Simm issue dealt with,' keen Michelle said just as Oliver's phone rumbled as he moved it from mute. 'D'you want me to take it on?' she asked. 'I check all Simm's records looking for a female customer and then a female partner?'

'Oh my word,' he said too loudly and dropped his voice. 'Message from Shona to me, copied to Jake,' he said quieter as he leant forward over the table. 'Leicester have come up trumps with two samples on the sweetener. One is Simm and the other...' he shook his head and pulled a face. 'What's been taking the time apparently. Belongs to a familial they've linked back to a woman in London who committed suicide back in 2016. A Miriam Lewis.'

Michelle Cooper sitting there with her eyes firmly closed was a picture. 'Do we take DNA from suicides, d'you know?'

'Not sure, but she says its linked to a domestic dispute.' Michelle put a lump of muffin back on her plate and peered up at her boss for more. 'Think we have the makings of a green light at last. Drink up, we'll get back and see what's cracking off.'

12

Mid-terrace fairly new build in town and Nicky Scoley had been a good girl. With the temporary Mabo Incident Room all packed up and everybody heading back inland, she was still by the seaside. What better than Fish, Chips and Mushy Peas for her tea with a strong cuppa?

This rugged but slim Richard Clifford who opened the front door for her was clean shaven and tidy even if he was wearing shorts, her Connor insists are only worn for playing sport. But then flip-flops should never leave the beach according to fashion experts, but loads do.

They went through the usual introductions he asked to be called Rich, before Scoley turned down the offer of a drink having had one with her meal.

'Tell me about Harry Simm,' she started with rather than just ramble on about the weather and all sorts.

'Not a lot to be honest,' was not a great start. Was a waste of time staring her in the face? 'Me missus got to know him first,' he went on fortunately. 'We bin here about a year or so, and she's after making a good fist o'doin' up the garden. Decided like women do, she wants some sort of central feature. Pal of hers suggests Harry Simm's Curious place in town'd be a good bet.'

'You knew him,' Scoley checked.

'No. Not at all. Off she toddles one lunchtime and when she gets home reckons he'll make something for us. Saturday morning first thing off we both go and I'm wearing me Mariners sweat shirt and bugger Lucy and the garden, this Harry bloke wants to talk about footie. Moaning he can't go Saturdays havin' to run the shop and that.' He grimaced. 'Wouldn' suit me I can tell yer.'

At that point the backdoor opened and in walked a young looking mid-thirties woman. Rich Clifford introduced his partner and explained Scoley's presence, sat in one of the armchairs.

'Just sayin,' Clifford says as she sat down on the sofa next to him. 'We're after that big sunflower thing Harry made when we first got to know him.'

'Wonder we ever got it,' she said sharply, sighed and shook her head. 'Codheads come first again!'

'Anyway,' Rich Clifford ignored the remark and carried on. 'We don't go to matches together much. I'm a season ticket holder and he pays at turnstile Tuesdays or Wednesdays coz he can't go on Saturdays like.' Scoley went to interject but he was far from finished. 'Gave me a lift once when me car's in for service.'

'I'm told you mentioned when you called, about the last time you saw him.'

'Fancy a coffee?' this Lucy asked Nicky Scoley and was on her feet.

'No thanks. Not long had one,' she lied. 'But don't let me stop you.'

'No point asking you,' she said down to Richard and walked off into the kitchen.

'Last time you saw Harry Simm?' Scoley reminds.

'Yeh,' he muses. 'Be that really wet Tuesday last week. Mariner's match called off and Harry gimme a bell. Says how d'ya fancy a pint?' He sucked in a breath. 'Not summat he'd normally do like on the spur of the moment.' He hesitated. 'D'you know I think the poor sod was lonely.' Clifford sat up straight and shifted forward in the chair. 'Look. Lucy'd got a couple o'her pals comin' round, so a couple of pints'll get me out the house for a bit. Might be footie on the tele there.'

'And you met him?'

'Got held up at work, so got to Book In Hand a bit late and Harry's full of it.'

'You've met there before?' the blonde detective asks.

'No. I normally meet me mates in The Louth, but Harry's a bit particular about his beer. Turn up an' he can't get it out fast enough. Reckons he's sat there suppin' and this sort of photographer's talent spotter just walks up. Offers him a chance for some photo and video work and…'

'Any indication of who it was?'

'No idea,' Clifford responded and shook his head. 'Been gone ten minutes when I turn up. Harry gave me the card and says he's gotta phone for an appointment.' Clifford pulled a face almost out of habit. 'Gotta say I was well pissed off missing out. Still am to be honest. Hardly an oil painting our Harry was he? No spring chicken an' all that scruffy shaggy hair like that Boris and stupid straggly beard,' he shrugs. 'Guess they must be in need of something odd, eh?'

'But he gave no indication who it was?'

'I was just gonna say. He'd not look like that if he was livin' with my missus.'

'No clue as to who it was? Scoley continued with. 'Tall, short, fat?'

'Look,' he sighed partly with frustration. 'Like he's as pleased as bloody Punch. Who it was didn't bloody matter all he could see was the cash register an' that. Not sure his funny old shop's doing too well to be honest.'

'On the matter of a woman not wanting him looking like he did,' said Scoley. 'What about women? He ever talk about one?'

Rich Clifford pouted before he blew out a breath as his partner walked back in with two mugs. 'Harry ever mention a woman?' Rich asked up to Lucy as she handed down a Grimsby Town mug.

'May have made some sort of derogatory remark at one point. An' took it he'd fallen out big time, got divorced or whatever.'

'Said something to me,' Rich Clifford slipped in. 'Sounded something like she's a daft ha'peth to me. Did well to get rid I reckon.'

'Name?'

Both shake their heads and sipped their coffee.

'That business in the pub,' Clifford asked his woman. 'D'you remember if I said what the name was?'

'Nah. Don't think so.'

‘He ever been here by any chance?’ Scoley posed.

‘Here?’ Lucy shot out.

‘That’s somewhere between highly unlikely and no bloody chance,’ said Clifford. ‘Not a bloody mate, just some guy we knew. Right?’

They did their best but at the end of half an hour there was very little extra to say.

Mid morning next day back in Lincoln Central, after Nicky Scoley had revealed everything the Cliffords had told her, Alisha was roped in to phone the pub Rich Clifford had said they went to.

At the same time Michelle Cooper was head down going through copies of Simm’s invoices she had obtained from the Economic Team. Their confirmation of no relevant SAR (Suspicious Activity Report) from his accountant was useful.

Under the auspices of DI Bristow her task was to hunt down female customers and then establish what relationship they may have. Male or female.

She knew she had to be very careful what questions she asked as she endeavoured to discover a likely candidate. She had been put off early on by a remark from Jamie Hedley when she explained her task.

‘And if Simm did touch-up a female customer and she was a cash sale no questions asked, how d’you fathom that?’

While she gets on with that, DC Sandy MacLachlan presented what he’s discovered so far to the team about the connection to a woman south of London.

‘This Miriam Rebecca Lewis aged 47,’ he opened with. ‘Lived a wee bit south of this Blackfriars station, south o’ the river. Worked at a Kentucky Fried Chicken and lived with a Stephanie Brammer and her husband. Brammer is an old school friend of this Lewis. According to the Met she’d been living with them for aboot six months having become separated from her partner. As luck would have it the Brammer’s were away on holiday when Lewis attacked this guy in the street one night. Arrested, charged, eventually went to Court fined an’ had a two year sentence suspended for two years. Days after the court case she jumps in front of a Tube train.’

'Jumped or pushed.'
'They say jumped.'
'While the balance of the mind,' Oliver Bristow grimaced with. 'Over the court case.'
'This be because she couldn't afford the fine d'they know?'
'Know of nae reason or at least nowt we've come up with,' replied Sandy. 'What they did discover is when the Brammer's returned from holiday this Lewis didnae say a word, and only discovered about it after she committed suicide. It was all in the local paper about her attacking the guy.'
'And he was who?' Oliver asked.
'Disappeared into the night.'
'Seriously?'
'Gave his name and address to the lads down there who arrested her apparently. Later when they wanted him as a witnesss for the inquest discovered he didn't exist. Naebody by that name lived where he said he did an' never had.'
'So he didn't press charges.'
'Witness and CCTV did for her, but they never discovered who the attacked guy was.'
'And she's connected somehow to Simm,' was Oliver thinking out loud. 'Long shot Nicky,' he said 'This Simm they're talking about? How else would he be linked? Looking for GPS from his phone back then,' Oliver continued with from his notes. 'You got dates and times?' he asks of Sandy.
'Nae bother.'
'Michelle?' he asked. 'Any news yet?'
'Tom, Dick and Harry. Best I've come up with is one or two women running small businesses, like a hairdressers. One bought a head from Simm made from nuts and bolts as a sort of statement piece for her shop window. Reckoned she had no partner when I asked and made a nasty remark about men.'
'Anything else?'
'Women on the invoices are few and far between to be honest. Get the impression it's usually men buying something for their partners. D'you know anybody who'd buy a dog made of wire for their husband?'

Maybe she'd have to admit Jamie was right. Cash sales were a major issue, but then defrauding the tax man was then more likely.

'Thanks for that,' said Oliver. 'Nicky. Job for the Tech Crime Team if you will,' he pulled a face as a reaction to the look he received. 'Long shot I know but as Jake says, what else we got.'

Alisha's call to the pub had proved as Michelle's endeavours had been. Frustrating. The publican knew who Simm was once he had been described. Not exactly somebody you'd not notice in a crowd. He turned out to be another claiming not to know him other than to serve pints to. He admitted who he now knew to be Simm since his death had been a major topic of conversation, and suggested he tended to be on his own. Just an odd looking sullen guy who'd sit in the bar now and again. At the most once a week. This Bill Arnold told her if he didn't look the unkempt way he did, he'd hardly be noticed.

When some of the early toxicology results landed on Oliver Bristow's laptop back at base on the Wednesday they were pretty much along the lines of what he was expecting.

Hush time descended as the DI stood up from the table he'd been allocated, smart phone to hand.

'Here we go,' he said. 'First things first. Lividity tells us, he died just where he was found. Not killed some place else and then dumped there. Few more difficult tox results still to come, in particular the sugar sachet's gone to CSI Leicester which says its not straight forward. But Shona suggests it could with luck be a primary signifier. Generally the PM's as we expected.' DCS Craig Darke had taken on the unpleasant task with them all having been stuck out at the coast and catching-up to be getting on with. 'Our Harry Simm had taken or was subjected to an immediate-acting benzodiazepine Rohypnol to you and me, or fluntrazepan if you wish to be technical,' Bristow read from his phone. 'It would appear the two mugs may well have been involved as Simm's stomach content amounted to nothing more than a cheese sandwich and black coffee.' he hesitated. 'Coffee and mug eh? If we've got that right, it was just an incapacitator, as cause of death was hypothermia. Not moved since death as hypostatis tells us. We may however get a bit of help on that score. With luck they'll be able to come up with what brand of coffee.'

'Already asked Sandy,' said Jake. 'Back there this morning to grab the jar for us.'

Oliver nodded his thanks. 'What do we know now?' he asked. 'Jamie. Bank, please.'

'I covered that guv,' said a dispirited Nicky Scoley before Jamie could utter a word. 'Sorted it through Connor. He photographed the bank statements for me and they're now on here,' she said tapping her laptop. 'Two accounts at Barclays. Bit old world having paper statements, but his personal account has a little over three grand. Nothing extraordinary going out or coming in. Salary from Curious Odds and Sods and gets paid in on 1st. Pays out for shop mortgage and all the usual Council Tax and stuff. Pays out a sum each month into an account at Nationwide, we need to get our hands on. Business account also looks pretty normal. No bundles of drug money paid in. No sign of laundering, but he takes cash out a lot which I suspect is him paying for the stuff he sells, like from that Pinhero woman.'

What she failed to announce was Connor back in Lincoln had attended what to all intense and purposes appeared to be an unexplained. It was, but the unexplained bit was why? Why had a sober twenty year old who never took drugs jumped from a five storey student block

'Anything on the phone records yet?' the DI asked Michelle.

'Waiting on the Tech Crime Team scouring his mobile. Requests gone in for provider data,' Michelle responded.

'Any news on his clothes?' Bristow asked.

'Still no clothes that can be easily attributed to the event, ' Jake offered. 'Unless you want his whole wardrobe checked for DNA. Apart from those in the wardrobe all we have are the pants he was wearing when found. Assuming nobody's ironed what he was wearing of course and hung it up. Linen basket had nothing more than socks, underpants and a few t-shirts.' He grinned. 'Had to be wearing more than that unless something funny was going on.'

Alisha was next. 'Facebook page in his name,' she started with. 'But its all about showing off his work with photos. No bad reviews or comments, but sadly also virtually no personal messaging. Snapchat account not been in use for months. Nothing to help, but Monday night the Twitter chatter started. Stuff like whats going on in Vicky Road, meaning Victoria. What the...pigs cars doing there? From one I've been given a note of.'

'Keep an eye on that, please.' Bristow said as he turned back to his team. 'Your thoughts Jake.'

'Got to say,' his Detective Sergeant said as he raised his eyebrows. 'It pretty much looks as though this was not random but also how I ask did everything fall into place by sheer chance? Especially the weather. He was home alone we assume. Nobody's mentioned seeing anybody or a car. Except with the shops shut it'd be expected I guess apart for a restaurant. A lack of witnesses on a freezing cold night, lack of local rumours nobody can plan for. No debts we know of as yet, certainly not drug related as Simm's not on any list the drugs lads have.'

'Could always be a drug debt and he's paid the price,' Jamie offers.

'Drugs barons are never that sophisticated, nor do they usually pop in for a cuppa,' were Jake's thoughts. 'He's not even got a cannabis caution.' Before Bristow can react he's back. 'What about burners?' finishes what he had to say.

'None Shona's team have come across as yet. Social media's still weak, but him hardly being socially active doesn't help. Time for a good kicking.'

'How d'you give him a kicking guv?' was Jamie.

'Not him,' said Bristow. 'The case. Visit his next door neighbours, a form of doing the door-to-door again. Making sure its more in depth than the cursory one Sandy quickly organized. Slip murder in their neighbourhood into the conversation. In these difficult times their sort are constantly worried about anything affecting sales. So, we light the blue touch paper and stand back.'

'Be a reason for what the weird and wonderful call room rise.'

'We need friends and family not just neighbours but they might just give us an entry card.'

'Want to stir the water, could try the people who supply him with odds and sods like the Pinhero female.'

Jake slapped his hands on his thighs. 'We doing this boss while the coffee's still warm?' Jake asked. 'Jamie,' he said when the boss nodded.

13

Hello again. How are you getting on? I heard mention of Harry Simm from Gloria when she first arrived at the Refuge. From what I was given to understand, initially his father owned the house he lived in. Got to be with his first partner in one of the villages close to Lincoln. Branston, Potterhanworth, somewhere out that way.

When Gloria couldn't take any more of his controlling, browbeating and bullying she threatened to leave him. Next day the bastard dumped all her clothes and stuff out on the street in the pouring rain.

Truth of course is she should never have given him any inkling of her plans. Just go. Prepare well, make plans, but go and don't look back.

She'd finished up in a Refuge for a while until she'd got her act together and found a new job. During one session with me. Gloria reckoned his old man gave him the house for Christmas.

Talking of Christmas I spent it with Ruthie's sister Amy. Her husband Karl and their two children. A proper family Christmas.

While we're briefly on the subject. One client I have to contend with spends Christmas Day with her family. This includes their two grown up kids, one hers, one her partner's and her ex-husband who she says used to bash her about.

I dare not ask too many questions as the whole concept is beyond my imagination. Save to say her brutal ex even turns up in time for breakfast!

Always wondered if after Christmas pud, wine and a few bevvies she suggests he stay the night rather than drive home. If you're wondering about sharing a bed. I'm *not* going there.

Now into the new year, it has been quite a while since any mention of Simm appeared in the media.

When Gloria'd finally had enough of Simm and walked out, he'd sold the place and moved to Mablethorpe. Taking with him a sullied reputation nobody would be aware of, before friends told her he'd bought that old shop and workshop.

The tricks pulled by some on the undermanned and beleaguered Police was not something with hindsight I needed to repeat. At the time with Miriam in mind, after dealing with Simm there was a degree of showing off whirling around and feeling impelled all part and parcel of the moment I experienced. A sort of victory jig.

Using the wreck of a car I'd bought in Miriam's name reminded me of the bad times in her life. Why in God's name had she been allowed to take driving lessons, when the moment she passed on the second attempt did that bastard of hers refuse to allow her to drive.

Apart from part of the controlling techniques having to use her own money for what turned out to be waste of time was just downright nasty and spiteful. What do you gain from such behaviour other than the desperate need for control?

I know I could have asked more questions of Andrea, but keeping her well away from my plans was a necessity. She needed to be oblivious to what I was up to.

Brendon Quinton when I was first told about him, had been just a bod working for the Council, living in a rented semi probably with the ubiquitous too-big telly plonked on a wall, with fairly regular habits. Or so I understood.

It had been difficult for me to meticulously plan what I needed to be ready for, when large chunks of a person's life are just blank.

Living out at Waddington was a bit of a pain, but not as bad as Mabo of course. Discovering early the first morning he caught a bus into town rather than driving, threw a bit of a spanner in the works.

Next day, I'd got on the same bus as him and when he got off so did I. Having seen him walk the same route for four days I took it to be his norm. Same stop, same bus ending up in the main bus station in Lincoln.

Brendon Quinton wore a suit to work and I guessed the bus was cheaper than parking. A bit of a pain for me to be honest. Having then to walk back to the bus station in order to catch a bus back to Waddo to pick up my car.

"Works for the Council" was about as much as I knew about a proper job as he'd changed employment since Andrea was getting battered by him, but she did tell me he was also a DJ. When the thought of going clubbing was about to consume me, she did mention local radio. With that news there was some consideration I gave to him not being at all what one would assume.

Suit, shirt, tie and polished shoes suggested important, but what if? What if, once inside the council building he changed into overalls ready to replace a light bulb, sweep the floors and undertake other maintenance tasks? Was he to some extent living a lie as he'd done previously?

Read about people doing that, to such an extent even their neighbours believe their friend has a career way above what is real. Really sad to think some people feel the need to live a life based on lies.

I'd even at one point considered double-checking up on him just to make sure by phoning:

"Lincoln Borough Council"

'May I speak with Brendon Quinton, please?'

"Can you tell me which department?"

What can you do or say if you don't know, or they ask who's calling, but end the call?

It was at times difficult to know how to play him when large chunks of his life were still a mystery to me. Where he lived in that semi provided a loud and clear message to say what he was *not* spending his time doing at work.

He could easy work in the Council Tax office, be a Resettlement Support Worker. Not the Chief Executive however as I've seen him on *Look North* spouting excuses about his lack of interest in climate change. Couldn't possibly be some highfalutin job, unless he had maybe a gambling or drink problem meaning some time back he'd lost his home.

That'd be before Andrea got to know him, unless he somehow managed to keep his problem under wraps as they often do. Was that what was behind his disgusting violence? The controlling, intimidation, the lies and deceit, not to mention being more than being a bit handy with his fists.

With all due respect to the nice people who live there, if he had a well-paid job surely he'd be outta there a bit sharpish. Unless this was some sort of political aspect by using the likes of Brendon Quinton to live the life of some poor residents the District Council take rent off. Was he in fact a Council snoop I'd heard of other places using? Interesting how a single male council worker was living in what could easily be home to a family in more need. Keeping an eye on the plebs could if it were true, be the reason behind it. A Council stickybeak a friend calls them.

My own database had provided me with a pattern of behaviour for Quinton as a respite from doing the same with Ross my third and most important in line. On Mondays Quinton tended to arrive home and stay in for the evening. Thus providing, an opportunity to do his chores. Washing and ironing more than likely along with watching *EastEnders* or some reality nonsense.

There is no way on earth I can sidle up to and have a word with a drinking pal in the Horse & Jockey and ask when Quinton washes his kecks.

Tuesday was different in that he didn't work. Or, worked from home as far as I could gather. To be certain would need me being parked up down his road for eight hours. Not going into work rules out many jobs like cleaning the toilets. Wednesday he was back on the bus into town just after eight. Worked at the Council offices and then by going through all the local radio programme schedules I knew what his eventual destination would be. That is unless he recorded his effort and they just played a tape. First up I watched him appearing at his local pub to meet up with two or three guys for nothing more than for him just a good boy pint and a natter. Be him putting the world to rights and moaning about the Imps.

Then as expected he jumped in his car and headed off back into the city and what had at one time been an old industrial building now a centre for business start-ups and Yellerbelly FM.

First time I sat in my car listening to his Night Train programme, I was surprised he'd ever been let loose on the air waves. With a voice sounding like he'd gargled with grit rather than mouthwash sounded more than a tad peculiar.

Sorry to all those who are into it, but hip hop to me is dire. All no-tune, unfathomable African-American youth lyrics born out of New York wrapped up in black politics seems to me. But then maybe I'm too long in the tooth for it.

For somebody brought up on the timeless offerings of Stock, Aitken and Waterman this other stuff would never be my bag. As they say.

Next two Wednesdays, at least I was sat at home listening in comfort as he raved on about music icons in between tracks. Sorry, but I've never begun to understand the idolization of these so-called celebs.

Thursday I thought he'd overslept or was working from home again. Then action. Spied him being picked up around half nine in the morning and followed as close as I safely could for as far as I dare. Out into the countryside and I discovered what appeared to be some environmental survey business going on. Be counting frogs or stinging nettles. At least that answered that question and I had an idea what he worked on.

Be one of those Environmental framework schemes nobody can understand or more likely dealing with some wildlife and nature conservation business. Be his role to discover a unique flower nobody gives a tinkers for, in order to divert the new bypass a mile to the west costing a good few extra million we all have to pay for.

Onto Friday back in the office, and after work I'd be waiting nearby for him to arrive home. Quick shower and change and Brendon was back on a bus, out and about in town. Time for more boozing but this time with a few pals. Most times three of them and once or twice two more were added to their ritual of nipping from bar to bar.

Have never begun to understand how some men can fill their bodies with eight or ten pints of what is basically coloured water. Then have room inside at the end of their sojourn to grab the inevitable kebab on the way home.

During my research I'd seen him stood in a queue for ages waiting to get served. Often wondered as I stood watching if he ever enjoyed a really tasteful Lamb Kopfte Kebab in a decent restaurant or anywhere without being stuffed full with all that booze. Looked to me like some sort of macho ritual.

Chances are he was never brave enough to tell all his mates he no longer wished to be dragged along the same boring scenario anymore, and just went along with it.

Taxi home was sensible and most times he shared with one or two of those he'd been boozing with.

Interesting to watch his routine, as boring as it was at times. Just when an industry report once again tells us more than a third of pub visits these days is alcohol free as the trend for moderation after the pandemic continues. Not for Quinton though.

Weekends were a real issue and not on the tactical list for the actual deed. This was when his Kia car came out and he was off somewhere all day on Saturday and Sunday or once or twice I'd noticed it was all weekend.

Following all the way was never really an option, in my car or the little runabout I'd bought for the occasion. I was never going to tag along behind miles and miles to wherever, driving too close as they do in films. Just twice having kept my distance and let him go on the busy A46 past Newark heading west.

What was that all about? Did he do hip hop on other radio stations someplace? Take his Night Train with him maybe? One far enough away where he had to stay overnight was possible.

At one time I did consider researching all local and community radio stations for sight of him and his programme on their schedules. If he used a different title and his name was not listed decided me against it.

I was still in need of information on him or with time in short supply to somehow get to know as much as I could. Quinton was certainly a sharper knife in the box than Simm had been and most certainly Ross was ever likely to be.

14

Never much of a reader, but Brendon Quinton had over the years come across quite a bit about people's sudden rise to fame on the net. Women talent spotted walking down the street, an actress approached by an agent at a bus stop. Every one an outlandish suggestion most of which he'd taken with a pinch of marketing salt.

Sort of thing he'd always laid at the door of PR gurus seeking publicity for their clients. Measles epidemic and some so-called celeb claims she once had the worse case of measles ever recorded, but doctors somehow managed to save her life in a desperate race against time. If it were not for them and the NHS she'd never have got that bit part in *Holby City*.

In Brendon's case it was never about everything going wrong for him. There had never been anything to go wrong. Now it had happened to him just like that, out of nowhere. Not a bout of measles. Being spotted.

Happening to a thin teenager in a mini skirt down in London on the Underground had over time become a legend. Being approached in out of the way Lincoln, had to Bren been a bizarre concept but to be happening to him was totally unbelievable.

It had never been a case of his luck having run out. It was never there in the first place. Broken home, single mum and a council estate had nowt to do with luck but more than enough ammunition for the bully boys at school.

There he was in the Wheatsheaf that Wednesday as per normal before he headed off to do his programme. Sat supping his pint of Tetley Bitter waiting for mates Mick and JJ to appear. Nodded to one or two he recognized as regulars and chatted to Will behind the bar as he poured his pint. Talk was about a woman from North Hykeham involved in a road traffic accident being charged with drink driving which was not particularly unusual. What had taken their interest was her being arrested before seven in the morning.

Knew JJ'd not be full of the joys of Spring with the Imps having lost again on Tuesday night. Off to Hillsborough the Sheffield lad regular as clockwork every other weekend. Midweeks were pretty much out with work commitments so Lincoln City got his cash.

Just sat there in his favourite spot watching the comings and goings as he supped a bit more aware of somebody, suddenly close by, looking down.

Quick 'Mr Quinton?' a brief chat, arrangements made to call on him, business card and inside a minute or two he'd been plucked out of thin air.

Since his wedding day this just had to be the best thing ever. Never admit it in a hundred years but he really was truly excited. New commercial radio station on the lookout for experienced young talent. Deejays away from the trend of plumping for the grey men Radio 2 had got rid of. This'll show the doubters, a happy boy said to himself sat there pint in hand.

How many times had he looked in the bathroom mirror since then? He'd always been pleased with what he saw and this special day was no exception. Knew there'd be promotional photos and media work for the station launch. Still had all his hair which had probably gone against quite a few others in the pub that evening, even those shaving their bonce for some reason. Daft haircuts were obviously a no no. Teeth good and white thanks to his mum and no beer paunch as yet. A strong nose he'd once been told spoke of better than average breeding.

Fancy folk'd not think that if they knew about his early life in that scruffy council flat, just him and his dear old mum doing two jobs to make ends meet. Had it not been for grandad Apedaile who'd coughed up a few readies from time to time, things would have been a damn sight worse. A young Bren was sure it was him and grandma who forked out for that smart as mustard decent school uniform when he went to Yarborough.

Not her fault he'd been an idiot at school. Mess-arsing about rather than head down learning and now just doing clerical and constantly moved from one place to another meant he was paying the price. But for how much longer?.

This was going to change things. Being told by that cocky bastard Arthur Kemp with a daft accent from Birmingham, he'd make nothing of his life was brilliant coming from somebody who at the pinnacle of his working life was measuring inside legs in a men's clothing shop. Like most of them these days, all choc-a-block with pretty boys.

This deejay work with great pay could easy see one of his visiting Gaming Championships dreams come true.

Brendon Quinton had always felt while living at home with his mother and this Kemp he was expected to pass off as his real dad, a distinct feeling of apprehension with regard to his sister's vulnerability. As a result it had been brother and sister seen out socially as a couple for quite a while. Rather than risk leaving her at home exposed to what that nasty bastard had in store. Now married to a good 'un she was no longer his direct day-to-day responsibility, yet the one always to keep an eye on.

When was the last time Brendon wondered to himself, when his life had taken such a dramatic turn for the better? Yeh. He'd done well from that mind numbing clerking job at Newark to end up at Lincoln. Had a girlfriend or two, then two nasty conniving women the less said about the better. More bad luck.

His name didn't help. Did his mum not think Quinton was odd enough without sticking Brendon in front? Over time he had gradually become Bren at junior school which inevitably with an unusual name changed when he got to Yarborough. All around him were three Chattertons, two Westerby's, a Pocklington, Brackenbury Dudding and Sardeson. Only one Quinton. 'Bren' was quickly ditched for Jail Bird. Was there any point in trying to correct the idiotic bullies' spelling of San-Quentin? In the hope it just might put an end to having Johnny Cash songs badly sung to him, in particular *A Boy Named Sue*. A tedious, boring and annoying form of bullying. Enough to get him into a few fights in the playground. Now it'd be a good name for radio.

Back to the real world and Bren was nervous and excited all at the same time, waiting for the sharp rap on his door and the ExpressMusicFM rep he'd met in the pub.

He'd not mentioned any of this radio business to anybody at work, especially to the cackling women. Certainly stayed silent in the Yellerbelly studios. To his mind daft rumours always came from frustrated soppy women and if it all went pear shaped then they'd make his life an absolute misery. He already suffered from their constant jibes, sarcasm and giggling when he walked in an office. Having egg on his face was something he'd suffered from too often earlier in life.

Knock knock on his door.

This was it. Time to show those silly cows. Heart racing with anticipation and eagerness he walked quickly down the short hallway to open it.

'Hello there.'

'Yeah. Come in,' handsome Bren said nervously as they shook hands and he pulled the red door wide open to allow entry. Smart suited and booted Bren stood back against the wall providing space to allow the big coated visitor to step over the threshold and then turn. 'Would you like me to take your coat?' he asked out of politeness.

'I'm good,' said his caller.

This was it, this was day one of a new life away from all the hassle and stress of boring work. Being shuffled about at the Council, getting nowhere fast he'd suffered from over recent years. This was the start of his trip to Singapore, that luxury hotel he'd looked at on the web. Maybe even a woman or two.

He closed the door quietly unlike most of his neighbours some of whom had taken to slamming as a sport.

He felt a hand grip his shoulder and as he spun back round Brendon instantaneously suffered a pain in his chest to make him grimace and gasp. When he glanced down a hand was pulling a knife from his chest. Then blood.

Mesmerized, confused and in absolute agony, he felt wobbly immediately just as he was about to strike out to defend himself. He screamed at more agony when the big blade was driven hard into his stomach. Brendon grabbed at himself to stem the flow to ease the pain, coughed up blood, slumped down to his knees, with his new future ending before it had begun, his back racked with pain.

15

Jake Goodwin had been first at work and in one of his self critical moods he suffered from sometimes he was just sat at his station pondering, looking all around wondering to himself.

He knew the chances were he'd have to move elsewhere. Kiss Lincoln goodbye if he really wanted promotion.

Thoughts of moving to goodness knows where would he knew bring him head to head with Sally. Working at Lincoln County Hospital. Senior Sister with a Matron post not far away, he'd never mentioned it to. Then there was young Tyler about to go to school. A move would take him into a strange environment. In addition of concern his Mum and Dad retired into the Lincolnshire countryside, long way from Betwys-y-Coed if he got a job somewhere like that.

He was always aware of chatter behind his back. Modern trends by the sackful appearing to change almost daily he allowed even if he was aware of them, to simply pass him by. At one time he'd made the fundamental error of asking Alisha why she wore two watches only to be told sarcastically one was a Fitbit. Any return from him was quickly scuppered with a couple more downstairs showing such devices as if that was the everyday norm. Mention of things such as K-pop he first thought was a new drink and then meme came along he had to Google, but still didn't understand.

Haircuts he'd never admit to any of the team was something Sally did for him with a machine she'd bought years ago. A lack of tattoos had once received the backing of his former boss who was very anti, especially for women. Now he was reluctant to ask Bristow and have him open his shirt to reveal a chest full. A hidden one maybe would suit him if they ever became mandatory but face, an arm full, neck and hands was never ever going to happen. Legs most certainly not as he never wore shorts, so there'd be no chance to show them off, the reason he decided so many do it.

He wasn't particularly bothered about being out of date with son Tyler not yet five, but as he got older knew the lad'll enter the world of bullies. A few times he'd been to Parents Evenings not as a parent as yet, but to give talks to the concerned in a Police glad-handing exercise.

Last time he'd noticed one or two father's in slightly offensive statement t-shirts and grubby shorts he'd never wear, let alone out of the house. Would Tyler suffer in later years from him being outdated and as some would suggest, badly dressed?

On the positive side he'd never introduce his son to the bad ways by taking him to a pub when only 17. Just what some do to establish a lifetime he'd never got close to, with a family of infrequent home wine drinkers.

Michelle was next in that day. She always had a small spray of artificial flowers on her desk, she changed from time to time. Sandy had a photo of his wife Rachel along with their kids Duncan and Kenna.

Inga Larsson when she was the boss had a photo on her desk of husband Adam and her parents all together. On a wall was a photo of her graduating from Bristol.

New man Bristow had nothing at all on his desk to further cause Jake concern.

Jake's desk was never pristine. But the Mouse son Tyler had given him for Christmas was just that. A mouse's face. Items such as a bottle of water he filled daily from the tap, and boring to some Salt & Shake crisps, he kept in a drawer.

Just a few weeks back around the time the News as it frequently did, was full of talk about solar systems being photographed as they were over 300 billion years ago. All about the time when some young woman during a request for witness information had said. "That's what comes of not being part of a TikTok group you can talk to in the bar."

Was he in the here and now and she from that solar system, or was it the other way round?

After morning briefing from Oliver with Nicky Scoley absent it was for Jake a case of working through all the Simm case actions. He was sitting back supping his morning coffee later when she returned. The blonde DS looked fed up and with a to go in hand slumped herself down at her station.

'Guess what?' she sighed as Oliver popped out from his office. 'Tech Crime Team have been going through Simm's phone, as you know. Checked out all the numbers he called back as far as a week previous. One odd-ball emerged when they tracked down who he'd called. Two minute call to a Sonja Sibbald. Expected it to be one of Simm's customers, but no. That's where I've been. Sonja Sibbald is a 63 year old in a nursing home suffering with dementia. According to staff as far as they are aware she's never had a mobile sinbce she's been with them and now she'd never fathom one. Good eh?' she said and sipped her coffee.

'Simm phoned somebody who not only has no phone,' Oliver mused. 'But can't use one if she had, and…'

'Got it in one,' Nicky reacted. 'Somebody has her phone. And guess what. It's the same number as the one on the business card Shona discovered upstairs. Atooz Photographic, she's already discovered as you know doesn't exist.'

'Keep on it please. Somebody has that phone. Relatives, friends. See who the nursing home can put you onto.

'Tried the number myself. Just no reply and doesn't even go to voice mail.'

Any other good news?'

Jake Goodwin head down peering at his monitor reading about the previous evenings arrests, a Code Red message out of nowhere ended his down in the dumps mood almost in an instant. Unexplained death, but to cheer him slightly this time just up in Waddington.

Time to grab all his bits and pieces, slip his jacket on, check his phone.

The DS had followed his Crime Scene Co-ordinator colleague along to the red front door, expecting to be shown the status of another cadaver despite Sandy's warning.

‘See what you mean. Think some grubby ditch somewhere’s better than this,’ said Goodwin, stood side by side with DC Sandy MacLachlan as the pair peered in the side doorway to the semi.

‘One thing’s for sure, this is never the same MO as Simm. Not cold enough for starters,’ he suggested on a sunny pale blue sky February morning.

‘Whenever I think of him sat out in that freezing fog it makes me shiver.’

‘He was unconscious.’

‘Even so. Just the thought of it.’

‘Better get on, Sarge’ said the Scot.

‘Not this way, not yet,’ was a warning from Pathologist Doctor Marcus Meller crouching on pads placed on the floor for him by CSI.

When they’d first come across each other in a twitten somewhere down south of the county Meller was close to being adamant he be adorned formally. Almost as if he expected it to be Mr Marcus Meller BSc (Hons) Edinburgh, to be addressed as Sir and genuflect.

Things had lightened since those days and their sense of humour turned out to be quite similar. Nowadays with some it was case of blue latex fist pumps Jake considered a remnant of Covid silliness.

‘Door-to-door boss?’ Sandy asked hopefully to Jake as he peered down once more at the mess that once was a white man.

‘OK, right.’ Jake nodded looking at what he faced. A man just caked in blood, took one more good look, turned and walked off back down the front path. ‘Witness d’you say?’ Jake checked with the uniform stood at the front gate. ‘Next door boss,’ he said pointing. ‘Woman called Margo,’ he pointed. ‘Offered us a cuppa. You might strike lucky.’

The road of detached small bungalows hardly spoke of wealth, prosperity and influence but certainly far away from sink estate status. Jake took the path to next door, but as it was partially open he tapped as he walked in.

‘Hello. Police,’ he’d announced just as a head poked out from what he realized had to be the kitchen.

‘Looking for Margo?’ he was asked.

‘Yes. I think I am.’

‘Through there pet,’ she pointed out. ‘Fancy a cuppa?’

‘Shouldn’t really, but…’ he grinned. ‘Why not, eh?’ Jake said to the thin woman and walked on into a lounge diner. Two more women were sat together on a two-seater worn sofa holding hands both looking up as he entered. ‘Sorry to disturb you ladies,’ he opened with. ‘Looking for who it was phoned us,’ he added as he waved his warrant card. ‘Police,’ he said gently. Jake looked down at the women in turn. He had a good smile when he decided to put it to use.

‘Be me,’ the elder looking of the two who’d quite obviously been crying.

‘Sorry to disturb you, but…’

‘Sit down, sit down,’ the other woman insisted. ‘You’re making the place untidy.’ Jake did as he’s been told although the place was not exactly pristine.

‘What can you tell me...Margo is it?’ Jake now seated asked, phone in hand.

‘Margo Leadbetter. Well…’ dressed in a plum coloured jumper and black trousers she cleared her throat. ‘Think I heard him come in, musta been around sixish, as I was just saying.’ She tapped her ear. ‘Think he’d bussed home, old car o’his gets him home bit sooner. Never go out before about half nine or thereabouts int’morning,’ made Jake realize she’d jumped nine hours and from him to her. ‘When the kiddies’ve gone to school. As I was going out to walk up to catch me bus, saw his door slightly open. When I popped me head in to tell him’s when I noticed.’ She shook her head, blew out a breath and spoke again almost at the same time. ‘Oh my word, goodness me. That was horrible. And such a nice man too.’

Jake recognized trauma and waited. ‘Then what?’

‘Went across to Audrey here,’ she lifted the second woman’s hand still clamped in her own. ‘Phoned Police for me; not up to it let me tell you. Phew! Too shaky after seeing all that. Goodness me yeah,’ sounded breathless. ‘Still a bit now.’

Jake knew this Margo Leadbetter’s home was next to last at the bottom of the road. Unlikely folk would walk all the way down the road and spot the door ajar except any visitors the woman might have had or those living opposite.

'And you had no reason to go out last evening,' he suggested, and Margo shook her head. 'And you had no visitors?

'No. Me daughters come at weekends so they can bring nippers along.'

With that the door opened more and the first person Jake had encountered walked in with a tray of teas. Heaps better Jake thought than the norm of being stuck in the middle of a damp field for hours and the cantankerous farmer not bothering to make a brew.

Cups were handed round to the two women and a mug was handed to Jake, he thanked the woman for.

'While you're all here, a couple of things. Is there anybody else you think we should speak to, and have any of you seen any strangers about the place at all?' The woman with the tea tray about to return to the kitchen went to speak before Jake continued. 'In particular what about unusual visitors next door?'

'One or two,' she said. 'But got to be a good week or so since.'

'How many of you have seen the body?' was without an instant response as they looked at each other with little more than a flick of their eyes. 'It's not a problem, just if anybody touched him say looking for a pulse we'll need you testing for DNA to eliminate you.'

'No,' said the two on the sofa in unison as their shoulders dropped and the tea lady nodded. 'All that blood...'

'Sorry,' said the woman with the tray looking as if she's in real trouble. 'I only looked. Obvious he was dead,' Jake would thoroughly agree with.

'That's fine. Thank you ladies.' Jake started on his tea. 'I'm afraid our forensic people will be next door for a day or two most likely. The ones all dressed in white, may wish to move you out I'm offering as a warning. They'll deal with everything for you. One good thing will be knowing your homes are safe with us about,' the women grinned at. 'Names and addresses please,' he said and produced a notebook he handed to Margo first and got on with his hot tea.

By the time Jake'd finished with the three women without leaving them with the impression they were not important enough to chat to, he returned to next door. At least to the doorway.

'Ah, there you are,' said a sarcastic pathologist Marcus Meller. 'Thought you'd gone for a tea break or nipped home.'

'Sorry no. Just been for a Full English. No way I can deal with this on an empty stomach'

Meller ignored the sarcasm. 'A Brendon Quinton early thirties. Appears fit and well apart from the obvious damage and colossal loss of blood. Two main arteries by the look of it. Medical connection possibly. Initial estimated time of death Sergeant?' he asked Jake. 'Some time last evening, probably one implement, sharp knife by the look of damage but it'll all become clearer when I get him back.' He stood up from a crouched position, holding his back as he did so. 'That's about me done for now. PM first in the morning do?'

'No problem I'll get DI Bristow to call you if not.'

'How's the ice man investigation getting along I heard about?' he asked as he returned articles to his bag just inside the door.

'Not, to be honest. Struggling to get to who Harry Simm actually was, let alone a list of his enemies. Obstinate public seem reluctant to talk for some reason. Why is the big question. Makes me think he's not quite who or what we think he is.'

'What did he do again?'

'Ran a curiosity shop if you like. An assortment of good bad and downright awful. Bit like a jumble sale.'

'Thanks for that,' said Meller as he stepped backwards out into the corridor in his blue nitrile shoe covers. 'That's me finished for now, body examined and its now ready for removal when CSI are done.'

DS Jake Goodwin stepped carefully past the body in the hall and undertook a quick recce of the semi.

The look of the main room was in two quite distinctive halves. Two-seater sofa with small low coffee table next door to it, facing a too big screen television and a log burner he should have chucked out ages back.

The other end of a pictureless room had all the gaming paraphernalia but with no big expensive chair he'd come across before. Bean bags. bean bags and more bean bags Jake could only assume was what Quinton sat on to game. An unusual set-up. How it was, would mean gaming at an awkward level unless that was purely for watching rather than participating. Bringing a chair in from elsewhere would make more sense.

There was only one real surprise in what had to be the master bedroom, there only being one. It was the glass fronted fitted wardrobes filling the whole of one wall for a man's room he decided was unusual. Bulk standard free standing wooden wardrobes was what he'd been expecting. Venetian blinds, two colourful rugs. A long wooden chest at the bottom of the red duvet and black pillow adorned bed. Two bedside tables with a touch lamp on one together with a Val McDermid novel. The other had just an alarm clock.

A quick check of the wardrobes produced clothes and shoes, but in effect what was a chest of drawers inserted into the wardrobe at the far end produced nothing untoward like a whip, handcuffs and rubber face mask he'd once come across.

Busy and bustling Shona Tate the Senior Forensic Scene Manager was Jake's next target before he called the boss back at MIT's base with an update.

'Anything for me yet?' he asked when masked up Shona appeared all decked out in the white suit, hood and mask at the far end of the hallway.

'Somebody's had a clean up. For the amount of blood all caked on his clothes a lot's gone walkabouts. Found a mop we've got for testing but they'd probably given that a good scrub as well. We're tackling the sink right now and the bath.' Jake could see in her eyes the frustration. 'Why do that?' she asked and shook her head. 'Why try to hide blood when one look at him's obvious, and could easy be on his toes and away?'

'Anything I can tell my boss?'

'Photos on their way to him, any time soon. Laptop and phone we'll check, then let Stevens' lads have a crawl about inside. Be here at least today and tomorrow.'

'Tech Crime'll need to check his calls. One you found in Mablethorpe had a call out to an old lady in a care home, who can't use a phone.'

'So I heard. D'you know this Brendon Quinton by any chance?' she asked Jake with a shrug and pointed down at the cadaver.

'No idea.'

'Got his work pass for the council, but no idea what he did. All the usual bits and bobs along with a business card on the side in the kitchen for ExpressMusicFM radio station. Ever heard of them?'

'No, but not really into radio these days since Steve Wright got dumped. Number?'

'Hang on,' Shona said and disappeared again to her left and returned with an evidence bag in hand. 'Here it is,' she said and read out a mobile number.

'Thanks,' Jake noted. 'Hang on a sec,' he said pulling out his phone. He called Tech Crime and spoke to Hari. 'Guess what?' he posed to Shona as he ended his call. 'Phone number's the same as the one for those Atooz people you found the card for in Simm's office place.'

'That'll be fun for you,' she smiled with. 'That you done?'

'Pretty much,' replied Jake. 'Need to report back and head for the council I guess, see who he was and what he did. You've got Sandy and the door-to-door team,' he pointed right. 'A Margo Leadbetter lives next door. Thought she heard the door close about six. Reckons he came home by bus, but no idea how she'd know. Then heading off out to the shops this morning spotted this door open.'

'Net curtain twitcher maybe.'

Sharon sucked in her breath noisily, with any face she pulled hidden by her white mask. 'Sometimes come in useful.'

'State he's in looks a vicious attack, but then angry does something to people.'

'More than just losing your temper to my mind.'

‘Our thanks once again,’ he hadn’t finished though. ‘Need anything, you know where we are,’ and Jake Goodwin walked off back down the path to the road, turned left to find his car all the while on the lookout for Sandy. Out in the fresh air by his car, mask off he called his boss.

‘White male, stabbed a good few times,’ he told his DI back at Lincoln Central. ‘Marcus Meller’s been and gone, says PM in the morning but he’ll message you. A Brendon Quinton in his thirties, and its pretty obvious he lives alone. Bit sparsely furnished and doesn’t look as though he’s used a paint brush in a good while. Works for the Council doing what we don’t know as yet, so I’m heading there now on my way back. Dog tag to gain entry but no job description. Somebody’s made an attempt at clearing up. According to Shona even the floor’s been mopped. Phone and laptop and guess what Shona found a business card for some radio station found lying about in the kitchen.’ He hesitated. ‘Same number as that Atooz.’

‘Brilliant! Need to see what Nicky’s come up with. Gotta be the same bastard.’

‘Name, number?’ Oliver Bristow asked for, and Jake read him the details from his notebook.

‘Heading off now once I’ve spoken to Sandy, see what this Quinton did for a living, without giving anything away if I can help it.’

‘Where’s he gone?’ Bristow queried.

‘Doing door-to-door locally up and down the road. See you when I’m done at the Council.’

‘Have fun.’

‘Yeah thanks.’

Jake enjoyed working with DC Alexander MacLachlan a great deal. A trusted and dedicated Scot. Sort of guy you could always have faith in. Inga Larsson had created a good team with Sandy and others such as DS Nicola Scoley who like the Swede when required could be all business with no girly shit.

16

'Energy and Climate Change Officer on a fairly good wack. Part of their Assets and Investments sector,' was Jake's answer to the question Oliver Bristow had yet to ask as he walked into the Incident Room. 'Woman I spoke to says he worked hard, fairly popular but knew little about his private life. Suggests he kept himself to himself pretty much. Two other people I spoke to knew he did radio and reckoned he was into this gaming business.' Jake grinned. 'Don't look at me,' he told Oliver. 'I've never even played Space Invaders.'

'Shona reckons they found a bit of a set-up in the spare room,' said Oliver. 'Job for Jamie,' he suggested as Jake slipped off his jacket to hang over the back of his seat.

'One thing,' said a seated Jake. 'Woman I spoke with at the council reckoned he earned around thirty one grand, plus expenses.'

'Fiddle in other words,' he smiled with. 'Jamie,' said Oliver across to him. 'Head for the Council, ask HR for his bank details, so we can see if he's short of cash,' annoyed Jake who'd just come from there.

'I'll make us way there.'

'Heard about people losing a fortune with something called Loot Boxes.' Nicky offered. 'Causing gambling issues.'

'Sorry?'

'Loot Boxes,' she shared. 'Apparently appear when you're playing a video game offering you help or whatever for a price. Know because Connor read about some dope losing ten grand.'

'Interesting,' said Oliver. 'Thanks. Could have been laundering maybe or anything else we can discover,' he said as Jamie slipped on his jacket. 'Into this gaming business could possibly leave him a bit short.' Oliver stopped for a moment to gather his thoughts. 'Could be a political stance we've had before with people working for some stupid cause, part of which is living well below their means. Being involved in Climate Change could easy be a secret protester and living a dank dreary life as a sort of personal punishment in the same way some of these religious folk behave. He'd know what the Council are up to sure enough. We need to know this guy, and somebody somewhere must.'

'Lived alone,' Jake started again, pleased he'd not been asked to turn tail and head back there. 'No signs of a partner according to Shona, means as yet we've nowhere to send the FLO team to. As you say, gaming obsession could be the reason. Woman next door is elderly,' he stopped to sigh and shake his head slightly. 'Not be nosy as she's hard of hearing,' was very much a normal Jake concern. 'But claimed she heard his door shut.' he grimaced with. 'Bit frail unfortunately,' he went on. 'My guess is, come tea time she's all locked up for the night, peeping out the window. Say unfortunately,' Jake pulled a face. 'Can't image by the state of him anybody could've done anything anyway, certainly not that old dear. Meller's even suggesting almost a professional job, or at least medical training.'

'Have you seen Connor's photos he sent through,' Oliver asked his Detective Sergeant.

'Not yet,' Jake replied. 'With all the mess in the hall I didn't manage to do a thorough check of the bungalow except for quick scan just before I left. Big telly, parquet flooring and all the gaming stuff. Shona said Connor was sending them across.'

Jake got almost wearily back to his feet and walked across to the new Holstein murder board placed in front of two Operation Galloway partially full ones.

Every time he saw Simm propped up in one of Connor's photographs he looked to Jake like the sort they make television programmes about. Sort who spend the majority of their time hunting in forests and swamps for the rarest of rare insects.

'That's what Shona's talking about. Look,' Jake gestured and tapped three graphic photos of Quinton 'The hall floor's been mopped leaving just a bit more blood dripping off his clothes. Her lads have got the mop and were checking the bath and sink as I left.'

‘What’s he hanging about for?’

‘Who?’

‘The killer.’

‘That’s what I’ve been wondering. Shona was asking the same question. Job’s a good’un, get outta there sharpish. But no, let’s tidy up shall we? Get a mop and bucket out, give it a good scrub like mummy told him to,’ was caustic Jake.

‘Are you saying we’ve got a second one who stops for a tea?’

‘No mention made of dirty cups.’

‘That a clue,’ Nicky Scoley posed, and the DI and DS looked down at her quizzically. ‘Whoever it was knew him. On the lookout for something? Been to visit before maybe, well enough to find a mop and bucket, add a bit of bleach to confuse Shona’s team.’

‘Now we got somebody concerned with DNA?’

‘Chances are, easy be somebody who’s been there before,’ Nicky repeated.

‘Or had forensic or medical experience,’ is Jake’s latest input.

‘To sit nicely alongside the stabbing being by an experienced knife handler.’

‘Could just be a fussy one,’ said Nicky. ‘Dare not leave a mess?’

‘One?’ just hangs in the air for the moment.

Oliver spoke directly to his senior DS. ‘Any suggestion of two, or more?’ Jake responded with a sigh and a shake of his head.

‘This means going back.’

‘See what Shona has to say when she’s finished. Good job team. As usual.’

Unknown to impressed Goodwin, Oliver Bristow used a system of praise taught to him by a former boss. Prioritizing short-term wins over long-term objectives can be seen as a mistake. Adding team praise for these short-term wins no matter how trivial they appear at the time, has in theory a long term effect.

‘One of these him?’ Alisha asked from behind Jake. He spun round and walked across, to peer over her shoulder.

‘No,’ he repeated three time before a ‘Yes. That’s him. That’s Quinton.’

‘And?’ was an impatient Bristow.

‘Next to nothing,’ said Jake initially as he took control of the mouse. ‘Follows the Climate Change Center, by the spelling looks to be American and likes stuff on Restore Our Earth Challenge and so on,’ he read from what appeared. ‘Nothing personal at all, other than the photo. Work and interest which look to be the same dominates. In a word, dull and useless.’

‘Keep checking, please,’ Oliver told Alisha once she had control of the mouse again and back to geotagging. ‘Did she look for a doorbell camera?’ Jake had no answer to as he tried hard to visualize the door. ‘You never know. One day our luck will change.’

‘Could be on one of Connor’s scene shots. I’ll check,’ Nicky offered.

‘We’re never not going to make mistakes I know that,’ said Oliver with one of his profound remarks he was adept at using. ‘But. If we’re not careful we’ll have the press parked outside.’

‘Coffee anyone?’ Jake checked as he headed for the door. ‘Carrying not buying,’ he grinned and was gone.

When Jake Goodwin returned with coffee and time to tuck into his cheese and cucumber sandwiches, it was time to down quills and listen just as Oliver received notice of Operation Holstein.

‘Brendon Quinton. Been at Lincoln Borough going on for four years. Moved from Newark into the position he holds. Or did. Gotta say it sounds pretty boring. According to the job description,’ he waved a paper copy. ‘He was assisting in the ongoing development and implementation of the Council’s Climate Change Strategy. Quinton in his role had particular emphasis on reducing carbon emissions of the Council itself.’

‘Brilliant!’ is Rufus Barrie sat closest to him. ‘Paying him a good wack just to look after themselves. What about us who pay taxes? Hundred thousand people can just go to buggery, eh?’

The team spent the next hour or more checking all the systems. No mention of Quinton on PNC or the DNA database or even links through other environmental websites.

'Did manage,' Jamie said on his return. 'To talk to a few he worked with. Seems popular enough but no great feelings of grief. However, one woman told me on the quiet he's just been passed over for his ex-bosses job. He'd gone off to Mansfield to be closer to where he was brought up and's got elderly parents. Our friend Quinton got an interview but he'd been beaten to the better role by some environmental enthusiast and protester from Wigan of all places.'

'Bank?' was inevitably Oliver Bristow.

'Lucas Moore down in the Economic Crime Team'll get what we need faster than us,' Nicky suggested. 'We phone his bank we'll finish up as number nineteen in the queue.'

'Anything else we know?'

'As far as I could judge, news of Quinton's death had not reached the office. One or two did remark how they just thought he was late for work or had somewhere to go, dentist and the like.'

'Thanks Jamie.'

'One other thing. Told me he does radio.'

'I was told that,' Jake reminded.

'What sorta radio?'

'Community radio. That Yellerbelly FM.'

'When? D'we know?'

'About to look it up,' satisfied his DI.

'Boss,' said Michelle when he didn't carry on. 'I can't find this NewMusicalFM place.' DC paused for a moment. 'Must be a list of all radio stations on Google. See what I can find.'

Oliver Bristow just stood there hand clasped to his forehead in an exaggerated reaction.

Nicky Scoley had got it right. DC Lucas Moore up in the Economic Crime office had got a copy of Quinton's bank statement in no time and being environmentally positive she'd nipped up to collect it rather than have him print off another copy.

Once she'd finished hunting down that radio station if that's what it was, Michelle Cooper was given the task of running through his account looking for anything untoward. Up in the Tech Crime Team they were working on Quinton's laptop and his mobile. DI Oliver headed down the corridor briefing Craig Darke their Detective Superintendent on the latest developments, to add to what he had already reported.

Back along in the Incident Room he called Jake into his office.

'Have a seat,' he planned to take one anyway. 'Just been talking to Craig. Asking if both cases are connected, being single men.'

'Seriously? That far apart?' Jake responded quickly. 'MO's totally different. Hypothermia and now a good old fashioned stabbing with what Meller described to Sandy as skilled, with a very sharp implement. Coincidentally,' he grimaced. 'It's missing.'

'Gay scene, drug scene?'

Jake Goodwin sat there hands on his thighs as he was giving the suggestion some thought. 'And how do we come to that conclusion?' he asked across the desk. 'No drugs so far, none in Simm's bloods.'

'That a link. Drugs and music scene?'

'Shona didn't mention drugs but might have come across some by now. But guess not or she'd have given us a shout. Gay? How d'we work that out?' was another query.

'Check his phone. Check for a few likely candidates. Maybe at work but...radio station's more likely.'

'Like the middle-aged and elderly women I spoke to?' was Jake's sarcasm. 'This Quinton, the Climate Change guru. What's the thinking from on high?' he asked. 'This some sort of green hippy commune idea with tree hugging and smoking weed, with a few gay didicoys just because he's into Climate Change?'

'No Jake not at all; but to be fair it's always possible,' Bristow grimaced and paused for a sec. 'This some climate change programme he does, d'you think?'

‘I put my bins out but it doesn’t make me some sort of eco professor or mean I’m on drugs,’ he immediately wanted too suck back in. ‘If you’re talking both, then we’ve got our work cut out with a gay killer on the loose. But first we need to establish if Simm and Quinton were in fact gay, and so far with Simm we know next to nothing, but I can’t imagine.’ He paused. ‘Just think what he looks like. Is that the normal image of the gay? Not the gay persona to my mind. Neat and tidy comes to mind, which he never was.’

‘Yeah, see your point.’

‘Is that why people are not coming forward, worried ‘bout being tarred with the same brush?’ was a question from Oliver in need of an answer.

‘I know gays but that doesn’t make me one and I don’t nip to the loo for a quick spliff. There’s more to it than that boss.’

‘Always possible.’ said the DI as he answered his own question. ‘And as our lord and master has given it voice time who are we to ignore it?’

‘Who am I to ignore it you mean?’ from Jake was greeted with a hint of a smile from his boss as the DS got to his feet wondering about the stupid voice time remark.

With so much going on, Alisha O’Neill when not keeping an eye on social media, had taken on making calls to those named on Simm’s PC. The Tech Crime Team had been delving into.

To start she got onto a dozen names of people listed in his accounts he’d done specific work for. They’d all arranged for Simm at one time or another, to create something for them such as a leaping Salmon for the centre of a garden pond. A rose arch of leaves and even a mushroom shaped garden table with two stools.

Not one of them knew him, only knew of him and had met him at most two or three times. Next up was Michelle Cooper with a couple of queries about Quinton’s bank account Nicky Scoley took back up to Lucas Moore looking for more in depth data.

Two of Michelle’s challenges turned out to be a life insurance policy and membership of some Green Grass charity.

Most significant was a regular monthly payment of £400 to a Wiktoria Golebiewska.

Tracking her down with a name like that had been relatively easy and it was Nicky who eventually made phone contact for early evening.

The one step forward scenario came into play when Oliver Bristow received a message from the Tech Crime Team and Nicky'd been sent to investigate.

Then another appeared when first Michelle admitted she could find no such radio station the card related to, but Jamie Hedley had come across Quinton's Night Train hip hop programme at 21.00 on Wednesday evenings.

'Darke boss'll love that!' chuckled Jake. 'He'll tell you in no uncertain terms they can hip off or words to that effect.'

Nicky Scoley put on a face as she walked back in. 'No news is good news, so what I have is news. Guess what. Telephone number for this New Musical radio station is the same as the old dear who owns the phone Simms rang. Quinton phoned the same number for close to a minute two days before his visitor.

17

Evening trip to a house in North Hykeham close to Lincoln, done as early as she could by Nicky Scoley, to avoid spoiling the whole evening.

When this Wiktoria Golebiewska woman had been reassured by the production of a warrant card, she proceeded to almost trip over herself with her eagerness to relate her story.

Probably due to nerves, being on her own and no previous experience of dealing with the Police in Britain, her initial summary had been very rushed. Almost as if she had decided in advance what to say and admit to, with forcing it all out at a gallop unnecessarily.

DS Scoley had managed to pick up on new markers. This female admitted to being Brendon Quinton's partner for a little over eighteen months until seven months ago.

That answered Craig Darke's query unless of course he was bisexual. Nicky was well aware Jake of all people had been tasked with searching out the truth. Sight of Jake visiting gay bars would be a sight for sore eyes.

Wiktoria admitted when Quinton was eliciting sympathy and demanding attention almost constantly, she had eventually begun to ignore him and his tiresome attention seeking. Despite that he had continued to try to control her before eventually becoming frustrated and violent. A slap here and there to start with, was then gradually upgraded. In response Wiktoria had then moved out to a Refuge in the city for a little more than two months, in order to provide herself with a safe environment to reorganize her life.

Wiktoria Golebiewska was young, early twenties at a guess and a good inch or two taller than Scoley. She was sporting fine eastern European features and her black hair was all mussed up and tangled up in such a way Nicky decided had to be deliberate.

Originally from Wloclawek in Poland, Wiktoria said she'd moved to Lincoln to study medicine at the university Medical School.

Since her break up from Quinton she had been living with a fellow student and her mother in their spare room which was where Scoley had tracked her down to.

She admitted getting to know Quinton initially through a Climate Science Center website and was particularly interested at that time in stuff on Restore Our Earth Challenge platform. Where she admitted she'd first came across Brendon Quinton.

Scoley had been offered a glass of wine when she first arrived but when she explained about being on duty and alcohol being an absolute no no, she took advantage of the offer of a can of Pepsi-Max.

'I'm sorry to bring this up,' she said. 'But we've managed to contact you after we discovered from his bank account he's been paying you £400 a month by Direct Debit. Could you explain that to me?'

Breath puffed out, sip of wine to help and a shrug before: 'So, will I get in trouble?'

'In trouble for what?'

'Taking the money off him.'

'If he organized a Direct Debit into your bank why should you be in any sort of trouble?' Scoley queried.

Sip more of the comforting white wine. 'So, s'pose you'd call it threatening,' she said. 'Managed to get away and moved into the Refuge for a while but he knew I was at uni and he approached me in the street, bullied me, threatened me with all sorts.'

'What sort of things?' Scoley knew from experience from talking to DCI Inga Larsson her ex-boss who'd become boss of the Sexual Safeguarding Unit, how that sort of reaction was not uncommon among narcissists. Often they are unable to accept how another person, particularly one they have known intimately, does not want to be with them.

'When we were together to get at me he was cruel to my little cat. If he didn't like cats why'd he allow me to take in a stray?' Wiktoria asked as if the DS had a ready made answer.

‘What sort of things?’ a concerned Nicky Scoley posed offering her an encouraging smile.

‘Threw the cat out at eleven and made it sleep outdoors in all weathers. Then he’d just throw Tiddles meat in the bin for no reason if something upset him and make her go without.’

‘Why? What had the cat done?’ asked Scoley angrily.

‘Nothing,’ she answered. ‘So, realized later this was all to get at me. Control me.’

‘Might I ask, how is this connected with you being in trouble?’ Scoley querid. ‘Seems to me he was the guilty one.’

‘When he kept pestering I thought I’d have to finish uni and go back home. The course is hard enough with out all this going on. In desperation told him of he didn’t stop I’d report him to the Council. Had his boss’s email address and said I’d spill the beans about his behaviour. Not sure I really would, but...’ she smiled temporarily. ‘Refuge wanted me to go to the Police but I couldn’t face all that business. Only approached me once since then to say he’d changed and would I take him back?’

‘The cat?’ was Scoley’s concern.

‘Gave him to a friend at uni. See her sometimes and she’s doing well.’

‘Thank goodness.’ Nicky had the feeling there might have been really bad news heading her way.

‘So, s’pose you’ll stop the money now,’ was a very disgruntled suggestion.

‘Not our problem. It’ll stop at some point of course. When the account runs out of money or when somebody closes the account.’ Nicky Scoley took a sip from the can of no sugar Pepsi-max. ‘Are you desperate for the money?’ she checked.

‘No. Just been giving me a big boost to save for a deposit on somewhere. Can’t stay here for ever,’ she suggested almost to herself. ‘She’s been very nice but it’d not be fair on Mrs Leadburn.’

‘Anything else?’ blonde Scoley wanted to know.

‘Wouldn’t put the heating on, even in winter,’ Wiktoria admitted. ‘Got me to sign things he’d not let me read and…’ she sighed wearily. ‘Had all that business of sign here and you can meet your pals. Come Friday night he'd got some other fuckin' reason to keep me in.'

'While we're at it, we could do with names of people he didn't get on with.'

'Be these gaming people s'pose.'

'What d'you mean?' Scoley slipped in. 'A form of betting d'you mean?'

'No,' was firm. 'Be these trips he went on to those big gaming competitions.'

'To compete?'

'No just to watch. Thousands go.'

'How often was this?' asked the DS.

'What he did for holidays.'

'What sort of places we talking about?' she checked for her notes.

Wiktoria thought for a moment or two. 'France...well Paris actually. Sweden, China I think plus...er, Manilla.'

'He still making these trips after he started giving you money each month?' Scoley sips again.

'So. Only know what people told me. See Brendon's off on another trip, they'd say and stuff like that.'

Time to change tack, Nicky Scoley decided. 'Also we understand he was after his boss's job when he left. Why d'you think he didn't get it.'

'Didn't know he had,' Wiktoria shook her head slightly. 'Be after I moved out s'pose.' She grimaced at the thought of it. 'Hardly ever met any of his workmates and certainly not his boss, but Bren was always saying he was a complete tosser. Got a feeling they were not too enamoured by him at the Council. Private sector would've got shot of him long ago. Possible they knew what he was like.'

Scoley had assumed the bloke from Wigan had got the job because he was better suited and maybe had better qualifications and more experience. Chances are the truth was it was down to Quinton's attitude. Sat there listening to Wiktoria she remembered Jamie talking to Quinton's work colleagues having left him uninspired by their enthusiasm and the more she knew about him told her it was a case of not speaking ill of the dead.

‘Yellerbelly FM,’ said Scoley. ‘Tell me about that.’

‘When I first knew him he did hospital radio but they wanted what he called too much soppy. So as not to upset the patients.’

‘Sorry? Soppy?’

‘Sixties pop. Wall to wall Herman’s Hermits and all that cringe stuff.’

‘Did you know he’d gone to Yellerbelly FM doing hip hop?’

‘Heard,’ she scoffed. ‘Not my scene at all.’

‘Next,’ Scoley said after a drink. ‘Sorry but I have to ask this. Where were you on the tenth of February**?**

Wiktoria hesitated to view a calendar in her mind. ‘Easy,’ she eventually came out with. ‘Back at home for my parents wedding anniversary. They live near Wloclawek. Poland,’ she tagged on the end as if Scoley’d not know. ‘You can phone them if you don’t believe me.’

‘Did he self harm at all?’ was next up.

‘No. But he did try to grab my attention and sympathy quite often by saying he was having a bad time at work.’

‘You think this was about not getting that job?’

‘Long before that. Told a friend of mine at uni how he’d been to the doctor with stomach problems soon after I walked out,’ had Scoley nodding.

‘Were there any other medical issues?’

‘Only the flu once but I think it was just a bad cold. Be that man flu they go on about.’ Nicky knew this man flu business is a proven condition. A weaker immune system leaves men vulnerable to harsher bouts of things like flu and the like and why they die younger.

‘So,’ she shrugged. ‘Had an issue with me periods at one time,’ she said suddenly. ‘Looking back now he couldn’t give a toss, apart from the fact it put me off sex. All this narcissistic business is what the refuge reckoned.’

‘Along with his coercive behaviour.’ Scoley was looking for a way out, having stayed longer than intended but it was certainly a sorry tale. ‘Do you by chance know of anybody else he’s been with?’

‘Not personally but I can ask about, now people are talking about him.’

‘As I’m sure you’ll appreciate we need to apprehend somebody for the killing or being involved in his death in some way.’

‘See what I can do,’ they locked eyes for a moment as she extinguished a slight chuckle.

Scoley slapped her hands down on her thighs and got to her feet. ‘Thanks for that Wiktoria. Please keep in touch,’ she said down handing over her card. ‘And if anything else comes to mind please just give me a call.’

‘Am I allowed to ask? How did he die?’

‘Sorry,’ Scoley sucked in a breath. ‘For the time being such information is not being released as not doing so may well assist in our investigations.’ She saw the look on this Polish woman’s fine face. ‘As it stands, we know what happened and the killer knows. Can we leave it at that?’

‘Yeh,’ was part of a sigh.

‘All come out in the fullness of time no doubt.’

‘I know we should never pigeon hole people,’ Nicky said to Oliver Bristow first thing the next day. ‘But to my mind Quinton working for the Council, dealing with the environment in some way creates a totally different picture from the one this....Wiktoria was painting. Not to mention this hip hop business for a couple of hours a week.’

‘You and me both,’ Oliver commented. ‘Would you not see a calm caring individual or is it a case of that’s the role the Council think suits him best, when nothing could be further from the truth?’

‘We know he had a gaming set-up in the spare bedroom but nothing lavish. These trips abroad though put a different perspective on it all.’

‘As well as dishing out £400 a month,’ he reminded the DS. ‘We sure the radio’s not paying him?’

‘Sandy’s heading their way, know soon enough. Spoke with Lucas one of the Economic Crime guys an hour ago. Apart from the £400 there’s nothing untoward apart from the usual living expenses and he reckons even that’s very tight.’

'How's he pay to shoot off to places like Manilla then?'

'Question I asked Lucas just now.'

'Have the women at the Council sussed him out,' Oliver asks himself as well as his DS. 'Somebody went on a date or two and recognized the bad vibes. After all from what you've been saying his abuse was in the main mental. Something his workmates might well recognize. Was the physical side he dished out later something they'd never come across in a date or two.'

'Beginning of the end for Wiktoria,' Nicky remarked. 'Once the physical appeared, seems to me.'

'People like him normally deny their faults, the controlling, beatings and all the rest of it. What if he realized if word got out he'd maybe lose his job, meaning his gaming trips'd be buggered.'

'Why he never as far as we know linked up with any workmates,' said Nicky 'Or,' she continued. 'Had he been disciplined already about his attitude to women, and knew what was in store if Wiktoria got to reveal all.'

'Is that why he didn't get his boss's job?' Oliver posed. 'What did you say she was studying?'

'At the Medical School studying medicine. She wasn't any more specific than that.'

'We can always check that out if need be.'

'And with HR at the council.'

When Sandy MacLachlan returned from YellerbellyFM he had little to offer, apart really for confirmation how as a community project they had no means to pay radio presenters or anybody else come to that.

A helpful member of the behind the scenes production team he spoke to confirmed Quinton did a weekly programme in an attempt to attract a younger audience. Yet admitted they knew little about him, apart from working for the council in an environment capacity of some kind and was aware of his first love of gaming. She didn't describe him as unsociable but confirmed he hardly mixed with other members of the team.

18

Hello there, it's me again.

Of course, no matter how much of a concerted effort you make, it can't be possible to think of everything or prepare for the unexpected when you step into the unknown as I've been doing of late.

As was the case with all Quinton's blood.

Struck lucky to be honest with that bleach I found under the sink. I know from what I'd come across during my gruesome bedtime reading, no matter how hard you try you'll not rid somewhere of all the signs of blood with a quick wash down.

It was never my intention to attempt to hide that from the Police, after all they had his body with big holes in it. My problem simply was how much had poured out onto the hall floor. There was never enough space between the pooled blood, his body and the front door to enable me to deal with what would be significantly bloodied shoes and the rest of my attire. You can't tell Quinton when you've plunged the knife in for the third time, *"Hey, take care where you're spilling your blood matey."*

Are the on line platforms doing enough to protect their users is a frequently posed question these days. Probably not but what I have to give them credit for is the amazing stuff you can search down.

Killing Quinton is a good example. I followed the instructions and did my best to repeat the video they called Stick and Twist. Bit like Blackjack. As directed I stuck the knife into his chest with the flat side up to avoid the ribs. Then in a movement I practiced at home, thrust it into his stomach and twisted it through 180 degrees they said guaranteed success. Knife dragged out as he grasps at himself, and it was simply a case of just pushing him over.

Washing the hall was the only option and thinking about it now I'm not at all sure there were any others choices.

Mopped the floor with bleach to create a safe passageway for me, and giving my shoes a good wash in the sink, stood on old newspapers I'd then taken away with me. DNA you see. Always on my mind.

Research into blood splatter was really involved. Talk of the direction of travel, impact angle and magnitude of force for a novice was a bit much. Guess Lincoln Police used infrared technology.

Talking of knives and stabbing, I see plastic knives and forks are to be banned. That'll mean giving children metal knives which will at least be good training for when they reach their teens.

Back to Quinton. One major plus was him living in Waddington and working in Lincoln. The city worries me. The undoubted tourist attraction, Cathedral, Castle with the Magna Carta plus other points of interest such as the famous Steep Hill. Along with the Brayford waterfront with 'Lin' meaning 'pool' centuries back make up a unique city to some extent.

Some modern elements of life in Lincoln meet my aspirations. Better awareness of the Brayford and what it has to offer. Plus such things as tables and chairs springing up outside a whole array of cafes and restaurants. I'm hopeful the downward alcohol demand trend and energy costs, will see a few tatty bars close.

The stories poor Andrea told to me during two sessions with her were difficult to take. Realizing I'd become aware of slowly becoming her release valve. Telling me in absolute confidence stuff the staff were not aware of, apart from the basic cruelty aspects. Think it was Debbie Parmenter who'd told her about me being the no blab one she could turn to as part of her emotional release therapy.

But then Debbie is one of those to my mind who tends to talk to impress. Couple of times I've kindly mentioned her young child. She told me her son was nine and to quote "means we're in his last year of single digits." Then another time talking about the poor lad as "having important cornerstones to his day." Whatever that meant.

I'd read how those who sexually abuse children rely on privacy and secrecy to ensure as far as is possible their secret is not discovered or reported.

I believe this had been the same with Brendon Quinton. Andrea had admitted how she'd eventually become too scared to do anything, as any perceived errors on her part would result in threats or worse.

In her case it was almost a case of left overs on Monday, Cheesy Chicken on Wednesday and a good battering Fridays when he got home from the clubs. Saturday morning she admitted more than once had become a regular insincere Sorry Day.

Apparently Quinton had demanded rough sex whenever he arrived home having frequently called at the pub on the way. In fact, reading between the lines it would seem sex was the payment he demanded for such simple things as her need for new basic clothes and a request to spend an evening out with her friends.

According to Andrea at family gatherings he had always been impeccable, acting as the perfect partner. In fact her oblivious mother was forever saying how lucky she was to be in a marvellous relationship with such a charming handsome man; compared with the one her sister was lumbered with. Quinton's way of ensuring and retaining the privacy he had need of as protection.

Another ghastly story she told me was about her birthday. She and Quinton had visited her brother and sister-in-law a few days before her birthday. As they were leaving Julia the sister-in-law surreptitiously handed a package containing slippers and pyjamas to Quinton.

A few days after her birthday during a phone call when Julia asked what presents she'd had Andrea commented on not receiving anything from her. Julia was adamant that she had secretly handed a package to Quinton when they'd visited. When she queried it with him he absolutely denied having been given anything. Both women decided the bastard must have binned it.

The time I'd taken in Quinton's hall dealing with his blood worried me. I'd expected to be in and out as fast as I could. Wig off stuffed in my pocket. Ditched the stupid stylized Peaky Blinders hat I swapped for a woolly big Welsh Rugby bobble one along with the bloodied big padded coat from the charity shop and stuffed it all back in the holdall. All part of my DNA avoidance golden rules to be used again. Enter as one, leave as another under cover of darkness. All that nasty DNA business had been and would continue to be an extremely important factor to bear in mind in every situation hereon in.

Got to admit now, even after dealing with Simm I was in a mess approaching Quinton's place. Sharp knock on his front door, stood back a step and glanced back up the road. Then was the moment to jump on my bike, to get away somewhere to calm my racing thumping heart beat. The red door opened. Too late.

At various points in my mission I've considered switching everything off. Rebooting and returning to offering exoneration. Continue doing the right thing, behave the way mother taught us. Knowing wrong from right and remain almost invisible to the world.

Where's the fun in that? Eh?

I had a need to return to normal life, my comfort blanket and all that business had delayed me. Leaving three hours blank on my appointments list had proved useful. False client names of course to make it look like just another busy day.

At least with Brendon Quinton news of his death had reached the wider public a lot quicker than Simm did. I'm wondering why of course. How come one was in the mass media within hours and another took ages? Maybe being out at Mablethorpe took it away from the limelight.

MURDER INVESTIGATION IN LINCOLN LAUNCHED

Lincoln County Police are investigating a death they describe as unexplained. Police attended an address in Waddington at 09.46am today and say officers will remain in the area.

The Leader has been advised of specialist teams are on the scene carrying out their inquiries and there will be a Police presence in the area for a least a day or two.

This remains a live investigation and the Leader understands four people have been evacuated from the vicinity of the property as a precaution..

Being the way I am I undertook a considerable amount of research about killing radio presenters. I'd have loved to have stabbed him live on air. Unfortunately my research never revealed to me how it could be done, satisfactorily.

My issues about attempting such a thing were all about my concerns for the unknowns.

I've done Siren Radio, the community station based at the University. I was invited in once to talk one morning about my gratis work with women in one of the local refuges.

Only people there at that time were the deejay and the charming producer. That was eleven in the morning. Who would be at a radio station when Quinton arrived for his nine o'clock evening show and who would lock up at gone eleven? Add to that the possibility of somebody popping their nose in at the most inopportune moment and I was full to overflowing with doubt.

The other issue was, doing it while he was on air would be in view of the public so to speak and how long would the cops take to arrive? Nice idea but not workable to my mind. Maybe in a grimy city somewhere with a choice of easy escape routes.

On the subject of radio and the media in general, I wonder why major news stories tend to be bunched together. We can go weeks with little else but boring and increasingly dishonest political diatribes. Then up pops not just one, but a number of un-linked news events. Yes, we've had Putin in Ukraine getting on for a year of course. Then suddenly that's all pushed aside to make way for the mystery of the woman out with her dog missing by a river, an awful devastating earthquake in Turkey and Nicola Sturgeon resigning, all one after another.

On the matter of media. Did you read about wet wipes still being wrongly flushed down the loo, piling up on river banks. In one instance apparently there's an island of them as big as a couple of tennis courts.

Why on earth are people still flushing them away, or not as it happens. Ruth and I never use them and I can't remember my mother, bless her soul, ever having them in the house. We rightly got rid of carrier bags, and to my mind we should do the very same with this pointless product.

Right then, enough of all that. Where was I? Oh yes, Quinton. He'd been easier than that objectionable Simm from my perspective. No need to be dragging a fat lifeless lump about had been a bonus. Changing the removal from this world system was as it turned out, well thought through. Trouble was, in return I had all that blood to deal with. A darn sight more than ever imagined I can tell you.

Not something we think about is it? How much sticky red stuff is slumping round and round inside us constantly. Certainly not how much you'd expect when it came pouring out.

Not at all like you see on the telly with a trickle of blood just oozing out from under the body. That'll all be part of that warning nonsense they keep repeating for people of a nervous disposition who shouldn't be watching in the first place.

Plenty of television programmes are gut wrenchingly dire at best. Six bronzed oily bodies desperate for sex on a foreign beach with a stranger they'd only once seen in a pub. Why I want to know, do we not get some geezer spouting about how utterly ridiculous and nauseating the following programme featuring the brain dead will be.

In my planning, I'd decided to move away from the need to undress an unconscious shit after hauling Simm from that old chair and dragging him out the back of the bloody shop. Now I'd got that mess in the short hall instead and questioned my reasoning as I got on with mopping furiously.

Was all that blood better or worse? Physically it had been a better bet. By the time let me tell you, I'd plunged that bloody sharp knife in second time it was all over and physical exertion hadn't really played a part for more than a few seconds. Adrenalin rush coming in was mighty handy I have to say.

Even so I'd expected this time to be less fraught. Physically it was of course, with no dragging a nasty shit's body about but mentally it is once more with me constantly

My question now in retrospect as I conduct my own wash-up, is should I have searched out a bin bag for his clothes or had leaving him as he was, all drenched in blood on the hall floor the best bet?

Time will tell if bloody cops come banging on my door before the reason for all this has been dealt with.

Been bad enough and time consuming getting past him and the mess on the floor to head for his kitchen to then give the hallway a good mopping before I'd changed my clothes.

Yeh I know. Those forensic folk'll discover blood in the cracks between the floor boards and blood splatter is it they call it up the wall will be obvious. This was all to make my escape less likely to be contaminated.

No matter how much stuff I'd added to my database as a novice at this sort of thing, I'd thought about the blood but not extensively enough. Then as one's brain does, up popped a welcome good notion to alleviate the problem.

In his wardrobe I discovered a pair of old trainers. Bit big for me but better than too big shoes. Tied them as tight as I could and with my blood wet contaminated shoes bagged it was time to leave. Escape the property hurriedly but not at a run to become obvious, down the path and out. Being the last bungalow down the bottom of the road meant hiding the bike round the back was easy. Undid the lock and I was backpack in place, on my bike and off.

Bike? You ask.

Been through the egress route time enough. What if I'm spotted walking away's the sort of thing I worried about at night. Yeh, wearing that big padded coat would have offered some disguise with that Woolly hat, but there was always a chance some nosy bugger'd see me sauntering past. Vision of even a bigger and bulkier me spread across the media was not my desire.

Car for obvious reasons with the likelihood of breaking down, getting pulled over or being crashed into, offered too many dangers. Out at Mablethorpe I had no choice. Back roughly on my patch even though I was up in Waddington things were different. Even so, in the city you've got all that ANPR stuff and CCTV stuck on every damn thing.

My bike is one of those mountain bike things wish I'd had when I was at school. Back home, hung it up the back of the garage now alongside Ruth's. Out of sight, out of mind. Give it a good clean some day soon. No. Give them both a good wash and polish so one doesn't hand a message to the cops.

Before I dealt with Simm this was all about planning, investigating and stalking. Now there are major concerns to consider regarding errors I may have made. Had Quinton not had a mop and bucket I'd have been on my hands and knees scrubbing and more besides.

Exactly what I have to consider with number three. What could happen if I get it wrong. What do I do if it turns into the need to bolt?

What if I'd walked into the radio studio stabbed Quinton on air and some bloke appeared out of the blue from the other studio?

Now its back to work, back to as normal a life as its likely to be from hereon.

Like so many people I have come across over the years, I was more that slightly sceptical about healing processes such as Reiki.

A birthday gift of a spa day. You know, one of those perfect escapes where they claim to soothe body and mind. Pampering treatments, massage, facials and all that business, a light vegetarian lunch and a meagre glass of fizz.

As a podiatrist by trade I've long since converted my third bedroom into a studio where I can tend to clients in peace. An offshoot of that had been regular elderly clients asking if I could manage home visits.

Now the spare room is for my Reiki clients and two days a week I'm dedicated to being out and about tending to feet. Controlling my appointments lists has meant I've been able to carry out my stalking and research, in the end dealing with Simm and Quinton without the worry of working nine to five getting in the way.

Bit strange how the customers for each treatment tend to be quite different. The pedicure business deals with both male and female, with most of them past middle age, and a number have diabetes where foot care is crucial.

The Reiki people, all women tend to be more full of themselves and I'm sure with one or two of the pretentious bunch attending for nothing more than being able to brag to their fancy friends over lunch.

This all means I can plan my visits and my energy healing business around the need to deal with as many men as I can muster pre and maybe post the Miriam target.

A thriving business and hobby I plan to continue for as long as I am able.

I've found it fascinating at times talking to people such as my regular clients.

"What have you been doing with yourself?"

"Been anywhere nice Jules, since I was last here?"

"Yes actually. Murdered a couple of scum bags. Anybody you want getting rid of?"

Hey, that's something I came across on the dark web. Might interest you.

Dark Net's not just for the Mafia, major crime gangs, big drug dealers and uni kids with nothing better to do.

Best if you look it up yourself, but access is gained through what they call a TOR. That's a network of volunteer relays through which your internet connection is routed.

Make no sense? Don't worry or dismiss the idea out of hand, there's plenty of step-by-step guides.

Now where was I? Ah yes. Talking about getting rid of somebody. There are websites on how to hire a hit man (or woman I suppose woke folk would insist on in this day and age). Some I must warn you are scams who take your money but don't carry out the execution. After all, who you going to complain to, Customer Services or the Ombudsman?

But, and it's a big but. Quite seriously there are people on line trying to hire a hit man. I'll leave it with you.

"Did you get away for a weekend?" I was asked three times after I got Simm sat down out the back of his shop.

Got to say I'm so grateful for the opportunity to talk to you. Without this outlet I'd be in a very dark world of my own making. Thank you for your interest. Now where was I?

Oh yes, I was about to say. At times it does feel as if I'm now living one life, I dare not mention to a soul, and everybody else is doing their stuff in another.

I do have to be very careful not to change my behaviour so alarmingly it focuses people's attention.

After Simm nobody even mentioned his death. Being across in Mablethorpe I think certainly helped. *Lincoln Leader* ran it for a few hours on their website, then took it down when something dopey arrived on the scene.

But to be fair, the coppers must have kept it out of the news somehow for reasons best known to themselves, so the average Joe Bloggs was not au-fait with what had happened. News moves on at such a pace these days, in Simm's case here today gone tomorrow was encouraging.

The no news pushed me towards social media in an attempt to gain an insight into what was going on. I do Facebook now and again, but even that gets on my nerves at times. I've never been able to fathom the reasoning behind some of the stuff people put on such sites. Why do we have grandmothers embarrassing their grandkids with gushing silliness about how wonderful they are, when in truth teenagers ignore old folk. Facebook, preferring instead porn or the likes of short-form of social media such as TikTok?

When I was young, relatives producing photos in an album of me aged 2 naked in the bath, was bad enough. At least they were not available to the entire universe as they are on social media to please the paedophiles.

Wonder who the cops have on their list of suspects? Probably family as they usually top the list with unexplained deaths. Be a few friends he'd fallen out with or maybe a customer. One ripped off by Harry with some ghastly overpriced piece of junk.

Number two was the complete opposite, with Quinton making serious headlines as a result of which I've had to become adept at generating a false face. Connections to Council and radio had to be behind the media interest. Wonder if their listener figures have boomed?

Got to say. What I've been up to is way out of my comfort zone and to a degree it has altered me, particularly with regard to getting a decent night's sleep.

I've had nights recently when I've gone to bed at around eleven, with my brain buzzing with everything. Fallen asleep and then woken up fully refreshed ready for another day only to find the alarm only says close to midnight..

Turned to tea recently as a before bed tonic, which is said to be sleep inducing and calms what they describe as 'monkey mind' with everything that's happened along with what I have planned running around inside my monkey brain during the night.

That's about all I have for you for now.

19

'Here we go, chop and change,' said DI Oliver Bristow as he strode back into the Incident Room. 'Sylvia down in Reception's just told me a Jodie Simm phoned, wanting to talk to somebody...in private. Back to Operation Galloway,' he said as he walked into his small office and after shedding his jacket slumped down in his black chair. Phone call made Oliver get back up and stood in his doorway. 'Coming in at half two,' he looked across the team. 'You got time to join me?' he asked DS Nicky Scoley.

'Yes guv,' she responded in the knowledge this was never a kind request. 'Lucas in Economics has just been on. I'll call on him after.'

Just before two thirty the pair greeted this medium height bustling woman with light purple tinted hair and ushered her to a soft interview room, where the DI formally made the introductions. No tea and sympathy to start as there had to be a reason for her wishing to talk in private.

Being told almost immediately by this Jodie Simm she is a hairdresser seemed a curious start, which had both detectives wondering what the visitor was making of their locks.

'How may we help you?' DI Bristow asked for starters.

'I think it's the other way round,'

'Please explain,' was calm and courteous.

'They tell me you're looking for relatives of Harry Simm.'

'We certainly are. And your link is...?' Scoley asked despite obviously being aware of the likely answer.

'Me lad.' But before either detective could respond she went on: 'Not many on us abaht see. Lots with an s on t'end.' Scoley had expected her to say husband or partner. Must be the coloured hair and a good splash of make-up making her look a good deal younger. Must be late seventies or older.

‘I’m sorry to say we do have an unexplained death of a man who from his credit card and business cards we believe to be Harry George Simm.’

‘That’ll be him,’ sounded very positive yet without a slither of grief in her voice.

‘Two things I’m afraid,’ said Bristow. ‘We need somebody to identify the body. Would you be able to do that for us?’ he asked as gently as the manual suggested. ‘And of course firstly we’d also like to learn more about your Harry, to assist us in our investigation’

‘Hmm. Gotta be done eh,’ Mrs Simm grimaced by pinching her mouth together. ‘Much damage t’him d’you know?’ she questioned as if preparing herself for the worst.

‘Post mortem tells us there were no visible damage,’ the DI hoped would be enough to satisfy the obvious motherly curiosity.

‘Blame it on Ally to be honest. Bless his soul,’ was the next gambit from the woman sat there on an easy chair feet together with clasped hands on her knees. Both Bristow and Scoley were eager to ask the obvious but refrained. ‘Look,’ she hesitated and drew in a breath. ‘Working for MoD like Ally did, couldn’t afford any scandal. No sleaze please what they said. Name in the paper or at worst t’ internet.’ She sucked in again, lifted her head and looked at Bristow as Scoley wondered whether or not she had a false teeth problem. ‘Paid her off, so now you know,’ she shrugged her shoulders. ‘Had to forego a decent holiday for a year or two but there’s no way we could have her smearing his good name was there?’

‘Excuse me,’ Oliver Bristow said when he was sure she had finished. ‘Can we go back a bit. Who are we talking about?’ he asked her. ‘Who is this Ally and who is the person you’re referring to?’

Sigh, slight shake of the head and breath blown out unnecessarily ‘Between you and me duck, Alistair’s me husband,’ she revealed. ‘That’s why I wanted a private chat so as not to have his name besmirched by all and sundry around this place and that. We all know what a mess the world’s in these days.’

'And you're here on his behalf?' Scoley slipped in, with besmirched still in her mind.

'Covid,' Mrs Simm said out of the blue as if it's obvious. 'Got it at that second peak. Now with all this nasty business turning up his memory needs protecting,' answered Bristow's next question.

'And the female?' Nicky popped in.

'Gloria Pickwell.'

'And she is who exactly?'

'Was. Harry's partner. Huh, not much of a partnership there,' she scoffed.

'Would you mind telling us what happened?'

'Look,' the woman pointed at Bristow who'd posed the question. 'T'be honest me lad picked on a wrong 'un. Not defending what he mighta done but she'd be forever gallivanting about with her fancy friends. No way to behave.' She stopped as if waiting for a reaction that never arrived. 'Into all this cocktails nonsense and went on what she called a cocktail cruise from one bar to another leaving me lad Harry stuck at home.' Breath blown out again. 'Harry reckons she coulda been into drugs too when she were out. All dressed up like some tart off the back streets.'

Both detectives had come across enough to know exactly the Friday night type she was talking about.

'The situation with her now is what?' Bristow posed, as he tried to fathom how Simm's ex partner's drinking habits might be connected to him freezing to death in his backyard forty miles away.

'Got a new partner in tow I'm told out near Nettleham some place, probably emptying another poor sod's bank account too, more than like.'

'Can we get back to your husband?' Scoley wanted to know. 'We take it Alistair is Harry Simm's father.'

'Of course,' was sharp. 'What d'ya take me for?'

'You say he paid her off. What exactly was that all about if you don't mind?'

'That bloody Gloria bitch. Threatening to go t'police and that. Came round one time telling us what'd been going on.

Him bashin' her abaht and that. Huh,' she shook her head and sighed. 'Didn't mention the money she was shovelling outta their account and chances are she was snoggin' some other bugger too, or worse. Ally calmed her down and then few weeks later she's bloody back suggesting all sorts so he gave her a wad o'cash. Had a word with an old pal of his who fixed her up with a pretty decent small flat in town.'

'What was Harry saying all this time?' Scoley checked.

'Denied it all,' Jodie Simm remarked. 'I'm sorry but me son was brought up better'n that. Me and his dad were an example of how to to respect women. Ran up debts as well the silly bitch an' I always reckoned she was just after more money.'

'Might I ask a couple of things,' was Scoley asking something she'd do anyway. 'Would you care for a cup of tea and, why has it taken so long for you to come forward?'

The pair waited. 'Knew like it had to be him. Not many Simm about. All go for the s on the end. Bit of a throw back from up north someplace,' the sigh returned. 'Please. No sugar.'

Alisha O'Neill had already looked at the name as part of her research. And was aware it was normally spelt Simms or Sims and in Germany seen as a form of Simon.

'But you didn't come forward.'

'Not in touch, sorry.'

'You didn't have to be in touch with him. I'd have thought the name might be a bit of a clue in the media coverage.'

'One o'the lads he used ta bugger abaht with, tracked me down like an' wanted to know if I'd spoke to Harry. Said he'd tried callin' but got nowhere.'

Nicky Scoley went off to order up three drinks and was soon back in the interview room.

'How'd he die then?' was not exactly what Oliver Bristow was hoping for, wanting to move on.

'Between these four walls,' he said with little hope of achieving silence. 'Sorry to say we can't go into specifics but in layman's terms, your Harry was drugged and sat outside all night I'm afraid.' Bristow explained gently as Simm sat there open mouthed. 'He didn't suffer according to the pathologist,' he added but was still not entirely sure it was true. 'He was unconscious already when he passed away.'

'Where was this?'

'In his shop.'

'He still in Mablethorpe?' Jodie Simm asked.

'Yes,' Scoley answered. 'Seems more than likely he invited somebody in he knew.'

'Ally it were, told him to bugger off when things got really nasty between the pair o'them. Sorry can't be doing with it. All me friends seem to play happy families and sort of old knees up but now it's all selfies at barbecues. Clients are always saying their kids are coming round, babysitting for the grandkids, going out for meals and that. Big Christmas do's of course. Me? I'm on me own and now got all this dumped in me lap.' Simm's head dropped a little. 'If only. How often d'we say that? If only he'd got wed to some plain Jane decent lass,' she managed with a tear in her eye and started on her tea. 'But no. Gotta go for all the glamour. Why d'blokes do that?' was prior to returning to the tea she drank down with gusto.

'We have to ask,' was Bristow doing so. 'Did he have any enemies you know of?'

'Only Gloria 'spose but it were all a good few years back, plus her brothers of course.'

'Brothers?' was quick.

'Danny and...Sonny they called him.'

'I don't suppose you have their contact details,' Scoley asked. Pen and notebook at the ready.

'Sorry, not sure I ever have. Huh, never met 'em like,' she sneered.

'And Gloria. Any chance you have her address?'

'No. Only what I bin told. Nettleham or some such place.'

'Gloria Pickwell was it you said?'

'Yeh.'

'On social media I imagine,' Scoley continued as she jotted down the name.

'On it all the damn time, never off her stupid phone. Unless she's changed or the new bloke put a halt to all her crap. Who they bloody talking to's what I want to know?'

‘Any idea what she does for a living?’

‘Make-up counter at Boots last I heard, but gotta be a good couple o’year back now. More maybe.’

The pair waited in case there was more. ‘Have you ever heard of a Miriam Lewis?’ Bristow asked eventually.

‘Who?’

‘Miriam Lewis,’ he said slowly and clearly.

‘No.’

‘What about Blackfriars, not far from St Pauls?’ Scoley checked.

‘What London? St Pauls?’ Scoley nodded. ‘Mean lives there?’

‘You tell us.’

‘No idea. London’s sorta place you goes for days out,’ the detectives wait. ‘Last time were a good year or two back went to an Ed Sheeran gig, before that…’ she paused. ‘Good long while back. Be Jersey Boys, reckon.’

‘Has Harry ever lived down there, worked there maybe?’

‘What? Had a shop you mean?’ she grimaced. ‘Could work the markets maybe. Mean he’d have to stay down there?’ and she shook her head. ‘Never been to this...Blackfriars place you call it.’

‘When was he with this Gloria?’

‘Be...let me see now,’ was time to ponder. ‘Gotta be 2015 maybe 2016 be the start of it all.’

‘And you’ve never heard of a Miriam Lewis?’

‘Like I said. No. Anyway what’s she got to do with anything?’

‘There’s a connection.’ Bristow said as he closed his folder. ‘Just one last thing,’ he added as it came to mind. ‘Did your son wear jeans can you remember? Blue denim jeans.’

‘Used to,’ she shrugged, struggling to understand the link. ‘Probably still does I s’pose, why?’ had her eyes pinched.

‘Just a thought.’ The thought had been a reminder in his notes about CSI having discovering minute threads on the mat just inside the back door. They’d turned out to be from blue Wrangler jeans. Problem was they had none of the clothes he was wearing to compare with.

20

Simple enough process for somebody as experienced with social media as Alisha. She soon came up with three likely candidates and a quick personal message about working with make-up brought up a positive.

It wasn't Nettleham as it turned out but close. Gloria Pickwell lived in Sudbrooke four miles north-east of Lincoln, a third the size of Nettleham a couple of miles away. Initial contact had not been as simple as Oliver Bristow and Nicky Scoley had hoped for. The DI's fall back suggestion was laid before the brunette about being pulled from work in an undignified manner in front of colleagues and the public. To which she reluctantly agreed to the pair calling, on her next day off.

A photograph on a shelf just below a big television screen of a highly tanned Gloria Pickwell arm in arm on a beach with a man said there'd been a change. He was balder, taller and lacked the straggly long hair and unkempt beard epitomizing Harry Simm. Money came to Nicky's mind and the detached house suggested she was never the sole owner, unless that is Alistair Simm really had handed over a shed load of money for her silence. Hardly rang true about an Armed Forces maintenance civilian, unless he'd won the Lottery.

No refreshments were offered and for some reason the pair were ushered through to the big kitchen to sit on uncomfortable stools against a breakfast bar.

Introductions made along with further explanation for their reason for the visit, brought an immediate reaction.

'So I heard.'

'But you didn't come forward,' Bristow suggested in response.

'Why should I?' the peach perfect make-up caked woman shot back. 'Nuthin' t'do with me for ages an' ages.'

‘Why did you ignore our appeals?’

‘Good bloody riddance,’ was out before her brain could stop her. ‘Sorry, sorry, um...’ she said as a form of apology and waved a hand in front of her face as if banishing the words. A complete nonsense Scoley could never fathom a reason for. ‘Look. What’m I gonna know eh?’ she said and dragged in a breath. ‘Look. Right funny buggers them Simm lot let me tell you. One time way back, Harry fell out with his sister big time for no reason. He’s in some local garden centre place and bumps into Cherie with her kid. Toddler he was then. Harry says to the little lad somethin’ like, “Who do we have here then?” and bent down to the little’un. She went absolutely ape shit, screaming in the shop.’ Gloria sat back arms folded shaking her head.

‘Why?’ seemed the only thing for confused and grimacing Scoley to say.

‘Coz according to her he shoulda known what her son’s name was.’ This glammed-up Gloria blew out a deep breath of frustration. ‘Crissakes! Sorta thing we all say. Who d’we have here then and stuff like that. Far as I know not spoken since. Sent Cherie a birthday card an’ nasty bitch sent it back.’

‘Shall we start with…’

‘Look,’ Gloria interrupted sitting forward. ‘His ol’ man was no better. Sort of tosser who’s all for King and country, calls him his boss and flies some RAF flag in his garden and never been in it. Just works with ‘em. What’s that all about?’ was close to being a rant.

And what’s waving your hand in front of your face all about?

‘The break up of your relationship with Harry Simm? Can we get back to that, please?’ Bristow calmly asked still trying to fathom a reason for such an outburst. ‘The why’s and wherefores. Before we move on to cash for silence and your brother.’

‘What?’ she gasped.

‘Harry and your relationship first up please, if you don’t mind.’

‘Nasty controlling shit that’s bloody Harry.’

‘In what way?’ Scoley wanted to know when the woman thought she’s said enough.

‘All the bloody usual. Bastard chose me friends, told me where I could go, who with and meet. Saw the bastard spying on me down the Brayford one time, checking up. Biggest problem was me short sleeved uniform in summer. Hard enough trying to hide marks on me face, but bruised arms is not much fun to deal with.’

‘He hit you often did he?’

‘Nah. Enjoyed playing games with me mind more. Did things like took my car keys with him when he went to work. Meant at the last minute I’m scrambling about and had to run and catch a bloody bus for work. Bastard thought that was fuckin’ funny.’

‘Did he give any reason for all this?’ Scoley queried.

‘Teach me a lesson, ‘ad to be favourite.’

‘Why?’

‘Meal’s not what he fancied. Running out of beer’s the worst crime when there’s an offy less than two hundred yards away, like. Said I’d showed him up in public, when he was more pissed than me. Got told one time he’d bragged to his mates down the pub about how he retained control. Said I loved it, reckoned…’ she sucked in a breath between her teeth. ‘Got a better shag that way, or so he reckoned.’

It occurred to Nicky perched up there, how all this was why his mates had not stepped forward. Chances are they’d had enough and were glad to see the back of him let alone influence from wives and girlfriends who knew the score.

‘These always his friends?’

‘Got friends at work o’course, but they’d all got a better deal than one I got. Few used to go out now and again,’ she pushed out a breath and shook her head. ‘Not me. Look. Never went out regular like with me girlfriends and once or twice when I did for hen nights and stuff, bastard accused me of havin’ sex with strangers.’ Kicked a giant hole in Jodie Simm’s version of the relationship.

‘Not a Friday nighter then?’

‘No bloody chance. He’s off lordin’ it round town, chances are ‘e was shagging left right and centre.’

‘What about enemies?’ Scoley queried.

‘Apart from me you mean?’ she grinned with. ‘One or two he didn’t get on with reckoned were sissies.’

‘Anything...?’

‘His word for gays.’

‘Oh right,’ said Scoley.

‘Thought all this trans business was just complete bollocks.’

‘Anything else you think might be useful to us?’ was better than attempting to comment.

‘Sexist through and through. Get a woman doing rugby on the telly he’d scream abuse at her. Said women footballers were just pissing about spoiling the real game and gays? Enough said,’ as she shook her head and blew out a breath. ‘One in a hundred’s gay so he reckoned, so why d’we have ‘em mincing on every programme and talking soppy?’

‘Couple more points’ said Nicky Scoley in need of a change of subject. ‘Did you approach the Simm’s for money?’

‘No,’ she admitted. ‘He offered like. Didn’t expect that at all. Went to ‘em for help, thought they’d be the best people like being family and that. Nice couple just got a bit desperate s’pose. Shock o’me life when he offered a sort of bribe. No idea they got a few bob stashed away.’

‘Tell me about your brother?’

‘What about him?’ Gloria asked.

‘Did you ask him for help when all this was going on?’

‘Lives in Dorset. Even so they’ve got a couple of young kids takes all their time. I’d never foist my problems on him. Got away in the end thank goodness and life’s good,’ she said happily and glanced all around the kitchen.

Scoley pointed to a photograph. ‘This you and…?’

‘Teddy,’ she said gently, a million miles away from her attitude to Harry Simm. ‘I keep asking mesen when people mention Harry, why couldn’t he be like Teddy?’

‘What’s with the long hair and beard?’ Bristow asked having just glanced at the photo of this Teddy.

‘How d’you mean?’

‘Harry Simm had hair down to his shoulders and a scruffy beard.’

‘News to me,’ she offered.

‘One last thing,’ was Scoley as Oliver Bristow wondered about Harry Simm almost being in disguise, and guessed this Gloria might well not recognize him. ‘Your former partner was killed late in the evening of Sunday 8th of January or early on Monday 9th. We’ll need an alibi from you, your partner and your son. Can we start with you?’

‘When d’you say?’ Pickwell tossed back as she slipped off her stool to check a calendar hanging behind the door.

‘Sunday 8th or Monday 9th.’

‘Mate of ours Trev’s into refurbishing old motorbikes and we meet up with him now and again out at Alford. That’s where we was that night,’ she said tapping the calendar with well manicured nail. ‘Don’t know what time we got home, but not be that late with work next morning.’ Seemed pretty conclusive but at the same time it reminded Oliver Bristow how close Alford is to Mablethorpe.

‘These people are who?’

Name and address they’d get Alisha to check and the pair were all done. For now.

On the way back to base talk between Oliver and Nicky was all about who was likely to be the real Harry Simm. ‘Read somewhere, people like him are emotionally destroyed at birth.’

‘What?’ was all breath.

‘Chances are he never did the kindness lessons at school. Have to wonder what his dad was like. Was he the same you think, but Jodie Simm’ll never admit it in a million years even if he was?’

‘Still no further forward,’ Nicky sighed. ‘But at least it looks as though we’ll get him identified and more’s sure to come out now.’

Two days later Jodie Simm attended the Mortuary to confirm the male cadaver was indeed her son, Harry George Simm. Oliver Bristow who attended with her at Lincoln County saw no sense of grief in the woman. Unless that would arrive and hit her once she was on her own. Alisha having checked the alibis Pickwell had given them linked to motorbikes, both checked out.

21

Nicky Scoley's lengthy chat down with Lucas in the Economic Crime team had produced more of the staple diet of more questions than answers.

He had not been able to discover any link between Quinton's bank account from which he was paying that Wiktoria a sum each month, and being able to afford to fly off here there and everywhere. In fact there were no outgoings for flights or accommodation. Time to relay that to the boss.

Unlike Simm, this Brendon Quinton was creating a bigger better storm on social media. At first the team wondered if this was all the environmental folk, fed up with trying to ban the wind and solar panel farms the country is desperate for. Turning their attention to using one of their own to get a message across. Unless of course Quinton was anti solar for some quirky reason and this was another sector doing their level beast to mark his card. Would somebody working for the council be anti wind and solar? It was certainly never the sort of subject he mentioned on his programme. Oliver Bristow on the other hand knew some Councillors most certainly were.

Helped also that he had been married rather than jumping from one partner to another like Simm had at one time.

The team had been through the various sources and had come up with a Helen and Jack Clement. Their initial approach had been met by a degree of reluctance but in the end Helen Clement nee Quinton agreed to a visit when her husband was home.

According to what they had so far, this Clement woman had been prior to Wiktoria Golebiewska.

DS Nicola Scoley and DC Michelle Cooper rapped on the door and when it was opened a stereotypical goon was stood there in vest, shorts and flip flops.

Nicky Scoley was an attractive young woman of two sides. As tough as old boots and the other version people come into contact with was always smart, intelligent and caring. Perfect for when situations require that particular feminine touch. But not that time.

'Yeh?'

At the sight of him Michelle so wanted to scarper. 'Mr Clement?' was Scoley's good cop.

'What of it?'

'Detective Sergeant Nicola Scoley,' she responded. 'We're here to interview your wife,' she added with her warrant card held up. 'With me here is Detective Constable Michelle Cooper,' Scoley gestured towards her colleague, warrant in hand.

'What abaht?'

'We're here to talk to her about a Brendon Quinton.'

'Dead an' good bloody riddance.'

'We need to talk to your wife if you wouldn't mind, sir.'

'Make a bloody appointment.'

'We have done sir, that's why we're here now,' was a more strident Scoley.

'You what?' he spat out. 'Hels!' he yelled back into the house. Within a second or two this woman smaller than both detectives appeared. 'Bloody cops 'ere reckon they come fer you lass.'

'Yes, yes,' said the brown haired woman as she gestured hurriedly for the pair to enter.

'Hey!' was close to a shout. 'How come I dunno 'bout this?' says unpleasant Clement as he planted a grubby fat hand on the far wall obstructing the officers.

Helen Clement blew out a weary breath. 'Because I knew what you'd be like.'

'Told yer before missus. I decide who comes in 'ere,' was more of his pleasantries.

'If you wouldn't mind, sir,' said Scoley and with obvious reluctance he pulled his arm away and the pair entered.

Shown into a small untidy lounge, the pair sat together on a small sofa 'Tea, coffee?' Helen Clement asked down. The message in her eyes was so easy to read for the pair of them.

'No thanks,' they replied almost in unison having seen the state of the place.

'Coffee,' came from uncouth Jack Clement stood arms folded in the doorway.

'I'm sure you can make your own, dear. These ladies are busy people.'

'Coffee, I said,' and without another word the embarrassed timid wife trooped off out of the room.

Something Nicky had never understood no matter how many women in Clement's situation she'd come across. So many of them never seem to learn. Meet one objectionable partner and then in time the downtrodden punchbag of a woman has linked up with another carbon copy moron.

'Nah then,' said this Clement still stood there arms folded legs apart. 'Whas this all abaht? You buggers know who did fer 'im yet?'

'We're here,' said Scoley as calmly as she could to this objectionable scruffbag. The sort in a vest who moan about energy prices. 'To interview your wife about Brendon Quinton. That's all. Nothing more.'

'What yer need to know? Bloke's a right bastard.'

'That's for your wife to tell us,' Scoley told him without adding, *and not you.*

'Another bunch o'bloody muppets,' he scoffed. 'He gobs in street is me missus responsible for that too, eh?'

'Sorry, sir?' Scoley said as she got to her feet. Always particularly protective of Michelle Cooper who had been badly injured once by a now behind bars waste of space unemployable ruffian who answered the door during a search for a missing child.

'Pair o'you got nuffin' better to do? Aint you got a murder to solve? Arrests some geezer an' give 'im a pat on the back? What about bloody burglars, kids on those scooters nearly basked into me old Ma? And all the piss head students rampaging round town Friday nights eh? Wha' about sortin' that buncha shit bags?'

'We're here sir, to talk to her about your wife's ex husband. Nothing else.' Before she sat down again Nicky Scoley provided her first warning. 'We'd ask you not to interfere if you wouldn't mind. Otherwise we'll conduct this interview in private.'

'What bollocks is that? This is my house missus.'

'We'll carry out this at the station if necessary. Do you understand?'

'I pays yer wages yer know,' made Scoley sigh obviously.

'Yes sir, we've heard it all before. Now if you wouldn't mind, please sit down and keep quiet.'

'And if not?'

'The choice is yours Mr Clement. Stay and keep quiet, alternatively remove yourself from the room or I call up a van to take you away. What'll it be?'

'Knew him as well.'

'That's good. We'll get round to that later.'

Jack Clement never did sit down and when his little wife appeared with a big white mug with an obscene slogan printed in red he stood there drinking. Noisily.

'Now Mrs Clement,' Scoley started as soon as the woman had settled down on a chair opposite. 'What can you tell us about Brendon Quinton?'

'What happened? Folks saying all sorts.'

'We have a long process to go through first. Now what do you think we need to know as part of our inquiries?' the DS asked.

'See this,' she said tugging down the neck of her pale purple nylon jumper. 'He did that,' although from where she was sat Scoley couldn't actually see anything.

'Are you suggesting he was violent?'

'Not suggestin' missus. Bloody was,' came from the dregs Clement stood there.

'What did we agree Mr Clement?' Scoley threw up at him. 'Your wife answers the questions unless you were there and you're offering yourself as a witness,' she turned back to Helen. 'Was this regular?' she posed gently.

'Hmm. Too clever by half that one, 'she says touching her neck. 'Only time what he'd done could easy be seen. Had to wear long sleeves for ages and to hide this,' she was back tapping the side of her neck. 'Have'ta wear polo necks even in bloody summer.'

'What else can you tell me about him?'

'Used to play mind games wiv me when I'd done somethin' to upset him' admitted Helen Clement.

'Such as?'

'Hid things. Like me credit card. Then blamed it on me, back to calling me a stupid cow and worse.'

'Am I right in thinking the missing items suddenly re-appeared?' was DC Cooper.

'Always. Like with me bank card, think it was. On the phone to the bank people when he claimed he'd discovered it. Snatched the phone and went on to tell the bank person I was a complete pillock and apologized for wasting their time.' She stopped to suck in a breath between her teeth, before releasing with a sigh. 'Kinda suggested I had dementia, and kept forgetting stuff.'

'What about monitoring your whereabouts?' Michelle continued with. 'Did he check up on you, even stalk you as we've come across in some cases. Maybe called at your friends on an excuse for a quick chat to see you were where you should be?'

'Not that I know of. Could have though. One thing's for sure he'd embarrass me in front of me friends. Then tell 'em things like I thought I'd lost me phone and he'd had to apologize to the insurance people which never happened. Yeh I thought I'd lost it for a few hours but obviously I didn't have a phone to call any insurance people.'

'On the subject of your phone. Did he have access to it?'

'Yeh. Knew the pin.'

'Insisted he knew the pin?' was Scoley's next question.

'Probly, now you come to mention it.'

‘What about finance? Did you have a joint account?’ Scoley checked.

‘Yes, but…’ never went any further.

‘But what?’

‘He did everythin’, said useless bitch like me’d never work it out.’

‘What about providing proof of purchase,’ Michelle joined in again and read from her tablet list provided by her old boss who’d been through this with women countless times in her new role.

‘Not with groceries and stuff like that, but with anything else really, specially stuff for me. Had to tell him how much I planned to spend. Then when I gets home he’d go on line and check what I’d spent. Usedta say things like “See you spent £24 on that crap jumper. Be a sort of reminder to me to be careful.’.

‘Not happen here,’ suddenly Jack Clement piped up still stood there. Before he poured the remnants of his coffee down his throat and plonked the empty mug on the coffee table.

‘What’ll not happen?’ Scoley decided was the best policy for now as he appeared to have calmed.

‘She manages all the money,’ he admitted. ‘Not good me wi’ all that business with computers and that.’

‘Anything else?’ Scoley asked Helen. ‘What about his job? Being connected to the environment and climate change how involved was he?’

Helen Clement grinned then smiled as she shook her head. ‘Just a job. Worked on Council Tax then heard of some new job going to do with that Climate Change business. Better pay that’s all. Read up on a load of stuff then pretended. Went to one or two sort of hard-core environmental group’s meetings to show willing. Think goin’ out and about he reckoned was a good skive. Sorry, just a job not a career or anythin’ he was interested in to be honest.’

‘What about being on the radio?’

‘Hear tell they call that bollocks music,’ both women ignored.

‘Never listened. Couldn’t when it were that Hospital business. Now I’d not give ‘im the satisfaction, thank you.,’

‘And in the end you moved on,’ Michelle Cooper suggested as Scoley’s mind linked what she’d just been told to the negative comments by some on social media. Where it appeared the trolls had sussed him out. Had his role been nothing more that local government going through the box ticking process to keep Whitehall happy?

‘Look. As ridiculous as it sounds h’d to keep reminding him what went in what bin. You know all that no black plastic in the brown bin meant for plastic nonsense.’ She sighed at the thought of him. ‘Just got fed up to the back teeth wiv it all.’

‘Environment issues you mean?’

‘No life with Bren.’

‘It’s early stages in our inquiries and we’re struggling to discover anything about his family. Do you still have their details by any chance?’

Helen blew out a breath. ‘Why would I?’

‘Fair enough. What about gaming?’ Cooper wanted to know. ‘Was he into all that then?’

‘Yeh. Stayed up all bloody night sometimes. Silly sod.’

‘What about trips abroad?’

‘Guess where I went on me holidays eh? Answer me that,’ was a question in no need of a reply. ‘Me sisters. Wanna know why? He’s off on some stupid gaming trip some place.’

‘Last but not least, do you know a Wiktoria Golebiewska?’

‘Ah maybe,’ she mumbled and looked at her husband again. He just about managed to grimace. ‘Someone reckoned at one time he was seeing some foreign bint. Student fink they said, no idea where from.’

‘But you don’t know her?’

‘No. Only bits and that what I heard.’

‘Thank you,’ said a smiling Scoley. ‘Appreciate it.’ Nicky Scoley was first to her feet followed by Cooper and they headed for the half open door. ‘Thank you Mr Clement,’ said Scoley sarcastically as she walked past him.

‘I’d get fed up to the back teeth living with a creature like that,’ said Michelle in Nicky’s Mini.

'Why do some women do that? Jump out of the frying pan into the fire. Cannot imagine what possesses somebody like her.'

'Imagine going home to that.'

'I'd not go home!'

'Could have been worse could've got a sniff of weed.'

'Or better.'

'Think we'll run him through the system. Really thought he was going to crack off at one point.'

Back at Lincoln Central they discovered the issue for the husband being so anti when up popped Jack Raymond Clement on PNC. Currently banned from driving for two years after being caught drink driving on the by-pass near the Whisby turnoff.

Nicky Scoley took it upon herself to brief the team on what she had discovered.

'This gaming business is known as esports, except it's never a sport. Big events with thousands watching with half a dozen on the stage playing. I can't imagine how anybody can get excited watching other people playing games.'

'Be like watching Tyler playing tiddlywinks,' Jake scoffed.

'Thought it was for kiddies,' said Sandy.

'Live Ludo's gotta be exciting!'

'When they were younger Jordan and Russell shared one of those Xbox things,' Nicky advised. 'Good few years ago my dad flogged it at a car boot.'

'I read somewhere,' said Jamie. 'This esports is being considered for the Olympics, but for a major problem. The esports bosses say applying the same anti drugs stance as other events will be impossible.'

'Here's something else,' Nicky added. 'Looked it up. Tickets for a big esports tournament or whatever they call them are around £300.'

'You're joking!'

'Tickets, flights, hotel, food and drink. That's why he needed the dosh.'

During afternoon briefing the Detective Inspector advised how he'd called Shona Tate the Senior Forensic Scene Manager to ask her to undertake another thorough search of Quinton's flat. He explained how he wanted to get to the bottom of him having little money left after paying his ex-partner a lump each month. Yet he was able to head off abroad a couple of times a year to gaming competitions.

'There's more,' he said. 'Jamie's had a phone call from somebody Quinton worked with at the council. Play it back please Jamie.'

"To be honest," said the voice belonging to a Trevor Garside. *"Just a squarish peg to plug a hole when there was a hint of cash coming our way. Due to a basic lack of interest Bren was unaware of some of the basics. Unaware of how we have a brief and fast closing window of opportunity to resolve a sustainable future for the planet. Nice enough guy at times but not wishing to speak ill of the dead, not up to it, to he honest."* Jamie stopped the recording.

'He's not finished yet,' and they waited.

"Bren had never for some reason understood legislation." the voice went on. *"Legislation compelling every one of us, councils included of course as a priority to prevent abuse to human rights. We are all falling short on delivering on our commitments and keeping positive reaction alive."*

'Is there any point?' Sandy asked as he sighed. 'In people like us asking what on earth that has to do with rising tides?'

'And they wonder why the poor sod wasn't up to speed when that's a brief resume of what I pay Council Tax for. Complete hogwash.'

'That's not all,' said Jamie.

'Please no!'

'Also been contacted by one of the women I spoke to, I guess didn't want to talk openly in the office. Apparently misogyny was a real issue when he was around. Told me it was often very obvious he preferred not to work with women and constantly critical of them in particular with regard to sport. Claiming at one time to have sent texts to the BBC about a woman introducing a Test Match wearing high heels on the pitch as she did so,' he read from his notes and stopped for a quick swig of flavoured water. 'Women's football,' he went on. 'Was another target, with emphasis on dizzy female presenters and commentator for women's matches but male and female are used for men. Apparently he'd once talked about men being criticized for wearing trainers to do the weather, but the women in comparison according to him looked like slags out on the pull.'

'Getting a better picture for once.'

Two days later Nicky Scoley's phone pinged and to her surprise it was Helen Clement with details of her former parents-in-law and not made any reference to her not knowing previously.

Turned out to be a landline and when she called to arrange to visit the person at the other end explained how they had bought the property from a Mrs Pauline Quinton but had a forwarding address up in South Shields.

22

Hello there, how you getting on?

With the intimate yet positive role I play in women's lives, at times it feels as though I'm their confessor. Hear a great deal of course like I guess hairdressers must do, about their lives. Including intimate revelations some seem willing to reveal to somebody they only meet maybe half a dozen times a year.

One woman I saw on a regular basis for a few months, I think because she had a desperate need to download her thoughts and fears was one I'll call Rhona.

At that time she still part owned the house she had shared with her husband who despite their separation was still living there and had no intention of moving out. He was free to come and go as he pleased, enjoy the home they'd built together while she and her two young children, who had to change schools of course, were trapped in a strange downmarket environment without the majority of home comforts she was used to.

Patsy Greenhall on the other hand has been a client for a good few years now and her chatter unlike others which are in the main topical, tends not cover a broad range of subjects.

She'll visit me before or after lavish holidays in the sun. I get all her talk about everything I'd personally never consider or go anywhere near. The amount they drink before they board the plane, what they scoff during the flight and from then on its all lying out in the sun and supping Sangria on these all inclusive deals they get.

Just the very thought of lying on an uncomfortable sun bed by the poolside just to get red sore bores me, let alone the thought of completely wasting two weeks of my life.

Holidays to me are always an adventure. Why go to Pisa and not climb the tower? Why on earth would anybody go to Egypt, stay at somewhere like gawdy Sharm El Sheikh, which could be anywhere with nothing but loads of sand and ignore the Pyramids, Valley of the Kings and actually not see Tutankhamun's golden mask close up for real?

I've been to the top of a ski slope in Norway but not skied down obviously. Watched baseball in Toronto. Panned for gold in Australia, saw a wild kangaroo followed by tea made over an open fire in a billycan. You can't get anything close to that in Ayia Napa.

Lurid stories I get from Patsy before she leaves about what she has planned which if you break it down amounts to nothing much at all.

Then on her return it really is a good twenty minutes sometimes of her boasting about parties in their rooms and how much booze they put away day and night. I'm quite sure the gets a sense of achievement from it all. A sort of badge of honour.

All this done as one big family outing. Six or eight of them and often a bunch of control kids thrown in.

As with so many things in life I frequently ask myself why. Why do some women stand with their legs crossed making themselves vulnerable, as if they need to go to the toilet. Why do younger people ride their bikes with their instep on the pedal to make the whole thing so much more difficult. Maybe its some fitness trend. Why do people dye their hair blue or green? I could go on.

Another is schoolteacher Brigit Arthur. Recently with her I've had to be very careful indeed. Bringing local news into our conversation including reference to Brendon Quinton had me treading very carefully. Was it Mark Twain who said "If you tell the truth you don't need to remember anything"?

Got to say I can put up with all these sometimes bizarre conversations. I'll show a degree of interest providing I can keep them well away from asking my opinion on local tragedies the media have now dubbed Yellowbelly Murders, I suppose that's due to his link with the radio place, but the Police have interestingly stated they are not linked, thank goodness.

One young woman got a bee in her bonnet about news reporters on the BBC wearing clothing bearing a manufacturers logo. Like reporting for News At Ten stuck out in a snowstorm somewhere wearing a North Face coat rather than a jumper his gran had knitted.

To this Felicity, as the BBC is publicly funded they should not appear on screen wearing what she says mounts to free advertising.

Something else which increasingly grates on me are these people who are permanently offended. Think it must have been around Christmas when somebody started a petition to stop that awful Katie Price woman appearing on stage locally with her so-called comedy act.

If like me you can't stand the woman, do as I do. Just stay away. Nobody is forcing you to buy tickets. After all as far as I know we don't yet live in a dictatorship where a few biddies can tell us where we can go, watch or do.

On the subject of bad behaviour, bullying comes readily to mind. I don't remember being bullied at school but maybe I was. With it not being such high profile as it is these days, maybe I just didn't recognize it as such. Guess I'll have snowflakes telling me off if I suggest its just banter.

Back to the here and now. There have of course over recent weeks been a great many pitfalls to avoid such as the casual normal everyday conversations. The *'What have you been doing with yourself?'* questions out of the blue I've mentioned before I think.

Other odd ball things pop up now and again. A new client suggesting she'd visited me on recommendation as part of her need to distress from the rigours of her career. When I asked about her life I was bemused by 'I'm a relationship director of course.'

I know a good few women who could use someone to sort out their relationships.

First. Why, of course and secondly what on earth did she do? Got to say, at one time when some silliness like that popped into conversations I'd ask, only to then be even more confused by the response. Nowadays ignoring is frequently the best policy.

As I sometimes do I called up my friend Google to check out Relationship Director. When it started going on about business growth strategy I knew enough was enough. This was another pretentious name like the ones they give to the bin men.

All that changing firemen to firefighters is just the sort of thing I find so utterly pointless. Yet, they refer to policemen and policewomen. We have plain and simple paramedics, doctors, chemists. Is the firefighter business a slight on women I wonder? I notice we still use mankind, man-made, management and maniac, but maybe that's stretching it a bit. Female models in shop windows are still manikins. So I rest my case.

I often think after a session with one of these women how there's a whole world of silliness going on out there I have no experience of whatsoever.

A while ago I decided rather than ignoring what people are writing about NFT's I'd never known what it meant. So, decided to give Google a job.

Turns out it means Non-Fungible Tokens, and I quote *"a digital asset representing real world objects."* Even 'fungible' made no sense to me. That so I'm told, is what they call a commodity replaceable by another identical item, mutually interchangeable. At least the 'dark net' makes sense!

One thing I have noticed to concern me greatly is, how infrequently their families were involved in their issues.

When sometimes I query how parents have reacted to the news, I face the oft repeated phrase about, how they've got more than enough on to be worried without their child's problems. The problems to my mind are not about busy parents, but their main obstacle is disinterested families.

Know this guy who when he was younger was an exceptionally gifted cross country runner. Was a county and inter-county champion and ran for Wales. He once told me sadly when we were discussing issues with families that not one of his parents or brother and sister (siblings some call them these days for no good reason), had ever watched him run.

Signs to me of a toxic family relationship he had to endure. Emotional neglect but for why? Is that down to pure jealousy?

Then on the other hand some of the mother daughter relationships you see are themselves not that good for the child. Providing them with an unreal sugary sweet image of the world.

We've all seen or heard about unseemly pictures on social media between fathers and daughters. Blonde teenage girl squatting on the floor in her pyjamas opening Christmas presents egged on by family, with the father sat there oggling with unhealthy thoughts.

Next time you see pictures of a father cuddling a girl in a bikini in the sea, you can see the total displeasure by the look in her eyes.

On the other hand walking down the High Street you seen countless mothers who never have control of their child. Yet on the other hand, fathers are quite the opposite.

23

Ahead of Nicky Scoley was one of those conversations nobody in the force relishes. Calling a mother about her son's death without knowing if the woman was already aware of when and how. Frequently, especially at night, totally ignorant of the fact.

Attractive Nicky in her early thirties, would tell you with true honesty how much she enjoyed almost all aspects of her role. Save for one. Breaking news of death to a parent or loved one.

She'd worked hard to get out of uniform, as the increasingly aggressive nature of too many on the streets she'd found difficult to cope with constantly.

Her move to DC had been worthwhile and she felt more comfortable. Even a spell down in Cambridge organized by the Darke boss to sharpen her skill set had improved her no end.

So often in the role she was heading for there and then, to gain the confidence and influence you are after, there is a need to tease it from them despite their distressed state.

Her day had started with another bout of nonsense they were all very used to. On her way in the Desk Sergeant told her about some scrag of a women arrested the previous night for ABH in a pub in the city. She was complaining according to Sergeant Steve Elvidge about her breakfast, but to her more importantly it seemed a lack of facilities.

In her cell overnight, she'd been demanding her human right to moisturize, exfoliate and sunscreen protection factor.

'If you're not careful, you can get a nasty sunburn in Cell 14,' Steve had quipped.

With that crass absurd nonsense still in her mind it very soon had to sit alongside news on her system the moment Nicky logged on. Two more people down south had been charged with conspiring to arrange the travel of a child with a view to harvesting her organs. How many other jobs, Nicky frequently wondered to herself, offered as much variety? From utter tripe one moment to appalling criminality beyond belief.

To Nicky, face to face had always been a bad experience but phoning had to be worse. The look of the person, their reaction their stature all came into play. This Pauline Quinton could easily be some feeble sick little woman or if she was lucky be more in control and robust.

The difficult call quickly revealed this Pauline Quinton had no knowledge of her son's death. The woman who sounded well and quite chirpy despite the news, had moved to live with her sister in South Shields after her husband died. South Shields Nicky then discovered was where Pauline Quinton's sister's husband had been brought up. Joined the RAF and met Brenda when he was stationed at Coningsby, about twenty five miles from Lincoln.

Quinton's father had died in the early stages of Covid in 2020 because he didn't like being told how to live his life by people such as Boris Johnson, and just carried on living life as normal as best he could until he started to cough.

Pauline Quinton admitted to Scoley she saw little of her son mainly due to the distance involved. 'Hardly,' she said. 'Somewhere he can just pop in for a cuppa,' sounded to the DS very much like an excuse.

When they get round to discussing friends and relatives who just might be able to provide assistance with their inquiries, this Pauline offered to look people up for her and call Nicky back. From the names she was given half an hour later, mainly relatives, the info was passed to Alisha to look at activity for any on social media. This resulted in a good few phoned interviews being carried out.

Shona Tate's major issue right from the start had been a lack of evidence. As far as they could discover it seemed quite possible the intruder had gone no further into Brendon Quinton's flat than the hallway.

The Senior Forensic Scene Manager had been looking for anything associated with his murder. Obvious stuff like a discarded weapon, blood, DNA, fingerprints even a cannabis grow or needles would be an obvious give away. Evidence of a visitor and a subsequent violent encounter apart from the stabbing, were simply not there. Nor was his home a ramshackle dirty filthy dive of a place. In fact too tidy by half had been another element to annoy Shona.

With her team unable to discover drugs, money or weapons. In the end Shona used a general purpose Cocker Spaniel.

'Ready for this,' said a strident Oliver Bristow as he stepped out from his office. 'Shona's just been using a sniffer dog almost as a last resort seems to me. He's came up trumps with a whole host of useful stuff.'

'He?'

'Jack the dog.'

'Oh right.'

'Cash amounting to £3,200 odd,' he read from his tablet. 'Amphetamines in a blue plastic bag and his passport. All deviously hidden behind the central heating boiler. Access they eventually discovered once the dog stood stock still, was by pulling up a thin wire from a pipe at the top to which blue plastic bags were attached. One contained a burner phone.' When Nicky laughed he stopped. 'What's so funny?'

'An environmentalist using plastic bags.' Oliver smiled his realization and shook his head. 'I know one way to store a phone is put it in the freezer, but what about heat?'

'Not if you never put the heating on.'

'Wow!' the DI exclaimed unusually. 'Of course. That's what that Wiktoria woman said. He never put the heating on claiming it was because he was totally against fossil fuels.'

'Guess it was the drugs he didn't want her to spill the beans about or find maybe. She'd tell his boss about the abuse. They tell us, we investigate and bingo! Forget the abuse but hey our Spaniel Jack can smell it.'

'How much we talking?' Jake queried.

'Clever. Not going for cannabis with the smell he'd have to deal with or crack for the world's idiots to smoke. All in 10mg tablets,' said Oliver from his screen stroking his beard.

'Our killer after drugs then?'

Oliver sighed. 'You tell me. But to be honest what else is there? Gotta be dealing surely, with amphets and a burner phone hidden away.'

'Sell Amphetamines to fund his life to some extent and in particular to allow him to afford to go abroad for the Gaming tournaments.'

The DI was nodding. 'Now we're getting somewhere.'

Lucas from the Economic Crime team eventually came back with answers. He'd put Brendon Quinton, into his banking system and only came up with three accounts with Brendon as a first name. Then without going through a lengthy and tedious process of entering Quinton he just put in the name Wiktoria. Out of nowhere up popped a highly likely Wiktoria Quinton in an obscure Irish Bank.

Lo and behold the account was full of cash in and cash out entries. Cash the team decide was for when he needed to pay for trips abroad.

Hard on the heels of that info was the early toxicology results from the post-mortem. Confirmation of some aspects surrounding the obvious stabbing, but interestingly advice that Quinton had no sign of drugs in his system. Dealer not user was most unexpected, but sensible in such a nasty world.

24

'Thank god we didn't book,' said a frustrated Connor Mitchell, CSI Photographer and Nicky Scoley's partner looking at his phone. Nicky in her underwear was across the bedroom from him. 'Just what we need,' he said reading the screen. 'Woman's been shot in Metheringham.'

'You what?' she gasped. 'Be serious!' Nicky exclaimed.

'Told you before, love. Want a quiet life,' Connor quipped. 'Work for the council.'

'Shooting in Metheringham? Really?' she glanced at her watch. 'You do have to wonder if this is some sort of scam. Pulling us away on some pretext.''

'Shires Coffee Shop in the High Street,' Connor advised, and looked across at his blonde partner.

'Coffee shop. This time of day? What time d'they shut?'

'Sorry pet,' he apologized. 'Been looking forward to it.'

'You and me both,' she uttered as her phone buzzed. Nicky sighed and shook her head. 'What's the betting,' she said picking up her phone. 'Here we go. Code Red.'

'Wonder where?' Connor joked.

'Ah well. There goes my Kathmanchu chicken.'

'Bloody looking forward to that Gurkha platter.'

Ten minutes later evening-out clothes strewn across the bed, they were in Connor's car, heading for Bracebridge Heath, the A15 and south.

The moment the pair arrived Connor's first photo shoot was obvious. Somebody or something had smashed the front window of Shires Coffee Shop. Stood leaning back against their car were two of the Armed Response crew.

'Medics in there and the local doc,' one of them told the pair. 'Best you stay out for now.'

'What cracked off?'

‘Owner was inside sorting out paperwork in the office at the back apparently, when bang.’

‘This time of day?’

‘What she reckons,’ he shrugged. ‘Walks out front to get a coffee of all things and bang. Window smashed and she’s hit in the shoulder. Made a right mess, not life threatening but not good according to the local doctor. Ambo on its way but you know how long they can take.’

With Jake Goodwin away on a course, Nicky found herself as the Senior Investigating Officer, until maybe the boss turned up. Maybe being the operative word.

The local bobbies had somehow fixed the mandatory blue and white tape to four traffic cones. Nicky and Connor pulled on their white protective suits from their black issue holdalls to put on in the Co-op car park. An incitent had been erected by the CSI team to hide sight of what was going on. Hopefully protecting the view from a small gathering of onlookers.

Without immediate access being possible, rather than just standing around waiting, Nicky Scoley went to check up and down High Street. Called in at the Co-op and spoke to two people hanging around waiting to see what was happening. They, like the staff she spoke to just heard a bang, then a car screaming away. Nicky took a note of their names and walked back to the scene but on the other side of the road. Quick check at the Pizza place who could add nothing and back to the scene.

At the war memorial there was a sign pointing to the church, one to a Swimming Pool and third to the Village hall. He or she could have come in one of two ways and from what the shoppers said, had headed out to her right as she faced Shires Coffee opposite. Cop car across at the corner to her left was stopping any traffic.

Nearest she and Connor had got to Metheringham for a while was stopping off for coffee one morning at Hanworth Country Park a mile or two back.

Treading carefully inside, Nicky realized immediately not to try to inveigle her way to gain a better view. The décor said it had probably been a village tea shop in its day and had converted itself into the usual Coffee Shop furnishings and serving at the counter systems to join the trend. Dominating as always, was one of those complicated looking auto fill coffee machines. There were some elements of old décor remaining but she doubted cake stands and doilies were still available.

Access beyond the counter with the doctor and the woman there, made entering what she assumed was the back office and stores impossible. Just a case of standing back watching as Connor continued to take general scene shots.

Nothing appeared to have been disturbed. No chairs or tables upturned. No scenes of crime, no blood, just that window and glass all over the floor.

In the open shop door strode white suited Forensic Scene Manager Shona Tate. 'Second time in a row,' she announced as she approached Nicky. 'Last week we were watching a bloody movie, now tonight...' she grinned as she shook her masked and hooded head. 'Lads been round the back, nothing but need daylight to be absolutely sure. Looks to me like it's easy gotta be a drive by.'

'In Metheringham?' was gasped by more than one.

'Not exactly Chicago is it?'

'This the local mafia then? Major Crime outfit, turf war maybe,' was Nicky attempting to lighten the mood.

'Or a bunch of bloody kids,' said Connor from behind his cameras.

'With a gun?' Shona chuckled as she said it. 'Are we serious?'

Once the ambulance had arrived and removed the woman up to the County Hospital. DC Sandy MacLachlan had also turned up to take on what turned out to be the unnecessary co-ordinating role between the various elements. Shona and her CSI team were then able to get to work. The process was to some extent short lived with no DNA or fingerprints to uncover. No witnesses they knew about. Even the few shocked neighbours who had gathered outside could provide next to no information

Sandy had phoned DI Oliver Bristow to suggest there was no need to call all the team together as he'd arranged with the Prisoner Handling Unit night shift to deal with any incoming messages. Connor and Nicky with their evening spoilt, agreed to stay put with Sandy until the front window had been boarded up, with a glazier ordered for the morning.

Only nosy parkers Nicky could spot now were this blobby big woman deep in conversation on her phone, with the local trolls having dispersed when the action subsided.

Nobody admitted to knowing where the shot had been fired from. Two or three assumed it was a car backfiring but she doubted whether most modern cars still do that.

One driver looked peeved through the open window of a Vauxhall as if expecting one of the young coppers to provide chapter and verse he could put on his What'sApp account.

From what Nicky Scoley had discovered from the few people out and about there had been nobody actually walking along the street at the time. No other traffic anyone could recall. How had they done that? Waited for it to go quiet, race hell for leather down the street and bang.

On their way home Nicky and Connor discovered even Mill Lodge the Beefeater was closed. Next on their list before they reached home, was to stop off at the County Hospital to be updated about the woman's condition. There they met her husband Ben anxiously waiting for news, who was able to provide information they then would set in place.

Next morning on arriving at Lincoln Central, Nicky Scoley was surprised to see all the team in the Incident Room save for Sandy, all hard at work as if they'd been there all night. She quickly understood Bristow had called them in early.

With Alexander 'Sandy' MacLachlan back down in Metheringham and with Jake on a course, the DI began his briefing.

'Very little to say,' he started with. '38 year old Gwen Abbott owner of Shires Coffee also has two other similar coffee places in Wragby and Horncastle. Married with two children and they live with her husband Ben, father of the children in Woodhall Spa. According to what little we can obtain from the County, she was shot in the left shoulder. Being operated on this morning and there may be a need for a degree of reconstructive surgery. Shires Coffee is closed. Glaziers will be there later today. Nicky please, if you would.'

'Pretty much as the boss says. Spoke with her husband Ben Abbott last night up at the County. He gave me some information. Then this morning kindly messaged me with details of senior staff who will arrange to clean the place up once Shona and the boys have finished and do their best to re-open.' She stopped to drink the coffee she'd got on the way in.

'To gain from the publicity,' cynical Rufus added.

'Called him early,' said Nicky ignoring the remark. 'Arranged for Jamie to head off down to the coffee shop, pick up Gwen Abbott's work laptop and then visit Mr Abbott at home to collect her personal one he told us last night she's got. Had her mobile phone in her pocket as it turns out, so he'll head up there to collect it for the Tech Crime Team.'

Some day very soon, they were experienced enough to expect something critical would be discovered on a smartphone, a laptop, a letter or diary entry. Some tat revealed on social media or a note stuck to the fridge door.

The Tech Crime Team geeks would deal with data from service providers, the internet, phone companies and emails.

'Thanks,' Bristow acknowledged. 'Think this might be a job for you,' he said across to Alisha. 'This is all a total mystery, most certainly out of place. When was the last time we had a shooting and you'll need the archives to find gun use out in one of the villages. Yeh, bit of shooting rabbits and maybe a gamekeeper or two. Be a case of eyes down on social media pick up what the grapevine has to offer.'

'Boss,' said Nicky looking at her phone. 'Local coppers are handling door-to-door.' she grinned. 'Be a case of butcher, baker and candlestick maker, and we were told last night most don't live over the shop, so to speak.' Just as Bristow was about to get in a word, she went on. 'Didn't even get a coffee. With no Nescafe, none of us knew how to work the big machines.'

'Michelle,' said Bristow seemingly unamused by Nicky's remarks. 'Background please on this Gwen Abbott and her husband. Rufus, take on Shires Coffee if you will. Anybody ever been there by the way?' nobody responded other than a shake of the head. 'Leave you with your actions I'm off to brief the boss.'

'Just a thought before you go,' was Nicky. 'Husband seemed keen to get the place open as soon as. Hint of money trouble maybe or taking advantage of the publicity?'

'Good thinking.'

'This might interest the Darke boss,' she quipped. 'With free coffee in the offing.'

'Boss,' said an anxious Nicky Scoley, on Oliver's return. 'While you were away, answered your phone. Surgeon found the bullet. Shona's sending one of her team up there for it.'

'That's proper progress.'

Alisha O'Neill was up next. 'Boss. News is starting to trickle in. One or two of the useless asking where they can get a coffee. Got one prat saying they'll not be serving Cookie Crumble Frappe or Kahlua today,' she had trouble pronouncing, 'Coffee Float means its a waste of time, but,' she hesitated. 'One of the regular bloggers heads her piece this morning with Cereal Killer Spree With Coffee, then goes back to some daft fashion silliness.'

'That's all we need,' said Bristow shaking his head. 'Please,' he talked to the ceiling. 'We've got two men murdered. Neither of them know each other that we know of. How in God's name can some coffee shop woman be involved if she is?'

'Another one in her own shop though, to go along with Simm.'

'That really all we have?' Bristow gasped. 'Dead Simm in his rag bag shop and this woman murdered for serving a crap Latte. You think retail is a serious link?'

Nicky Scoley caught Michelle's eye and both sensed what the other was thinking. Bristow was struggling badly. She kept comparing him with Inga Larsson and was forever asking herself what she would do differently in this case.

'Hypothermia, stabbed and shot don't really go together,' Rufus offered.

'One froze to death, one stabbed with a kitchen knife and now we've suddenly progressed to Heckler and Koch have we?' Oliver sarcastically posed to Rufus. 'This what you Yellerbellies call natural progress?'

'We get a serial killer jumping from one to another every chuffing time?' Nicky offered. 'Their MO's usually better safe than sorry.'

'Gwen Abbott' said Michelle. 'She and her husband Ben both originate from Derbyshire. Married with two children and he's the Service Manager at a local Fiat dealer. Nothing on PNC for either. Trying to track down where and when they married, if they did.'

Nicky and Connor had warned Ben Abbott the CSI team may well wish to search the family home. He at first had seen somewhat disgruntled with a degree of insolence about him. In the end accepted the inevitable. There was nothing he could do about it, search warrant or not. Better that than they big red key his door in.

25

As soon as was possible DS Nicola Scoley was despatched to Lincoln County Hospital up on Greetwell Road for a short brief initial chat with Gwen Abbott.

She was sat up in bed with her left shoulder bandaged and padded and Nicky imagined she normally looked brighter than the pale woman before her. Introductions completed, a warning about length of stay from the Staff Nurse and she had her notebook in hand.

'Could you please take us through events from your perspective?' Scoley posed kindly.

Quietly and with an opening sigh Abbott began her story. 'Got three coffee houses, and obviously can't be at all places at once. So,' she said and pushed out a breath of weariness. 'Have this system where in the main I operate from Metheringham being the busiest. One day a week I visit the other two just before my staff lock up for the night to carry out my own form of stocktaking. Not actually counting how many packets of biscuits we have and all that. Rather its an opportunity to talk to staff and discuss issues without being disturbed by customers. They leave and I stay on just to give the business a once over. How clean is everything are stocks at the correct level all that sort of thing. Always need to bear Environmental Health in mind.'

'Then what?'

'Just felt thirsty, had a busy day and walked out front to grab a bottle of the flavoured water we sell a lot of these days, and bang,' she just held her right hand up and across to place gently on the bandages.' Scoley waited. 'Utter confusion. Thought something'd happened to the machines, shoulder in excruciating agony and I'm just totally confused slumped down on the floor.'

'Anybody come to your aid?'

‘Who was there? Luckily it’s my left shoulder and somehow pulled my phone out. Pressed 999. Just managed to scramble to my feet and staggered to the office in agony to find a seat, blood dripping down my arm.’

‘Then we arrived?’

‘Yeh,’ she said and eyes closed she breathed heavily. ‘Stupid really, somebody passing by mighta come to my aid, ‘cept I was hidden round the back. Anybody about must have decided some yobs’d just smashed the window for no reason as they do, like scratching people’s cars.’ She sighed wearily. ‘Usual jealousy from the work shy I guess.’

‘Did you know the window had been smashed?’

‘Not until I was struggling to get through the back and noticed it. Still didn’t know I’d actually been shot by a gun. Convinced even now, that was shock and confusion. Brain said it had to be the coffee maker, eyes told me the window’s smashed. Grabbed a tea towel, did my best to stem the flow.’

‘Any idea who?’ Scoley asked in hope aware her time was limited.

She shrugged as if she didn’t have a clue. ‘Doesn’t bear thinking about, what if…?’ she blew out a breath, ‘Shot me you mean?’ Abbott asked.

‘Yes.’

‘How would I know? It was dark an’ I wasn’t in any state to just nip out and have a look,’ tended towards sarcastic.

‘Enemies, business rivals, any ideas?’

‘Seriously?’ she asked. ‘I sell coffee not cocaine,’ she smiled for the first time but carried an air of annoyance.

‘Anybody you’ve upset maybe, or your husband.’

‘Ben?’

‘Possible.’

‘Don’t talk wet,’ was livelier than she had been at the outset. ‘He works with Fiat cars, he’s the Service Manager, not the second hand Salesman who sold somebody a dodgy motor and they’re getting their own back,’ she said with her lips pressed firmly together to make her point.

‘Maybe he’s fallen out with somebody but has nothing to do with cars,’ Scoley suggested carefully. ‘Be useful if you could ask him when he visits. Bit short on clues so far to be honest.’

The Ward Sister was heading their way. ‘Thank you Gwen,’ said Nicky Scoley as she stood up. ‘That gives us something to be going on with,’ she said as she slid her notebook into her bag. ‘Probably need to speak to you again. Think of anything give me a call. Promise?’

‘Yeah.’

‘Day or night’ the DS added, handing Abbott her card as she smirked.

Back at Lincoln Central Nicky briefed the DI and the team about what Abbott had said which was hardly a great deal more than Nicky and Sandy had surmised from what they’d seen on the night.

‘Another few inches and this’d be murder,’ Oliver Bristow said seriously to the whole team once she’d finished. ‘That’s the route were heading down. Most women are murdered by men they’re in a relationship with remember. We need to know all about her, so allocations. Nicky,’ he said for starters. ‘Will you take charge of the case overall, please? To that end first and foremost start with this Abbott woman. Basic victimology to be honest. Rip her family apart. Husband, boyfriend, close family. She having an affair? Who are her managers, what do we know about them? Young Barista could easy be her fancy man. She’s got a previous relationship trying to gain retribution, maybe? Does she have kids and if so are they theirs or hers or half and half with someone we don’t know. This day and age they could be anybody’s, even adopted legally or otherwise. You okay with that as well as holding the umbrella?’

‘Yes boss.’

‘Good. Now, Alisha,’ he went on quickly then changed his mind. ‘Before we move on anybody comes across a name,’ he told the room. ‘No matter how irrelevant, you feed it to Alisha who’s already started to scour social media. Alisha,’ he returned his attention to. ‘If you want to use the Tech Crime Team upstairs and need any assistance with their procedures

I'm sure Nicky will lend a hand. Michelle I want you to give Nicky a hand but taking a look in particular at the finances of the family. Big mortgage maybe,' he said switching his attention across the room. 'Where did the finance come from for the first coffee shop? Did an ex set her up in the first place and now wants his money back? Are profits really so good she could open two more or is that all on borrowed money? Borrowed now means big interest rate rises, she's buggered, and can't afford to pay it back. Borrows off some loan shark money lender to tide her over. Can't pay back now with the energy crisis hitting along with the rest of the financial mess were all swimming in. Then heavies arrive, with a warning shot.'

'Guv,' was Jamie Hedley.

A sharp 'Yes?'

'This a bit far fetched? Gun in Metheringham's a shocker but are we seriously introducing a couple o' ne'er-do-wells demanding their cash back for a coffee shop?'

'You got any other ideas?' was unlike the normal calm Oliver. 'Coming to you don't worry,' he said pointing at his Detective Constable. 'Right, where was I?' he checked notes. 'Sandy's still liaising with Shona and in conjunction with her they're looking at the bullet and linking it to a gun of some sort. Jamie,' he said. 'Please lend a hand as and when of course but basically I need you to carry on with Simm and Quinton. You could keep an ear open for mention of either of them being linked in some way to this Abbott woman.'

'How?' Jamie asked. 'Thought the media were on the serial route not us.'

'We're not,' Oliver told him bluntly. 'But you must know this world of ours can at times come up with a few surprises and the odd shocker. I'm with you, don't see how, but if either of them or somebody connected to them gets even a mention make sure you're onto it. Just come from Darke and the words reputation and force are inevitably being mentioned more and more. Time to get digging and don't let me hear the press talk about a whodunnit anymore. Your job is to find the one or ones who did all this. Thanks team. Heads down.'

More than twenty four hours had been spent delving into the Abbott family, their relationships and their business affairs. From Nicky's perspective it seemed to be going the same way as the previous two still remaining to be solved: Simm and Quinton. Now Abbott, right out of the blue and she could sense Bristow was struggling.

They now knew, 38 year old Gwen Abbott and Ben Abbott her husband three years older, had been married for 13 years. Both born and brought up in Derbyshire. He in Draycott and Gwen in Breaston nearby. She'd been to Nottingham Trent University gaining a degree in Business Management and Marketing and Ben had always worked in the motor trade. They had two children nine year old Bethany and Karl almost two years younger.

What had so far not come to light was how their move from Derbyshire to Lincolnshire had happened or why.

With no link so far to Simm and Quinton, Jamie had been delving into Shires Coffee Shops, resulting in him discovering fairly good profits for the past four years during which time they had quickly gone from one shop to three. Bank loans for the Wragby and Horncastle coffee shops were not overwhelming, but further inquiries had revealed all three shop premises were rented. He had been unable to discover involvement of anybody else other than Gwen and Ben Abbott.

Nothing from Michelle other than an average mortgage on their three-bedroom home in Woodhall Spa they'd bought three months before they opened the first shop.

Oliver Bristow put that down as a marker against her name on the board. Most people he knew of, struggled to buy a home what with estate agents and solicitors, moving costs, new carpets, curtains and all sorts not to mention the actual cost of moving. Add to that taking on a mortgage for a shop within a tight time frame had to be something to seriously consider.

The real results were slow in coming and as is the way these days it was Alisha and then with help from Nicky and the Tech Crime Team things were starting to reveal themselves.

From Alisha's viewpoint checking social media basics had been somewhat tedious with Gwen Abbott using Facebook and WhatsApp extensively both for her own personal chatter but also to promote her business. Her marketing degree were being put to good use so Nicky reckoned.

Young Hari Minstry up within the confines of the Tech Crime Team had been a considerable help to Alisha by delving into seemingly anonymous messages left on the Wragby Shires Coffee shop social media pages.

He was as close to being normal as any in the Tech Crime Team. Joining straight from university by what most members of MIT and beyond considered must be a geeks snatch squad.

Worst of the bunch but also the best was ASBO: Adrian Simon Bruce Orford, who for the most part only drank hot water and chewed on liquorice. Lived with an 'aunt' nobody had ever been able to confirm was an actual relative, except she looked a good ten years older.

There were no hideable secrets from the likes of Hari. Hard drive, a write-blocking device and in no time he'd have a byte-by-byte forensic copy.

He had quickly discovered somebody had shared a nasty complaint about both product and service. Suggesting a Cappuccino had been both cold and bad tasting, along with complaints about staff attitude and lack of cleanliness. Problem was it was not aimed at Shires Coffee and had purely been copied to Gwen Abbott for information, she had tapped *Like* to.

The sender had tried hard to remain anonymous but Hari's expertise revealed a system he'd come across before, where the messaging is in fact a circle. Where as hard as you try you end up back in the same place. Previous experience told him to investigate all those also included as having received the message and go down their paths individually. Everyone finished up at the same site.

Evening briefing and when it came to Alisha O'Neill's turn she was the only one with something unusual. She explained how Hari had taken her through the process until they were left with one name. He suggested this might well be the original instigator of this particular circular messaging. Somebody somewhere had engineered a block creating a return to sender automatically. Once connected there was no way out, although time permitting he would continue his search.

'Ready for this,' she said and walked to the Abbott board and wrote: DOMINIQUE NIQUENIQUE, turned and looked at the Major Incident Team. Alisha waited, fascinated by the looks on people's faces.

'Well bugger my boots!' Jamie exclaimed.

'Gotta be that er, song from way way back,' Nicky offered. 'Bit of an oddity, by…'

'Better'n that,' Jamie interrupted. 'Been looking at other local independent coffee shops just in case I can fathom some sort of connection and one of them's owned by a…' he checked his notes. 'Dominic Archer-Lees. Dominic? Dominique?'

'Next thing,' said Alisha. 'Hari suggests he needs sight of a mobile connected to Shires Coffee. Preference is for a smart phone though. He knows of a system obtainable through an app which provided him with access whereby you have the option to hide or unhide messages on mobiles. He asked if we'd come across a reference to Ph,' she stopped to smile with all eyes and ears on her. 'He assumed it has nothing to do with,' dusky Alisha checked her scribbled notes. 'Potential of Hydrogen, it…'

'Hark at you!' introduced sniggers.

'Ph of course is a measurement of alkilinity and acidity, He reckons its social media shorthand for phone,' added to the good humoured remarks. 'According to ASBO somebody has seriously expressive tech skills.'

'Jamie,' said Oliver after giving Alisha a silent clap. 'Let Alisha and Hari have everything you've got on this Dominic guy.'

Alisha set about her new task in discovering all there was about this Dominic Archer-Lees. Sure enough on his Facebook page top of his list of shortcuts was as Jamie soon discovered CuppaCoffee in Dunston. Looking at his own page there was nothing untoward other than a considerable amount of banter with friends about CuppaCoffee. That page was just as one would expect. Photos of cups of perfectly pictured stylish coffee, an array of delicacies and good reviews.

Much to the chagrin of others it was SIO Nicky Scoley along with pretend girlfriend Alisha who headed for Dunston and afternoon coffee.

If anything they found the place too stylish with glass topped tables each with an underlay of a cake photograph to add temptation. All good enough apart from uncomfortable wrought iron chairs one associates with outdoors. Product photos adorned the walls and with service good, to Nicky it was rather over the top in self-marketing. The coffee however tasted as good as you'd find anywhere.

Coffees drunk and a few moments to allow customers to leave.

'Time for a word me thinks,' Nicky Scoley whispered as she got to her feet. 'Dominic?' she asked of the tall big shouldered young man at the counter.

'Sorry. Reps by appointment. Only two of us, can't get away and…' a Warrant Card brought him to a halt. 'Oh,' and his look altered.

'Need a chat.'

'Yeh right. All yours Claire,' he called to the redhead serving a woman. Both of them dressed in navy blue polo shirts sporting a white cup graphic with *Cuppa* printed in white above it. 'Follow me.' The follow was round the counter and into a small office come storeroom next door to the toilets. Scoley took a seat and he followed suit leaving Alisha to stand, a concern for Scoley. 'Right then,' he sat with forearms on his knees. 'How can I help?'

Was this another racial slur making the coloured woman stand or him just being impolite and acting the boss?

'If I came across...Dominique niquenique, does that mean anything?' Once more his facial expression changed dramatically.

'Er, well sort of.'

'What,' Scoley asked. 'Do you mean by sort of?'

'Had a run of bad reviews over a good few weeks now. Then got a really nasty one from what you just said, this

Dominique niquenique whatever,' he stopped to chuckle. 'Didn't pronounce it like you. Anyway, whoever was suggesting drinks were disgusting and cold,' he stopped to sigh and shake his head. 'How can coffee from the machine,' he gestured back out the door. 'Be cold for crissakes? Service was slow, prices too high apparently.'

'From this Dominique?'

'Yeh, but. Tried to reply but just went round in circles, like every name copied or liked on each message linked me back to this Dominique whatever.'

'Next question. Do you know the owner of Shires Coffee Shops?'

'Well sort of. Not know exactly, more like know of. Any idea hows she's doing? Nasty business, gotta say.'

'Think she's making good progress.'

'First thing I knew, one of me mates phoned said she been shot and reckoned it was murder.'

'Badly wounded.'

'Still bad. What's wrong with the world eh? Bloody kids I s'pose.'

'Answer me this. You're mid-twenties right?'

'Twenty-seven.'

'At twenty-seven you own this I understand,' Scoley glanced around the room.'

'You been checking up on me?' and kept his smirk to himself.

'Only because one of our Digital Forensic guys looking into Gwen Abbott and Shires Coffee came across a forwarded social media message she received containing a few bad reviews aimed at you.'

'You're joking!'

'From that discovery to you is pretty much how it works,' said Alisha down to him. 'With a case as serious as this we go down all sorts of avenues.'

'Explain how come all this is yours?' Scoley this time gestured around the room with both hands.

Dominic frowned. 'Easy. This place was a thatched cottage back in the day owned by my grandmother,' sounded plausible.

'She turned it into a tea room, had an extension built on the back here' he gestured. 'Where she lived, you can't see from the road. My old man, her only son's got his own business and suggested me. Left it to me in her will and I updated it. Had to borrow a few bob off me dad to put in the new equipment and that.' He smiled. 'Think back in her day it was probably just a kettle and teapot.'

'You live over the shop so to speak.'

'Yeh, why?'

'Just wondered.'

'Don't get any o'your stupid PC ideas.'

'Sorry, sir?'

'I'm not a bloody poof with pretty boyfriend waiting upstairs for a kiss.'

'Didn't say you were,' had Scoley wondering why on earth that had raised its head. 'And you're in competition with Gwen Abbott and her Shires Coffee chain,' she managed as her brain dealt with the previous remark.

'Hope you're not suggesting...'

'Again Mr Archer-Lees. I'm not suggesting anything,' stopped him.

'Look,' he said sitting up straight and taking a deep breath. 'She's got three in local villages. Metheringham, Wragby and Horncastle, s'pose you know. Those without transport and the cost of petrol means loads can't get for a coffee to places like she's got. Always knew in somewhere like this I'd not go into battle with Costa. So, always been the plan to be after a coffee van once this place was up and running and I'd built a bit of a name. Sort of van to tootle round two villages a day. One morning, one afternoon. Do all the small places same every week with no shops at all, do it regular for folk gagging for a decent coffee.'

'And the last thing you need is bad reviews.'

'Seen small places go to the wall with a dozen bad reviews by jealous idiots. But,' he shrugged. 'Way o'the world with all them…'

'Trolls.'

'Yeh them.'

'So. You'll not know Mrs Abbott?'

'Not unless she's been in here snooping.'

'Thank you for that,' said Scoley suddenly as she got to her feet and Alisha O'Neill stepped aside to allow her DS to leave. 'If you think of anything pertinent to this case Dominic,' please don't hesitate to get in touch,' and offered him her card. 'Good day to you.'

Quick word with the boss and the pair headed for Lincoln County Hospital, spoke to a kindly staff Nurse who offered them a quick five minutes.

Gwen Abbott was sat up in bed reading from her Kindle. Left shoulder still heavily bandaged. 'Hello Gwen. Me again. Sorry to disturb you,' said Scoley as she reached the bed. 'Just a quick word,' she added and simply picked up an Android smart phone from the table. 'Just need to borrow this for a day or so.'

'You can't,' she said. 'Hey! Put that back, you…'

'Can't what?' Scoley shot back down to her. 'You ever get those calls where this,' she waved the mobile at Abbott. 'Rings and then there's nobody there? This needs checking. Somebody must have known you'd be at the cafe that evening.'

'I need that. Got a business to run for crying out loud.'

'I'm sure your husband can get a cheap one of the market if you're seriously that desperate.' Scoley waved the phone again. 'Our forensic guys are pretty quick, we'll have it back to you in no time. Have a nice day,'

'You've not heard the last of this!' she shouted back, as Scoley leading the two detectives walked swiftly from the ward thanking the staff on their way.

26

Andy Ross was busy cutting back bushes down the side of the front drive for Mr Whilley. Didn't know, in fact had never known the old boy's first name. Alas the balding clean-shaven unfortunately was in a wheelchair. Not sure he'd been like that all his life and Andy often wondered what it must be like for the poor sod and others like him. At least he had the capability somehow of managing to get in the car and the wheelchair folded up in the back.

His missus could deal with dead-heading the roses, hoeing weeds from the borders and spraying stuff on the paths. These attractive mature bushes and an Acer tree in their drive was something he'd tended to for a good year or two now. Unsightly when in a poor state but a delight to the eye when he'd finished with them.

Always annoys Andy when people concrete over their garden to save themselves a job and create a flood risk at the same time.

From chatting to the Whilleys' he'd discovered they had two grown up children along with grandchildren all of who they reckoned, lent a hand with anything more than that.

That day was different. Almost as soon as Ross'd turned up in his van, and helped by folding the wheelchair for her, the Whilley's had headed off out in their car, across the city to the hospital. Reason unknown but then it was none of his business.

Mrs Whilley had asked him to keep an eye open for Amazon as they were expecting a parcel, but with working out the front anyway that'd not be an issue.

First up had to be that lovely Acer in desperate need of a tidy up, and made to look its best for visitors. Job done, he went to his van sat on the tail gate poured and sipped coffee from his flask and chewed on a Snickers when he heard a voice.

'Hello there.'

‘Sorry,’ he said as he was approached. ‘Owners are out for a bit, thought you might be Amazon,’ he realized probably not by the small vehicle. ‘Be away for an hour or so.’

‘Not them I’m after.’

‘Oh right.’

‘On the lookout for somebody like you,’ he was told as he went back to sipping his coffee.

‘What d’you need doing? Anything within a twenty mile radius for big jobs. Early Spring down to climate change I guess. Already mown a lawn or two and we’re not in March. Just a bit of a mow’ll need to be closer to be honest.’

‘Sorry. I’m Jules. I’m from a horticultural website and we’re looking for gardeners to help advertise a whole range of products for our sponsors. Range of hand tools, cloches, hedge cutters like you have there. Wondered if you’d be interested?’

‘Er...yeh...but, I’m nobbut a gard’ner.’

‘Doing a good job there I have to say. That’s the whole point, trend is for reality figures, men like you who have the looks, stature and expertise. No need to show you how to handle a lawnmower. See you’re busy so I’ll leave a card. Give me a bell and I’ll arrange for a better chat, go through the process with you and arrange the next step if you’re interested.’

‘Oh right,’ he said as he put down his plastic cup, stood up and took the card. ‘Somebody recommend me?’ he queried.

‘Just visiting the area on another matter spotted you and to be honest you’re just what we’re looking for. Happy with that?’

‘Yeh sure. What will it involve if you don’t mind me asking?’

‘Videos in the main these days, plus promotional shots. Might even be a bit of radio work.’

‘Fine, thanks,’ an amazed Ross grinned nervously. ‘Thought you were another after an early lawn mowing.’

‘Thank you…’

‘Andy. Andy Ross.’

‘Thanks for that, hear from you soon Andy.’

Andy just stood there coffee in hand he then downed in one go sat back down on the tailgate to get his head round what had just happened.

By the look, that was someone from another world. Probably a big city dweller, one of those with flower boxes on a veranda outside some plush apartment.

He sat there pondering rather than getting on with the work. Slight breeze blowing but for the time of year it was quite mild.

Andy Ross looked all about. Still had the majority of the work to do, and by the time he finished the Whilley's place'd look trim and tidy once more with a boost of enthusiasm.

Nice village, just the sort he wished he could afford to live in rather than that crummy flat with no garden save for that small triangle out the front he'd filled with roses. Gave old Mrs Gumbrell something to do; dead-heading the roses as he'd taught her.

Village had a string of three shops next door to each other. Fruit and veg, the Whilley's told him was some sort of community venture. Grocer next door once had been a Post Office and then third along was a cafe. More of a bakers really selling bread, rolls and cakes, forced by the coffee boom and a need to diversify, to add three small tables and two more outdoors in summer.

Andy sat thinking about his future, after what had gone on with a second cup full. If there's money in this video business maybe it'll pave the way to moving somewhere like this. Garage for the van and his gear so he'd have no need to pay over the odds for the lock-up. Local pub'd suit him fine and require no more than a casual stroll home. Better place to invite women to, had to be a real bonus.

Never been invited indoors by the Whilley's. Best he'd managed was last Autumn when they offered a mug of tea when he was done, sat out on the patio. Somewhere like their bungalow would suit very nicely. Be an idea when he got home. Have a look to see how much the place is worth.

Time to get on, and as he started work on the trio of bushes in a need of a good trim, that coffee shop shooting came to mind. There's him thinking of moving to a village and suddenly he remembered spotting a breaking news story.

Woman shot in her own coffee shop. In the States anything like that hardly seems to be out of the norm and Andy guessed doesn't even make the local media so commonplace are such hideous events. In Metheringham was an altogether totally different business. That'd liven the place up, but where it happened was thankfully a bit too away from where he fancied moving to.

Drinking two cups full, sat there idly thinking about that modelling business meant he had only about a cup left and it was mid morning.

First bush done, quick step back to admire his work and he was back to it.

How can you get served a coffee so bad or so expensive you have to pull out a gun? He wondered to himself. Some he'd had before these pucker coffee places opened had at times been pretty grim. Not now surely.

Didn't know the poor woman but then why would he?

Thinking about the increase in crime especially all that organized crime and drugs business, how had it been allowed to happen with a supposed to be tough on law and order, Tory government?

Was that because those making the laws never come across the aggressive drunks, fraudsters, the on-line con merchants, drink and drug drivers? Where they lived would always be given everything their community needs at the drop of a hat.

None of that leveling up business for them. They were already sitting on a pretty high perch and druggies, vicious scoundrels, bigots, racists and homophobic shits of this world were never seen shopping in their beloved Waitrose.

Last of the big bushes, then it'll get easier and the Amazon man had not been seen.

In the complex world of Andy Ross, there was always a chance he would in the end turn down the offer. *Nobbut a gardener* was how he saw himself and used that as an explanation of his reticence with people. Finding others to his mind light years better than him in all respects.

Never an expression of being an experienced landscape gardener from somebody able to craft an unattractive space in no time, faultlessly producing a creative unique design and practical environment.

The deep dark negative unpredictable thoughts had been with him all his life, and at times controlling him.

The photographic and media business popping up out of the blue like that, produced his initial thought of *You can't mean me* almost instantaneously.

At his lowest ebb he had been known to almost tell people he was hopeless and not worth employing.

Time to get on. Had to be that tall hedge up next in need of a good trim.

27

What on earth's going on? I ask you. My daily routine pretty much follows the same pattern. After showering, getting dressed and having my midweek Granola breakfast I then clean my teeth and check my list of clients for the day.

Next regular task which has stayed the same for years, is to just check the news for the day. This starts with the BBC News website which today was like it is most days. Politics and some tragedy somewhere in some far corner the world. Floods out east, another shooting in the States. From there its a simple click or two across to the *Lincoln Leader* website to see what's happening closer to home.

I'm lucky living within the city boundaries, but I often wonder how folk out in the villagers cope when the news is almost entirely Lincoln city based. How do they get to hear what's cracking off in their community. Chatting and gossiping down the local Co-op or village store probably. Be the only reason some go out at all sadly.

Back in the day of course, we used to have a paperboy stuffing the newspaper through the letterbox full of yesterday's and we'd have to wait for the local evening paper to get anything close to home.

Now what I faced this morning was in front of me at the click of a button. Five stamp size pictures across the top above the headline. Fred West, Peter Sutcliffe, Dennis Nilsen, Harold Shipman and Perdro Filho a Brazilian maniac. All serial killers strung along above *Our Serial Killer Strikes Again.*

That was bad enough but then a goon at the *Leader* was suggesting Simm and Quinton had now been joined by some woman in a coffee shop they reckon'd been shot.

Excuse me. This has got bugger all to do with me. I was at home last evening watching that new female cop drama on telly with Ruth. Anyway why would I want to shoot a woman?

Where on earth d'these idiots think someone like me'd get a gun? Do the cops seriously think I carry a loaded pistol in my jacket pocket just in case? Just in case my coffee's cold, service is a bit slow or they've run out of porcupine syrup.

Now it's good and bad news when you think about it. For the next couple of days, innocent chatter with my clients will all be a case of *What do you think about that poor woman? In a coffee house too. Can't believe it, been there twice with my sister. She's got two kids they're saying.* Then some will add on some quip about Simm and Quinton already dead, to make life difficult.

The good news? Take's the pressure off me a bit. I'm still planning number three the cops've stupidly replaced with this barista woman. Means they'll be busy again but heading off in the wrong direction with any luck.

In quiet moments I often wonder what will be going through my mind when and if the coppers land on my doorstep with all their Miranda phrase they have to spout. Sat in a cold cell somewhere without any creature comforts, what'll I be thinking? *Should've kept out of it you idiot. Whata bloody fine mess you've got yourself into. For why?* What will jail be like, and the shit bags in there'll not be worth thinking about. And the food? Be worse than the awful Irish Stew and Tapioca pudding we had at school. Time to stop all this maybe, but then I think of Miriam and something inside pushes me on for just one more. Particularly as I've never found it easy on the living side of a close death. Maybe just maybe this coffee shop woman has given me more time.

Got Cynthia Whittleton at two this afternoon. The coiffured dyed hair sort who'd win any Gossip of the Year competition. She'll be full of it mark my words. I know now for certain she'll claim to have met the woman certainly at that Shires Coffee place. Probably met her at a pretentious summer ball where she and her self-opinionated old man go to be seen and get their photos in pretend snooty magazines.

To be honest she just might have been poking her nose in and got to hear more than I know. Might be prudent to strike now while our Police are otherwise engaged dealing with a gunman. They've got to take this business very seriously, as I imagine there'll be mounting pressure for action from the public who will be more concerned about where this killer. Gun in hand, might strike next.

Fortunately my last today will be Rose Williams who'll talk about nothing else than the cutest, most beautiful and well behaved grandchildren in the world and what they've been up to. She'll forget to mention precocious, but inevitably will keep saying "my lovely" from the moment she walks in the door. Why not just call me Jules for crying out loud? But then that's got to be better than 'duck'. Despite all that nonsense, with her concentrating on Louis and Lyra and ignoring the gunman, it'll be a case of thank goodness for small mercies. Got Frances later in the week saying how coming to me allows her to decompress. Or does she mean decompose?

I've done my due diligence, spent hours observing habits and locations. Noted the visit of friends and those I assume to be relatives.

One thing for sure, I'll not need a gun.

If I remember rightly it had to be a good four years sis had stuck it out being with Jack Somerton, who on the surface had then seemed a pretty decent bloke. Until that fateful day when this repulsive blonde scraggy bitch in a dirty strappy top was at her door with more than a degree of insolence accusing Miriam of stealing her husband. How different her life could have been without that silly bitch.

Been the rebound had done for her with the shit. Good looking guy, all the charm in the world but with a vicious streak to be wary of.

Reason why women had fallen for Brendon Quinton was obvious from first glance. Being seen out with him and the jealousy vibe from all and sundry would be working at full pelt.

Andy Ross is a whole lot different. Gardener handyman, the sort who advertise in those magazines they drop through your letter box on an all too regular basis. Mow your lawn, trim the hedge, rotovate borders You know the sort of thing. Always remember Miriam saying he was good at it, but on the downside stayed up late to watch horror movies. No idea if he still does but he certainly enjoys a pint or two. I've spotted him going in the

Walkabout in town. Thursdays I noticed he stays home, probably in readiness for his Friday skinful. To his credit he catches a taxi after drinking in town, but Friday is his Black Swan night, means he can walk home. Has to be, rather than getting pulled up by the cops with their *"Take a deep breath. Keep going, keep going, keep going..."* routine. Not been able to get close to him of course save for that quick chat but there's been no sign of drugs, but no doubt the inevitable post mortem toxicology heading his way will check that out.

Thinking back now there were moments over and above the actual killings I remember vividly. Chances are it will be exactly the same with Ross.

Double-shot Americano, Cheese Toastie and a Biscotti biscuit to dip one Wednesday lunchtime, I'd thoroughly enjoyed when stalking Quinton. There he was just sat back happily people watching from High Street Starbucks. Unbeknown to him, somebody was doing exactly the same. He was in somebody's viewfinder. Mine.

Don't know about you but it's not something I ever think about. Who are the people on a bus or train? Why are they there, apart from the obvious? What are they doing, where are they on their way to or coming back from, and as in my case who are they keeping an eye on? Has to be a lot of that for these private investigators.

One thing's for sure I now realize I spent too much time with Simm. Put myself into a position where he could have sussed my delaying tactics, felt something wasn't right. Quinton had been over and done with quickly, and another had gone to plan.

I've always given freely of my spare time. Usually helping out where I can after major tragedies and helping care for people under threat. Done all sorts over the years but have never reacted to the adverts you get on the telly about coughing up a few quid. Trouble with that is you never know what your cash is being used for. Tragedy in Afghanistan we're all supposed to feel guilty about if we don't chuck money, and off it goes into the hands of the Taliban. Better to my mind to be more practical. Helped with that Ukraine business, helping pack clothes into boxes. Even drove a van to a major collection point. Food Banks is another area I've been able to offer assistance. Their existence in the UK in 2023 is an utter disgrace. Total failure of our society where we allow people to earn millions for doing little more than driving a car, being an influencer or dabbling in drugs.

On that subject, I think it was Maureen Coates who during one of her sessions mentioned reading about ITV making tens of millions from *Love Island* merchandise. Items such as pink and white water bottles costing £20. Made me wonder if some of those at the food bank were the very same as those guzzling from their newly delivered bottles.

Having a career where I can choose my own hours suits me to the ground. Pretty sure I'd not be able to go through with this all if I had a job with stipulated hours

In the case of Ross, when I've done with him he won't be able to. Wriggle that is. The plan is, when he answers the door to me, wearing a blue coat and ushers me in I'll stand aside to allow him to close the door behind me. When he turns to lead the way all those hours watching You Tube will prove invaluable and more than likely I'll never have spoken a word apart from an initial greeting.

I've always had the option if things become difficult of saying thanks but no thanks, or just leave the whole concept open and never make contact again.

This time on the Thursday night I'll knock on his door and say hello when it opens. That's something which came to mind last evening. Each time out of courtesy I shake their hand as a welcome, but in fact it is also a goodbye. Anyway, as I was saying, I'll allow him to close it and walk past me. Then I'll tap Ross on his right shoulder and as he turns slightly, slit his throat from his left to right with one hand, push hard with the other to see him stumble and fall. In an instant so I've read he'll be in pain, gasping for breath, trying hard to stop the blood pouring from his neck. That'll be what we call the end of a load of old squit.

According to the sites I've studied time and again, he'll try desperately to speak incoherently, a desperate plea for help, even according to one snuff killing I watched, the guy pulled his phone out to call for help as red warm blood poured onto his hands.

According to another video I watched, his mouth will fill with thick blood, virtually drowning him.

I was worried for a while about another stabbing and went through a whole host of scenarios. One I was hopeful of using for a time was something called Dicoumarin used in the treatment of Thrombosis as an anticoagulant. Then during my research it was suggested it can result in serious sometimes fatal uncontrolled hemorrhage. The words 'can' and 'sometimes' were enough to put me off. I'm not hanging about waiting for him to die and anyway how do I give it to him?

I'd even tapped friends on their right shoulder to discover their reaction as part of the planning.

That vile nasty bastard responsible for the suicide of my only sister is next on the list. Once dead, first thing I'll need to do will be to pull the plastic bag from my pocket, slide in the bloodied blade in exactly as I've practiced using blood from sliced liver and maybe give him one last look.

Practice makes perfect they say and of course they're right. Time and again I've locked our front door, dressed in the clothes I've got for the event, sharp knife in pocket, gloves on and then gone through each stage. Now I'm pretty much pitch perfect.

Next time one of my clients asks have I done anything interesting I could always tell them what I've actually been doing in my hall twice or three times a day.

Next up will be my quick escape before some nosy bastard turns up at the door. Turn, open the black door, step out leaving it slightly ajar. Pull off my big black coat, turn it inside out, unfold my hat from the pocket, adjust and walk off. From there it'll be a case of turning quickly left, then left again two floors up, push open a glass panelled door with my elbow, walk calmly down two flights of concrete stairs to the ground floor, turn right and out into the dustbin area and away with a completely different look. Black hair, wearing a grey coat and jeans witnesses will claim.

All my clothes as usual I'll burn in my garden incinerator with rubbish I've accumulated when I get home.

Then at last it'll be all done and dusted. Job done and folk'll need to find somebody else to mow their lawns.

28

'This is more like it,' said their DI after Nicky had revealed the outcome of an hour upstairs with Hari Minstry and others in the Tech Crime Team of computer geeks.

'This has to be revenge' said Oliver Bristow. 'Stupid woman engineered her pals to write obnoxious reviews about CuppaCoffee, she saw as a major challenge. Somebody somewhere gave her a helping hand hiding the so-called reviewers with that roundabout system Hari's come up with I don't pretend to understand. To further cover their tracks we also now have phone messages which are obviously the Ph link.'

'What's the charge guv, sending nasty messages?' did not go down well.

'Far from it. Waiting on our Economic Crime Team upsetting the apple cart this morning out at CuppaCoffee going through his accounts with a fine tooth comb.'

Jake hated it when Oliver Bristow went off on a tangent without any mention to the team. From a few things he'd gathered the DI suffered from having to face DCI Inga Larsson's record from when in his role and Craig Darke himself before her. Was her name being throw at him every time he briefed Craig Darke about a total lack of progress?

'S'cuse me guv,' he felt was necessary. 'Aren't we also looking at Shires Coffee to see if her business has been affected? With a drop in sales being the reason for her and her mates to give him a good smacking on line?'

'She's the victim Jake. Yes she may well have organized the bad reviews, but she didn't shoot herself. Ask yourself this, who else that we know of could have wanted her dead?'

'How d'we know this was not some kid taking a pot shot for fun?'

‘Because,’ he checked his tablet. ‘The bullet retrieved from Gwen Abbott’s shoulder is a 9mm Parabellum,’ Oliver read slowly. ‘According to ballistics, it’s German and used just prior to and during World War Two. Reason why its taken a while to track down. We now know it would have been used in a number of weapons back then.’

Jake found it very difficult to stay calm but could sense the mood of others around him. ‘What now?’ he managed rather than what he wanted to say.

‘We wait.’

‘Murder, suicide.’

‘Really?’ Oliver responded sharply to Jake.

‘Worth thinking about while we wait. What’s the chances after a big bust up, except her husband didn’t have the guts to stick it in his mouth when it came to it?’

‘Not a happy bunny,’ said the DI just after he’d finished his Coronation Chicken spread sandwich lunch and a banana, up to Jake Goodwin stood in his doorway. He pointed at his Detective Sergeant. ‘Tread carefully is the command from up above, so no rushing in where fools fear to tread. No Armed Response, just a gentle search by Shona’s team first thing. Well, actually earlier than first thing. Darke boss is worried about a gang turning up in Dunston all fully kitted out and armed to worry the shit out the locals.’

‘Looking for?’

‘The gun.’

‘CuppaCoffee we talking about? How d’we…?’

‘Cafe in trouble, sales have dropped by twenty five percent since those crap reviews began.’

Jake had spoken to Nicky on the quiet about Bristow keeping things to himself. The Blonde DS’s opinion was with all these cases piling up to damage his reputation he’d decided to go solo, see if he could solve one of them. Either that or with Simm and Quinton still live acts he was offering some respite by taking on the shooting.

'Where would he get a gun from? I know I keep saying this about this case, knives are bad enough but d'we seriously have young men carrying guns around our villages?'

'All the time we have the internet anything's possible.'

'Do we know how CuppaCoffee was doing prior to Abbott's malicious messages?'

'Doing okay. Sales increasing slowly. Nothing fantastic but on the plus side, according to Liam in Economics.'

'Well enough to buy the van?' Jake could only grimace at.

A case of waiting for Shona Watt and the team turning their attention back to Simm and Quinton and what little they had to go on. Social media had dried up, but that was expected the moment something else took people's attention in the ever changing world.

Jake was a little put out to say the least. DI Oliver Bristow was taking pride of place along with DS Nicky Scoley for the interview with this Dominic Archer-Lees. He was dressed casually in a checkerboard shirt of blue, red and white with grey chinos. CuppaCoffee cafe and living quarters had been searched too early for him to be decked out in the coffee house uniform.

Bristow did all the introductions introducing Archer-Lees to the tape along with Samuel Mackinder his solicitor, but Scoley reckoned the chances are it was his father's.

Jake at that time was sat back with a coffee and his Tunnocks' Caramel Log in the Incident Room thinking to himself.

Yet again it was the same subject. Was now the time to leave the work he had enjoyed so much for a good few years and move onto pastures new? Take on a role similar to the one Tigger Woods now enjoyed in Intelligence Gathering. Be more office based but at least there'd most likely be no traipsing across fields at the crack of dawn and getting muddied up to the eyeballs. Dealing with hostile farmers and folk with dogs.

Yes, Inga Larsson had dealt with some issues personally but he and the team had always been aware of what line she was undertaking to investigate. Bristow on the other hand was too reserved, too remote for his liking and just went off and reported back after. How much else had he been doing they knew nothing about? What had he discovered which by rights should be on the Murder Boards?

'Where shall we start Mr Archer-Lees?' Oliver Bristow in a navy suit, asked in Interview Room 3. 'How about you tell us about the vitriolic messages you received on social media. Not you personally of course but your coffee house business?'

'Jealousy.'

Bristow waited. 'Could you please explain what you mean?'

'Didn't like me venturing onto her patch. Like one of those turf wars the druggies have.'

'Is there not room for you both? After all, you often get Starbucks and Cafe Nero in the same street, and other dotted about close by, like here in Lincoln.'

'You'd think so. Good few miles. What crabby old ladies are going to bike further than the end of their street just for a coffee?'

'Do you know Gwen Abbott or her husband?' Scoley asked this irritatingly cheery guy.

'Only from going in their place when I was getting set up. Just checking out the opposition. Not the only one I poked me nose into. Never spoke to her. Not seen him that I know of. What's the chances her old man's some rich bugger and she's just playing at it? Needs to keep going so she can brag to her fancy friends'

'What was your reaction when you first received the messages?'

'Messaged back to suggest if this Dominique person would contact me we could discuss the problems.' He shook his head and shrugged. 'Done all the customer care business in the past. Never did hear. Thought a voucher for a couple of cups mighta sorted it.'

'Did you know who this...' Scoley had to read. 'Dominique niquenique was?'

'No idea. Mates took the piss, saying sounded like me going trans.'

'When your…'

'Look,' said Archer-Lees pointing at her to stop Scoley as she tried to digest what he'd just said. 'Kinda guessed it was a piss take with a name like that being so soddin' close to mine. But what can you do? Bet you lot get loads of bollocks sent, eh?'

'When your attempt to resolve the situation amounted to nothing,' Scoley continued with. 'What then?'

'Tried with the second one, even mentioned a voucher I seem to remember,' a true fact both Bristow and Scoley knew from his social media messaging. 'This is all I need,' he sighed. 'Doing okay making inroads into the cash for the van I'm after. Could easy be some silly sod with a sort of pop up cafe in one of the poky villages me van'll not visit.'

'Dominic,' said Oliver Bristow as he sat up straight to give Nicky time to consider the reasoning for gays and transexuals to have even been mentioned?

'Look,' Archer-Lees interrupting as he went on pointing at the Detective Inspector. 'All this shit carries on I'll be losing everything after all the hours I put in. Bloody hard work painting and decorating an old place like that. Reckon some of the work Gran had done was awful to say the least. Be bastards conning the poor old dear.'

'What old dear? Dominic,' Bristow quried.

'Told her before,' he said gesturing at Scoley. 'Me gran.'

'Did you shoot Gwen Abbott?' was an unexpected shot across his bow.

'Talk wet!'

'Can you think of anybody who might have wanted Gwen Abbott dead?'

'Thought you said she aint dead.'

'More by luck than judgement. The question still remains Dominic. Have any of your pals opened a book on it maybe?'

'Now you're talking daft,' he said breezily

'How come then, our Crime Scene Investigators discovered this in your shed?' A serious Bristow questioned as he lifted an evidence bag from the floor and plonked it onto the table. 'For the tape I am showing item C14 in an evidence bag. The object inside is a Walther P38 German made hand gun, along with the

9mm bullet surgeons retrieved from the shoulder of Gwen Abbott. Ballistics report D9 confirms the bullet has been fired from this gun.' Straight faced Bristow just sat back and folded his arms, waiting. Alarm written all over Archer-Lees' face as his solicitor whispered to him.

'Might I ask for an adjournment in order to talk to my client in private,' the solicitor asked.

'Teas alright?'

'Er...yes thank you,' replied the solicitor who looked at Archer-Lees for guidance. 'Make that two please. One sugar for me,' he ordered.

'And me.'

Oliver Bristow moved to the empty Interview room next door when Nicky Scoley went off to get two coffees and the two teas. On her return the DS delivered black coffee to the boss first, placed her mug on the table and took two teas to the pair next door.

Nicky Scoley had in her file yet to be opened, data and a resume from the Economic guys about the two coffee businesses.

Shires Coffee Shops had begun to feel the crunch initially back when having recovered from the initial horrors of Covid the energy prices rocketed. Not only putting her own costs up but that of all her suppliers. Petrol and diesel had been passed onto her just for starters. Then when the surge in food prices were added to the mix customers had less to spend on the fripperies of life. Stay at home, invite your friends round became for many the order of the day. Put on the Tassimo and in quick time Lattes and Cappuccinos were pounds cheaper and ladies who meet were still able to enjoy a gossip.

The Economic team's delving had shown CuppaCoffee not doing much better, before suddenly the publicity on line appeared to be about to sink him without trace.

Fifteen minutes after the drinks arrived and Oliver Bristow was keen to move on. Introductions procedure repeated and they were back to business.

'Might I ask,' was Mackinder the solicitor first up before Bristow could start. 'How are we to know where that old gun came from? According to my investigation that type was never around for that long and manufacture ended when the war did. My client most certainly wasn't even born then and to be honest neither was I.'

'There are people who keep such items as a hobby. Good trade on line I'm told.'

'And to substantiate your claim, how are we with that?' short bald pasty faced Samuel Mackinder posed with hint of a smile.

'How about we try this,' was Scoley, removing a photograph from the folder Bristow had given her during the break for the pair to scrutinize.

'And?' was the best Mackinder could manage.

'For the tape, I've shown Mr Archer-Lees and his solicitor Mr Mackinder a photograph item 14A, a Walther P38 in a lawn mower box where it had been covered with grass cuttings. I am now showing them,' and she slid another photograph from the folder. 'Item 14B is a crime scene sight of the lawnmower in position in the shed belonging to Mr Archer-Lees. Both photographs taken by Crime Scene Investigator's Photographer Connor Mitchell.'

'Might I ask?' Bristow offered to the pair sat opposite. 'What do either of you imagine are the chances of a jury accepting a suggestion of it being normal practice for a lawn mower complete with an almost full grass box being wheeled into a shed without being emptied?

'Fingerprints?' was no answer.

'Not on the gun,' Bristow was willing to admit.

'Thought not. How you getting on with DNA?' the solicitor scoffed.

'We don't discuss all the evidence we hold as you know only too well.'

'I'll take that as a negative as well. Anything else? Bit like a penny dip.'

'Your client tracking Mrs Abbott's phone?' Bristow shot back.

'Of fuck it!' stopped the pair trading. 'Accidental death's best you'll get outta me,' Dominic suddenly exploded with.

'Dominic,' said Mackinder. 'Please…' he pleaded.

'Forget it. Thought I'd make sure she'd get the message smash her windows. So bloody what?'

'But you shot her in the shoulder Mr Archer-Lees.'

'How was I to know?'

'You were to know because you knew she was there, most probably on her own at that time. We've got ANPR marking you down as being in the area and to be more specific in the village on CCTV. We have you checking her phone locality. What we don't have I'll admit, is where you got the gun from. But give us time.'

'Between now and coming to court,' Scoley slipped in.'

Dominic Archer-Lees physically slumped down and the DS was expecting him to cry before he somehow managed to pull himself together.

'Was me grandad's me dad reckons,' he responded quietly. 'Found it in the attic when I's clearing out,' he blew out a breath as if that was a great weight off his mind. 'Dozen bullets too. After what happened threw rest in bin.'

'Could you tell me why Dominic?' was a motherly Nicky Scoley.

'Place is going bottoms up, with all that shit going on. Not like having a fuckin' threat posted through me letter box. This is internet for all the bloody world to read and laugh about. No flames without fire eh?' he stopped to shake his head and look down at the grey table. 'Trouble is folk in small places've got bugger all to talk about. Some o'that shit the bitch put out was headline news to people round me. Remember stupid stuff about dog poo on the pavement, and' when's the chip van turning up, is what they take as important news in their sad lives That and some total nonsense going off half way round the world. Some o'the oldens'd not realize that stuff is made up or just a pack of lies. According to the world they've lived in, lies wouldn't be tolerated.'

'Could I just say in his defence…'

‘Look. I’m not a killer,’ stopped Mackinder. ‘If it’d been a bloody brick I’d not be sat here now.’

‘And Gwen Abbott would not now be in the Queen’s Med waiting for a further major operation on her shoulder, young man.’

The world wide web being both a magnificent encyclopaedia of giant proportions or a swamp inhabited by sickos, went through Scoley’s mind.

DI Oliver Bristow joined Nicky Scoley back in the Interview Room once Archer-Lees had been charged with Attempted Murder and taken to a cell crying his eyes out.

‘Wouldn’t you have thought a bright young man like him would have planned what to do with the gun? Plenty of places even the Witham’s not that far away.’

‘Probably had some plan in mind I guess, but maybe not,’ said Bristow as he collected his things together. ‘Then when the news of her being shot appeared on his phone while he was eating his Cornflakes, panic could easy set in.’

‘Some crummy sites even announced her death.’

‘Isn’t that what’s good and bad about all this technology. No Editor to check what’s going out. To spike all the garbage. If he’d had any sense he’d’ve decided to lie low, be as normal as possible. Be in a hell of a state opening the coffee place, worried sick he’d been spotted, so do his best to make it like any other day dishing out cappuccinos.’

‘Don’t know yet if he was on foot, or this was a drive-by.’

‘Co-op CCTV shows a car dashing past, no people except a customer.’

‘He that good with the gun d’you reckon, firing on the move?’

‘Here’s a thought,’ said Nicky. ‘Is he left handed? Driving and shooting out the passenger window’d not be easy with your right hand.’

‘Driver. Now there’s a thought.’

‘Thought his hiding place would be good for now, even a day or two. Clever idea though. Except for one thing. The gun dog,’ Nicky said with a big grin.

‘Just shows you,’ said Oliver as he was about to leave. ‘We’ve got the brains and all the tech but he’s the one with the good nose.’

‘Drugs, cash and weapons means that’s some nose. Connor even got a great shot of the dog sat there stock still, asking this what you’re after?’

Oliver Bristow files in hand just stood there looking down at Nicky. ‘Got one at last, thank goodness for that.’

‘You been under pressure?’ she dared.

‘And some,’ he shrugged.

‘Not had the Darke boss popping along for a free coffee lately told me something’s up.’

‘Have a word will you, see if we can do her for fraud or whatever we use for social media crimes these days.’ Was not a response to Nicky’s statement and told a story.

Why would this guy not open up? Why was everything a big secret? Why keep the French vineyard a secret until Sandy was after more wine? They’d never have heard he had a holiday home had Mablethorpe not popped up out of nowhere. No talk of friends. Things he does, places he goes. Not even a whisper about a boyfriend, girlfriend, partner. Economic guys secretly checked his home and discovered it belonged to a divorced Sylvia Bristow, they assumed has be his mother.

Nicky knew Jake was planning to see what he could discover about him from Grantham.

29

When Jake Goodwin walked into the MIT Incident Room next morning he was greeted with an instruction from Jamie Hedley.

'Darke boss wants to see you.'

'Any idea why?'

'No. Just popped in looking for you, said ask him to see me first up.'

Jake dropped his bag beside his chair. 'Bristow in yet?'

'I've not seen him,' said Jamie as Jake walked out and headed along the corridor.

'Morning Jake,' said Detective Superintendant Craig Darke.

'Have a seat,' he said and got up to close the door. 'First thing, your DI is away and will be for a few days. Like you to take over as you would, if he was sick.'

'Is he?'

'Is he what?'

'Sick.'

'No, no certainly not. Working away, special ops if you like. You alright with that?'

'Special ops if I like?'

'Is there a problem?' was up a notch.

'No, it's just that…'

'Just what?'

'All this secrecy business.'

'What on earth are you on about? What secrecy?' Darke asked as he shifted in his chair.

'We know nothing about him. How long's he been here and between us we know next to nowt.'

'What is it you want to know?' was strident Darke.

'Is he single, married, divorced? Where's he live? Where's he come from apart from Grantham. What's his track record and when we ask folk down there they claim that don't have a clue either. Grantham guys reckon he was just foisted on them out the blue when there were no vacancies.'

'What difference does it make Jake if he used to be a beat copper in Knodishall and is divorced with eight kids?'

'Sorry sir, but its all part of being a team.'

'I'd appreciate your focus Jake, but if you'd rather bother yourself with unnecessary nonsense perhaps I'll find somebody else.'

'We know you're an encyclopedia on pop music.' Jake knew this was probably the last thing he should be doing but now was the chance to maybe get a move away. 'Most of us have met Jillie a few times and Holly. Know you started off down in Staffordshire. Well aware about your first wife. Working alongside you I know how good you were running MIT. I've been to Inga's for lunch a time or two. Meet up with Nicky and Connor. With Bristow think the best any of us have managed is a coffee once. Found out about the vineyard by chance, and the place by the sea when he turned up at Mablethorpe out the blue. Had Simm not been murdered would we have ever told us? Hobbies, what's his interest, family and…'

A loud 'Thank you Jake,' stopped him. 'Enough now.' and Jake wondered what was to follow. 'Need somebody to run MIT for maybe a week that's all, but if you're not up to it, just say so…'

'Course I am boss. It's just that none of us have a relationship with him, like he's permanently hiding something from us.'

'I think the best thing you can do is head off back and continue the good work we're used to from you. If I'd said he'd flown to Spain for a week to get a tan, or his mother's sick my guess is we'd not be having this conversation.'

'Except,' Jake dared. 'That'd be true to form, not saying I'm off to Spain next week.'

'Back down in Staffs my old boss down there saw work as work and play as play and never the twain shall meet. In the office it was a constant head down and work. Not half an hour's chat about football, ten minutes work and tales of how pissed we got at a barbecue. Always possible Oliver has come from that sort of environment and its what he's used to. Understand?'

'Yes but what do I tell the team? Tell them he's in Seville and when he comes back without a tan, then what?'

'He's away for operational reasons. Another force are using his expertise.'

'Fair enough,' said Jake with no desire to continue a discussion he would never win.

'We understand each other?'

'Yes, sir.' But unexplained expertise was another concern.

'Good. Now what do I need to know?'

Back down in the Incident Room he explained as best he could about DI Oliver Bristow being away for a week on an operation in need of his expertise. He got exactly what he was expecting.

'Where's he gone?' more than one wanted to know.

'What you on about?'

'What expertise?

When Detective Sergeant Jake Goodwin pulled into the cul-de-sac off Woodfield Avenue he had already been made acutely aware of major issues concerning the discovery of a man's body in a flat.

He was familiar with the fact some of the so called 'council estates' fringing the city had reputations for crime. Every city has, but any reputation foisted came from half a century or more back. Something now not deserved.

In this day and age Jake knew a whole different array of decent folk lived there, many by choice. This was never home to a sad and often unruly underclass. A world of homeless, winos and on another planet druggies was certainly not where he found himself that morning. A real mix of property types, large and small, owner occupied and rented.

Stepping from his car and heading towards the three-storey block of flats a voice from the CSI white van pulled him up short.

'You'll be lucky Jake,' made him look. 'Be better off getting a coffee,' said Willie one of the Crime Scene operatives he recognized. 'You'll not get in for ages. Right mess up there matey.' The driver lifted up a cardboard coffee container as a gesture.

'Costa just off the by-pass,' a colleague suggested.

'Thanks for that,' Goodwin responded as he walked on. Better poke my nose in or they'll mark me down as absent on the register, he decided.

Jake walked on past two police cars, three people he recognized. One he didn't as he strode up to the door in the corner. He signed in and under instructions nipped up the concrete stairs to the top floor. Christ, he wondered on the way up. What now? Had control said his throat had been cut, or some poor sod had cut his own throat?

Congregated together up there when he'd gone through a glass-paneled door and turned right were DC Sandy MacLachlan his co-ordinator colleague stood there back against a windowsill, arms folded. With him was Shona Tate the Senior Forensic Scene Manager leading her CSI team, with one of them stood alongside. Both of them kitted out in white. Similarly dressed was Nicky Scoley's partner Connor Mitchell the Crime Scene Photographer stood cameras round his neck, waiting.

'Can't get in yet,' said Shona to stop him. 'Doc's with him now but there's no room to gain access and we've got the place streaming with blood.'

'Thought aboot a ladder,' suggested Sandy jokingly. 'Except bloody winders all closed.'

'What do we know so far, if anything?' Jake asked in an attempt to start his investigation.

Sandy looked down at his notebook. 'Postman, came round here noticed door shut, when he pushed the post, it opened. He shouted then saw…' he checked. 'Andy Ross, according to his mail,' he said as he picked up a white envelope from the windowsill. 'Phoned it in just after 10.30. Waiting on more stepping pads comin' so we can get in without walking the red stuff all over the bloody place.'

‘That’ll be a good while,’ said a frustrated Shona stood leaning back. ‘Doc confirmed death immediately. Throat cut,’ she pulled a face as she sucked in a breath.

‘Called Nicky with the name and address so hopefully we’ll know more soon,’ was how Jake had been given the Code Red.

‘She was onto the Council when I left,’ Jake responded, leaning back against the wall, arms folded. ‘Apparently some of these places are owner occupied, and others rented off a housing association. What about neighbours?’ Jake asked as he pointed to a brown wooden front door to his left.

‘Did a quick check round when we couldn’t get in. Nae reply there,’ big Sandy offered. ‘Woman downstairs reckons they’ve gone away to a wedding but has no idea where. First one there,’ he pointed round the corner to Jake’s left. ‘Nae reply. Same women reckons its a young couple most likely to be at work. Two on the floor below heard and saw nothing, third there looks to be another out at work. Bottom floor’s where this...Mrs Gumbrell,’ he checked. ‘Lives. closest to the front door and net curtain she can peep through. Next one’s empty and the last is another we assume to be at work.’

‘Team back at Central getting residents names off the council.’

‘One o’them’ll no doubt turn up soon enough to get in the way.’

‘Been told Jamie’s on his way,’ Jake told the waiting crew. ‘He can organize door-to-door when extra bods get here.’ He glanced right to look at the partially open door and what looked like Dr Marcus Meller crouched down over a body. ‘How long d’we reckon?’

‘Give him ten minutes, quarter of an hour,’ was Shona responsible for all access. ‘Need to create access when the steppers arrive. Easy half an hour. If you wanna nip off, we’ll keep it safe. He’s not going anywhere.’

‘You had coffee? Jake checked with Sandy seeing two empty cardboard coffee cups on the windowsill behind her.

‘Our mistake,’ Shona admitted. ‘Here first but soon realized it’s a job for Marcus to deal with. Sent the lads off.’ she shrugged. 'They forgot about Sandy. Sorry,' she apologized to him and probably not for the first time.

'C'mon,' Jake suggested and gestured to Sandy to follow. 'Half hour max. When Jamie Hedley appears, tell him we need door-to-door doing first up.'

'I could do with one,' came a familiar voice from behind the almost closed door. 'That you Jake?' Meller's voice asked.

'What's your choice?'

'Working with this mess,' he sniggered. 'Americano, two shots.'

'Anything to eat?' Jake called back.

'To be honest with the state of this, wish I'd not had breakfast.'

'Will do.'

Sat in the car park at the Costa Drive-thru away from any big ears, Jake had by then briefed DS Scoley back at Central and the pair began to pool their thoughts on the scenario as far as they were aware.

'Darke boss is running this past the OCG lads just in case it sparks something. Turf war maybe with another stabbing.'

'My brain is asking if Bristow knew this was coming and ran away on purpose?'

'At least this time there's an excuse for him not being here.'

'Don't know if you could see, but the poor sod was face down facing away from the door one hand the doc says still clutching his throat. The other looks as though he was desperate for his phone nearby in congealed blood.' Cool as you like Sandy sipped his welcome strong coffee.

'Operation Galloway guy was frozen to death but that's about all. With Holstein, Quinton was stabbed in the hall but we found cash and drugs. Question is,' was Jake surmising. 'Are these two linked? Serial killers tend to go for the same safe methodology.'

'Except Quinton was not known to the drugs lads. If that's what somebody was after, why were the drugs still there?' Sandy queried almost to himself. 'This as far as we can tell has similarities to Quinton '

‘Tit for tat turf war maybe,’ Jake offered. ‘Somebody stepping on toes up top of the city. Now this them getting their own back in Birchwood.’

‘Using the same hit man,’ was not a serious suggestion.

‘Without further info that’s what I’m thinking too.’ Jake drunk more of his coffee.

‘Neither of them are Mr Big living where they did surely.’

‘Be OCG poking their noses in next.’

‘How would you get away from there? You had a chance to have a scout round yet?’

‘Front door with a back door at the bottom leading into a yard with the bins.’ He held up his free hand. ‘Simm front door closed but not locked, back door open but slumped outside. Then it was door ajar for number two and this one. Postie actually claims it was closed but when he went to poke a letter through it opened, means it was only pulled to.’

‘To all that gore.’

‘Why only pull the door to?’

‘Noise maybe. Loud click without the key.’

‘Network of cut-throughs between the blocks is one way, or alternative is to head off across the open grass area towards the shops or head straight for Jasmin Road, the church and away.’ Sandy pulled a face. ‘Be too obvious you’d think?’

‘Cop shop over near the Co-op.’

‘Not twenty four hours, but we could at least check.’

‘Not if it was last night. We got a time from Meller?’

‘Not yet. Folk next door away and body tucked round the corner. Could’ve been there ages.’

‘Darkness always buggers everything,’ Jake sighed and sipped his coffee. ‘Car outside maybe?’ he suggested and pulled out his phone. ‘Jamie hi. Can you ask about unusual cars, please? Somewhere like that with a quadrangle for parking be all the usual ones. Some clever sod may have noticed something different. You might get lucky and come across some old petrol head who can’t sleep, knows all the cars and how many horses. Has Meller given a time yet do you know?...Okay, thanks. You got a team together yet?’ He asked the DC. ‘Great. Wont be long.’ Another quick sip and back to

Sandy waiting for news. 'Got more troops than he expected, door-to-door up and running now.'

'Big estate.'

'Yeh. Could be he went the opposite way back up the road, across Woodfield on his toes away through the woods…'

'In the dark?'

'Good point. If he managed it he'd more than likely finish up near Damons and the petrol station. Car parked up there at the Motel maybe, is one to think about with their CCTV.'

'Stayed at the motel's another option,' made Jake sag. 'Booked in like everybody else. More CCTV,' Sandy said as he made a note. 'Sure to be.'

'Arrived and booked in. After dark makes his way across, does the deed, back the same way for a beer in the bar…'

'We'll need all cars for every stayer for all day.'

'We need to remember all this,' Jake chuckled as he scribbled. 'Trouble is, out onto Doddington Road, dark or not dark he'd easy stroll down and just before the crossing nip into Hartsholme and away. Good pathways. No cameras. Reckon you could manage it even in pitch dark?'

Scot Sandy pulled a face and supped coffee. 'If he parked in the Park car park we're pretty well buggered.'

'Long way though to go unnoticed. Even a fair bit of traffic at night, means dash cams if we're that lucky.'

'Did whoever's responsible know the next door neighbour'd conveniently be away? Need to check them out pronto.'

'Except the busybody neighbour says they're away.'

'Useful,' Sandy accompanied with a grin.

'Keep asking myself what's going on. One after a bloody other now this one,' was a serious Jake Goodwin. 'Been talking it over with Sally, wonder if this is what I want anymore.'

'Get away with yer...'

'Hear me out please,' was abrupt, 'Know there's more crime and not enough coppers, but the world's gone mad. So mad in fact we're getting more than our fair share. Just got Archer-Lees banged up as they say and wham bam this drops in our lap. Plus,' he went on before Sandy could speak. 'What's with the boss going off on some tangent we knew bugger all about?'

‘Be fair Sarge he was to some extent responsible for discovering the gun in the grass.’

‘Not just that. What about that holiday home he never mentioned one iota about, we’d not know anything about had Simm not frozen to bloody death and he turned up within ten minutes. What about the wine eh? Why not say, hey me mum’s got a vineyard in France rather than you wondering if you could get more from Aldi?’

‘See what you mean,’ Sandy said when he’d drunk a bit more.

‘Know I don’t go, but if we chatter about the Imps he never joins in. Thought he might be into cricket. No chance. Never any mention of boyfriend or girlfriend or going on holiday except for weekends out at the coast. Strange guy.’ Jake glanced at his watch as Sandy drunk.

Non-involvement was always to some extent frustrating with the need to get on with the clock ticking. This was a bad one.

This was murder number whatever popping up in a row. Where was the boss’s interest? Had he turned up first at Mablethorpe purely because the Darke boss knew he would be at his holiday home?

‘Somewhere, somehow there has to be a link unless we think this quiet county has suddenly been hit on. Think we can discount that Archer-Lees.’

‘Ages are no help. Simm fifty odd and the others in their thirties and far as we know don’t know one another.’

‘Except for a weak drugs link. Simm single with previous partner we’ve spoken to. Number one ran that grotty shop, two was some sort of Council eco bloke and what now? According to locals he’s a gardener. With age differences between first and last hardly possible they went to school together, and Quinton was dragged up down in Stamford anyway.’

‘Drink up, better get back.’

On the short journey back to the crime scene Jake was still wondering about the DI, or reasons why not. Had he been forced on Darke by those above? Did the Grantham man have friends in high places? Does such nonsense still exist in a modern police force?

Parked up fifty yards away they were booted and suited and ready for it.

At the flat, Dr Marcus Meller had kindly waited for them and welcomed the coffee, probably his reason for staying put.

'Professional job by the look of it,' he said as Jake approached the Home Office Pathologist in the short corridor before the wooden sapele front door.

'In what way?'

'Slitting some poor devil's throat's not a simple as it sounds.' Meller paused to take his first welcomed drink. 'This'll all be in the report to Craig. Briefly and don't take my word for it. This was quite possibly carried out by a hit man.' Jake's eyes flick towards Sandy. 'To be sure of death the procedure is if he was right handed would need to start from the upper third of the neck on the victim's left side walking away from you and end up on the right hand side. Findings so far are compatible with such a system.'

'Why professional?' Jake asked stood with Sandy, Shona and two of her team in the passageway listening.

'Homicidal cut throat by a right handed person from behind, severing the left carotid artery. My guess is the victim had half turned to his right therefore making it easier and more accurate by offering up the entry point.'

'Professional you say?' Shona queried as Meller drank his coffee. 'Not the sort of thing many people do for a living or go to college for.'

'You'd be surprised,' Dr Meller chuckled. 'Previous experience for one. Means you could ask HOLMES about previous slit throats. Alternative and more likely is someone with practical use of a very sharp thin blade which leads me to think butchers and abattoir, slaughterhouse workers.'

'Time of death?' Jake slipped in he had need to tell MIT about.

'I estimate say between eight last night and midnight or just after…'

‘Thoughts we’ve been having are darkness provides a good escape route from here.’

‘Toxicology,’ a slightly disgruntled Meller continued with. ‘That’ll follow the PM of course, but unlikely to make a material difference to the findings so far. Stomach contents and alcohol levels could be more use to you than me.’ He drunk down the rest of his coffee he’d not offered to pay for. Jake had remembered he drank black the preferred drink of serial killers. ‘I’ll phone time for PM but likely tomorrow,’ with that he handed the empty cardboard cup to Jake.

‘Phone me. Our DI’s away.’

‘Thanks for that,’ was at least some sort of acknowledgement. Meller grabbed his black bag and walked off round the corner. ‘Have a nice day!’ they all heard.

‘Ambulance on its way apparently,’ Shona advised as she read a message on her phone. ‘Warned them its an horrendous mess and to come prepared. Don’t want blood dripping down the stairs.’

‘We’ll leave you to it,’ Jake suggested and nudged Sandy to lead the way out. ‘While we wait for access,’ he said to his co-ordinator. ‘How about we look for Jamie, see what he’s got so far and find ourselves an old petrol head who knows all the cars off by heart.’

Maisonettes facing onto the central square looked their best bet with windows looking out.

The pair stepped out the back to where the dustbins were corralled to have a look and met two of Shona’s team, emptying the contents of each bin for a search. Seemed they’d drawn the short straw but it got worse when they admitted the next block they could see also had nine bins.

It took longer than it should have done going door-to-door close to the scene. Most they spoke to knew very little more than it was an unexplained death they’d got from the *Lincoln Leader* website or from *Lincs FM* or *Radio Lincolnshire* news.

One or two they spoke with claimed they’d been in the kitchen at the front making a cup of tea during the course of the evening but had not seen any car lights. Before it got dark nobody’d seen a strange vehicle. All a long shot not working to their advantage.

Once the cadaver had surreptitiously been taken away to the mortuary and the congealed blood had been removed, access was possible. By the time Jake and Sandy returned to the crime scene Shona and her team were well into their systems.

Andrew James Ross. Employed full time as Handy Andy Gardener according to business cards they discovered. Phone in the kitchen lying on the worktop close to a tray with two mugs, a plate of Hobnobs and two or three mini milk pots. SIM card removed to stop external interference had been bagged to go to the Tech Crime Team for them to extract vital evidence from, with luck.

'Shona,' said Jake calmly stood in the kitchen. 'Remember Harry Simm? He had a cup of coffee with nasties dropped in it. Was there anything like this?' he pointed to the mugs. 'Set up for that Brendon Quinton, do you remember?'

'Washed up mugs I seem to remember with Simm,' said the Forensics head honcho as she stared into Jake Goodwin's eyes and he nodded. 'Assumed coffee as there was no alternative anywhere. Not sure about Quinton. I'll get Alfie back in the office to pull up Connor's photos. You thinking…?

'If stab victims Quinton and this Ross had refreshments all set out it'd point us in the same direction.' He pulled a face to prepare her. 'Hit men are all about routine remember.'

'So they tell you on the course,' she smiled and sniggered with. 'I'll get Simon onto that and bear in mind we might need to be on the lookout for Rohypnol.'

'He'd be in a bad way, slit throat, staggered a pace maybe two and totally vulnerable.'

The flat was nothing to write home about. Not quite as prim, proper or as tidy as Quinton's place, but still okay.

Kitchen was dated and Jake was pleased to notice no dirty dishes his Sally could not abide. No discarded bits of food, no takeaway boxes but not heading towards house proud any time soon.

He was pleasantly surprised by the contents of the fridge with plenty of fruit and veg. Then when he thought about it a gardener was more than likely to have the right food.

This marked him down as different from Simm. No mention of drugs discovery so far made the media's serial killer theory less and less likely.

Eggs, cheese, milk. A whole array of stuff to make a good mixed salad, plus spuds and veg for a good few days. Jake even came across jam, mayonnaise, coleslaw and butter.

One interesting sight was pointed out to him by Shona was the walk-in cupboard just inside the front door. Chockablock full of an assortment of domestic items including an ironing board, coat hooks full of jackets and Winter coats. Right at the back a cabinet displaying a whole range of Scotch Whiskies on the top.

Jake's first thought was to give Sandy a shout but then remembered Scotch was not his tipple. At last an insight into the world of Andrew Ross.

The side-to-side lounge had all the furniture congregated in the centre rather than one end to relax and the other to eat. Carpet could have done with a good shampoo. No dining table so assumed eating was confined to a small drop-down table in the kitchen. Either that or he scoffed on his knee. Toilet and bathroom clean to show he'd been brought up proper.

Spare bedroom was in effect an office come store room. There was everything from small box files and a laptop to a dozen hand held gardening implements cleaned and laid on old newspapers. Why were they not where the bottles of whisky were on display?

This made two living in acceptable conditions and only Simm fitting his own unkempt grimy image.

Jake had been reminded by something he spotted on tele about the Beverley Hillbillies being close to the same image as Simm. There was little point in mentioning anything as it was doubtful whether any of the team would have knowledge of a programme and characters his dad had enjoyed.

From what he'd seen of the area and what he'd been told previously it appeared to him that some people have a problem with perception not one with actual reality. A case of rumour and innuendo more than likely off some grubby social media site.

30

Is it me or is this all getting well out of hand? See that lad who owned a coffee shop's got done for attempted murder. That's ridiculous. What's wrong with young people today with all their angst? Some scientist recently tried hard but failed to justify it all by suggesting this is a side effect of that Covid. That's utter nonsense too, it was going that way long before all that business.

Be interesting to find out what that was all about when it comes to court. Think that's youngsters' problem. Where d'they get their info from. All totally unreliable sources as possible, I once read.

How have we got ourselves in this state? Why do these kids go out at night with a phone and a knife? When I was young I probably had a hankie and packet of fags. Don't even have hankies these days they tell me, just wipe snot on their sleeve. Arguments about what's on their phone or pictures they've taken I've read about time and again. Phone snatching, plus drugs of course seem to be here there and everywhere these days. Woman disappears in tragic circumstances and within days there are cretins on site taking selfies. Such stuff I find acutely difficult to comprehend the reasoning.

How many times do you hear of cars being stopped by the coppers and first thing they sense is a wiff of cannabis? Can't all be the scrotes of this world as coppers call them. Have to be normal law abiding citizens. If that's what their stupid parents are up to, God help the kids.

Quick snort rather than afters at dinner parties I read somewhere. Sorry but I'd much rather have Apple Crumble and Ice Cream, or that Banana and Caramel Parfait Fudge and Dulcey I was treated to one time.

All the everyday poncy gits who should know better. Chances are of course I may well have clients who think nothing of sniffing a line in the lavvy. As long as they don't do it in mine before they leave.

Read this morning the poor coffee house woman who got shot's had two operations and hopes to be back running her business in a while. Drug gangs and folk like that I can sort of understand being out of their mind half the time but shooters over being served a poor cappuccino and stale blueberry Muffin? Be gun fight at the OK Coffee Bar next.

Why didn't I just hand all this over to the local coppers? To be honest I reckon they've got more than enough on their plate these days. Big help to me though with all this other stuff muddying the waters.

Expected more on law and order from the Tories, but alas that all went out the window when the Police numbers were slaughtered. When was the last time you saw a copper down your street?

Brexit next up, then that Covid business they got all arse about face. One of the highest death rates in the world and some Boris fans claim it went well! Now it means the lads down your local cop shop don't have the numbers to deal with stuff like this.

Bit like that Rotherham child sex abuse business and coppers in fear of their jobs unwilling to take action with the possibility of racism hanging over them, so they say.

So, I'm doing my bit until the police get up to strength. Good to see they've put some foreign woman in charge at Lincoln County for female issues such as sexual assault and increasing booze laden domestic abuse. Why a foreigner? Thought Brexit put paid to all that. Have we really not got anyone of our own, or is that about this female, black or gay diversity business and being politically correct?

One thing I can't get my heard around is civil servants being taught not to use phrases such as "I'm visiting my Mum and Dad" as it is gender inappropriate. Whatever that means.

For countless years I've felt I should do something about the way women are treated. Sorry, but I've never been into all these banner waving marches no matter what they're protesting about. Getting involved in something like that could so easily see me finish up on the wrong side of the law. In some cases I remember there were photos of badly dressed scantily clad women trying to bash policewomen. What was that all about?

Getting angry by writing to the media's always been a complete waste of time as they select only the ones fitting their own political agenda or likely to boost readership.

Don't know enough about social media to use that. Apart from the checking I've needed to do recently, I just see it as a scurrilous menace responsible for so many ills in our society. Wouldn't know what platform is best and with so many of those trolls about you never know what it could lead to.

To be honest I'm not really sure what half of the stuff means these days. Couldn't fathom recently when I read something to do with the increase in incels. Apparently and I sort of quote: they are members of an online subculture defining themselves as incel which is short for involuntary celibate, claiming to be unable to establish a romantic liaison. Almost as bad as that absurd woke business.

Then of course we have the Word of the Year 2022. 'Goblin mode' which turns out to be two words appertaining to greedy behaviour. Why not just say so?

As humans of course we all have out own particular likes and dislikes and matters to thoroughly annoy. Take the use of mobile phones in dramas on the telly. You either can't read a word, or when the texts are important to the plot the phone's not there long enough to read it all. Please don't get me started on characters seeing people who've been dead for ages.

Water is another of my gripes. Why on earth do intelligent people pay an arm and a leg for bottled water? Its a proven scientific fact that normal tap water is purer and better for you. In test after test the public chose it against that other nonsense.

Music is so bad these days I hardly bother with the radio and BBC Sounds I assume is maybe what they call Radio One these days. Bit like people talking about Malware which could be like Tupperware for all I know. Why doesn't anybody explain what's going on anymore?

Of course there are those who regard me as not being with it. Being 'off grid' as they stupidly say. I tend not to follow trends, and certainly not that Prince Harry film and biography. Even had one clown suggest as a result of what he said he would make a perfect King.

Couple of weeks ago a new client at the end of the procedure said: “Don’t want to use the C word but I feel so calm.”

To my mind the internet serves us, but harms us at the same time. Gives us the opportunity to read a book less than five minutes after we’ve ordered it. Groceries delivered every Thursday morning at ten, but at the same time provides a service for some old folk to be scammed out of their life savings and women abused by trolls.

Having said that, there’s no way I would be doing this if I’d had to go to the Library and borrow a book about how to kill. Read about stabbing as an art form or one about how poisons work and all the stuff I’ve discovered on the net. Get a look or two from the Librarian without a doubt.

Away from the web. There have of course been instances which have made me really angry. What I’d never considered before was how in time of conflict women become the prey of non-aggressors.

The situation in Afghanistan is well known of course. I’m talking about situations such as when Russia invaded Ukraine. Millions of people managed to escape to Poland and beyond. They were mainly women and children with the men staying behind to fight.

The sex trade predators were quick of the mark and set up camp at the borders faster than the refugees apparently.

On the lookout for tired, homeless, destitute attractive young women with or without children in tow. Unable to speak or understand Polish the sex bandits were there waiting scouring for suitable women to join their evil trade.

Leaving the utter chaos of war behind them some women were grateful for the opportunity to start a new life. Poland was just the main border but they were being shipped far and wide and what’s the chances some finished up over here? Even Lincoln maybe.

Teams of traffickers always having been active in Ukraine in times of peace was something I knew nothing about, and the chaos of war made life for them so much easier.

Bemused and dazed beautiful young women arrived at railway stations in a totally confused state and starving to be greeted by both men and women offering help.

Having escaped through a war zone and being welcomed how many would even consider the likelihood of sexual exploitation that the offer of accommodation for them and their family may be the price to pay?

I have no words to describe how their whole ghastly experience may have been like.

I suppose I got angry but did nothing about it as they were women thousands of miles away. When the ghastly behaviour of ill treating women landed on my doorstop more and more it was time to set my plans into motion.

Long before number two on the list had been dispatched, I'd spent what time I could, out and about stalking the next. This one similar to Quinton had a fairly set routine which is probably true about most of us.

With Ross it was proving difficult to get to know much about him, over and above what Miriam had said on the phone when things had got really bad.

How many times had I beaten myself up for not heading down south and dragging her back up here? Thoughts of what that could have meant are the making of nightmares.

As you know, each time I've gone to the trouble of burning my own clothing and in the case of Simm even his. Apart from his underpants with red love hearts on them that is. Means I've been scouring fresh suitable clothing from charity shops, and paying by cash. The stuff to wear for Simm I got from a place in Newark. It was a trip up to Sheffield for Quinton and finally wore a pretty decent coat I got in Scunthorpe.

For the trip up to Sheffield I'd arranged to be free of appointments on my wife Ruthie's day off that week. On the way there as I often do, wondered how many small out of the way places have a bridge with a toll you have to pay like at Dunham Bridge.

Tram from Meadowhall into the centre then a stroll around and checked three charity shops for a suitable coat and eventually discovered what I was looking for. Job done, back to Meadowhall for a wander around and we grabbed a Chicken Platter at Nandos.

We sat enjoying our food looking at folk strolling past as we did so. New hobby of mine trying to guess what secrets these anonymous people hold. What about him, is he in an adulteress relationship his loyal wife knows bugger all about? Has that one with a pair of stupid white high heeled boots been nicking money out the till at work for years? Doubt any of them had murdered one or two and planning another.

Not something I'd given a moment's thought to before all this business took hold of me. Serial killers leading a normal life.

Next time you're at the supermarket stood there in one of the cold aisles deciding whether you want Fig or Strawberry Yogurt. The person next to you with a similar dilemma could easy be planning to throttle somebody next week or bash them over the head with a shovel.

What I already knew from back in the day was that shit Ross at one time was by chance another working for local government with a role in Lincoln Borough Council.

Don't know about you but its the sort of role in life I still refer to as a bin man, no matter what oddball name Personnel (or should I say HR) give them this week to continue with their politically correct money wasting obsession. Or what colour lids they put on the bins to confuse us all.

I often wonder how much it costs to make such irrelevant changes. Like turning Schools into Academies for no good expensive reason.

Him being a bin man meant he was no feeble plumped up. Dragging those bins about is not easy work and he'd be more than capable of holding his own. Given a chance.

Too much blood had been the main issue with Quinton, but a similar way of dealing with it looked to be a good bet again. Forewarned is forearmed they say.

Of course I have insider information on this one being the target for all this business. Been very satisfying in the knowledge of the good I've done for society even if I've not rid Europe of sex traffickers.

Looked to me by that stage as though Ross my main target from day one, my personal bulls eye will need to be the last.

Research tells me the people I've been dealing with have in-bred nasty issues. One physical and one mental but in the case of Ross he had both in spades.

I realize of course how this could all come tumbling down around my ears. Chances are if I'm not careful I'll be sat in a cold cell wondering how I could have made a fundamental error after all the meticulous planning I've done. It's not as if I just knifed some abuser down some dark alley in town. Been years in the making and then it could so easily all turn turtle in a few moments with blue lights flashing and Ruthie sobbing.

My wife is not the sort to nag and fully understands why I need to do this and why now. Just that she probably feels left out. Working as hard as I do and then off out and about spying on these nasties is taking a toll on me, but I know Ruthie has my well being at heart.

Think one of her problems is she comes from a really nice close knit family. Her parents are still alive and forever off on another of those big riverboat cruises across Europe. She also has a brother and sister, both married with kids.

Simm and Quinton I went for happened to be the two worst cases I'd come cross of domestic violence regaled to me by women at the refuge invested in me in the quiet of an evening. Miriam of course once I felt confident and practiced enough was the reason for doing all this while I'm able.

All these cases in recent times of women such as Sarah Everard being abused and murdered had brought the whole matter to the fore. Naturally big sister Miriam simply had to be on my list.

31

Jake Goodwin picked up his phone and saw the name *Inga Larsson*. Knew without her rank would be her private mobile.

'Good morning madam.'

'Jake,' she responded. 'You free around one-thirty for a chat?'

'Guess so. Anything I need to know first?'

'Not really.'

'Good. One thirty it is.'

He turned to Nicky Scoley. 'That was Inga wanting a chat. Anything cracking off you know about?'

'Does she really need our help with all the stuff going on up here? Why not change hats and go back to MIT mode?'

'This is all yours at half one' he said spreading his arms wide.

'Thanks.'

'Thanks Jake,' said DCI Inga Larsson when he walked into her office and closed the door behind him before sitting down on one of three chairs facing her. Bigger posher office than the one she once occupied down in MIT.

'How's it going?' he asked.

'Fine, but I was going to ask you the same question.' Jake frowned.

'Bit up to our ears in it if I'm honest. Got three now but they're all different in many respects so we're not, or should I say the boss is not, willing to go down the serial killer route.'

'Any reason?'

'Don't ask me,' he shrugged.

'But Jake...'

'Look,' he sighed. 'Could be out of order, but he plays it all too close to his chest fort my liking. Frequently its a one man band we're not allowed to know anything about. I'll be honest Nicky and I can't fathom him at all'

'You *and* Nicky?'

'Yeh.'

With that the DCI who was once the DI responsible for the Major Incident Team picked up her phone and Jake waited. 'Nicky' she said. 'Inga. Any chance you can pop down and see me for a minute or two? Thanks. Put Sandy in charge, it won't take long' she looked at Jake. 'Nicky's on her way,' she said as if he didn't already know.

In the intervening period Jake sat pondering what was going on as Larsson chatted about Sally and Tyler as well as ordering up another coffee.

'Come in, come in,' she said to DS Nicky Scoley as the door opened. 'Have a seat. I've ordered coffee.' Inga then turned a page of a notebook in front of her and looked up. 'Can we get something absolutely straight for starters please? Fortunately I know you both extremely well and trust you implicitly by means of sheer experience. What we are about to discuss does not go any further. Understood? And I mean that.' The pair nodded.

A still bemused Jake mumbled 'Yeh.'

'Thank you,' she looked past the pair of them. 'Good timing,' she said as the door opened and one of Larsson's team walked in with coffees.

'Thank you,' the ever polite Swede Larsson acknowledged. She waited until the door was closed. 'Here we go then,' she said sitting back. 'Detective Inspector Oliver Bristow,' she hesitated. 'Currently assisting another force with his specialist expertise and that's where this story starts. Few years back he was plucked from another force as the powers that be...yes Jake?'

'Which force or doesn't that matter?'

'To be honest from what you are about to learn the less number of people who are aware of facts the better. Anyway, he then undertook an undercover role for a major force,' she winked with, 'if you get my drift. That role, combined with his particular expertise led him to be involved with a seriously major organized crime investigation.' She stopped to take a drink and Nicky followed suit.

'Why weren't we told about this?'

'That will become clear.' She hesitated almost as if she was plucking up the courage. 'He's a super recognizer. Oliver Bristow has the ability to memorize and recall thousands of faces, often having seen them only once. That acute ability when you are also undercover on the outskirts of a OCG is super useful, and so it turned out.'

'And that's what he's doing now?' Jake wanted to know.

'Not exactly, but assisting with a case up north. Down south it was a CHIS (Covert Human Intelligence) role combined with his recognizer skills. This time it's a case of helping out. The reason he's been with us for a while now and not been taken away as he has this week, is what I'll come to next.' Inga returned to her coffee. 'Appreciate now why this is all behind closed doors?'

'Sure,' said Nicky with Jake still trying to fathom.

'It gets worse,' Inga admitted to her two former close colleagues. 'His evidence in the case at the end of the operation was absolutely crucial, and we're talking Old Bailey six week trial. In so much as a bizarre event was organized. During the trial with Oliver giving evidence from behind a screen, the Defence barrister made a real issue over the matter of him stating what and in particular who he had seen which implicated the top OCG bosses in the dock. The supercilious QC suggested his recognizer talent was nothing more than a figment of imagination.' Inga sat smiling and shaking her head. 'The Prosecution in response set up a gathering of a hundred random people chosen by the Defence into which they placed the twelve members of the jury. Oliver had been allowed, wearing a balaclaver, to spend thirty second looking at the whole Jury sat in an empty court. At the gathering of a hundred and twelve drinking coffee and eating cake, he walked in and picked them out one by one in the order they were sat on the benches.'

'Fu..!'

'Yee gods!'

'That good eh?'

'Super Recognisers are about one percent of the population,' said Inga. 'Having significantly better-than-average face recognition ability, even years after seeing it very briefly.'

'But why's that such a secret?' Jake asked. 'I met one years ago.'

'Because all five got sent down for more than twenty years each for extortion plus importing and dealing drugs, one with murder added got thirty eight and subsequently a price was put on Oliver's head.'

'You serious?' Nicky gasped.

'Ten thousand quid.'

'Shit!'

'One attempt was made on his life soon after the case came to trial, and he now has a metal plate in his shin. Oliver Bristow is not his real name. He has a new birth certificate, new passport, new credit cards, everything in fact. The Oliver Bristow you know is a new man. Name he chose from a character in a novel apparently. The real person he once was, no longer exists in any way shape or form. In fact to also protect him his mother has metamorphosed into somebody else.' Inga checked her notes. 'Uses her middle Christian name and her son's new surname. All this elaborate transformation is for two reasons. His recognizer talent we want to keep, and the cost of protecting him for years would if he left the Police, be extortionate and full of risk. Anyway he would rather be a copper than a security guard at Sainsbury's. This way it's easier to look after him and his talent. Thus he's away right now for a few days recognizing people.'

'Doesn't go to crime scenes because?' was good old Jake.

'Could easy be a set-up. People we're dealing with would simply kill some poor soul if that meant Oliver would turn up at the crime scene. Bearing in mind as far as we know they're still looking for the person he was, not the man as he is now.'

'Is the vineyard true?' Nicky asked.

'Absolutely, but. His mother was not left the vineyard in a will until after the major court case. The copper the OCG could track down had a mother who was a midwife living in the south east. All that has helped with the subterfuge. One sad thing he knows he can't have contact with his father who had divorced his mother, and sadly he was in a relationship with a top copper's daughter which has also gone for a ball of chalk.'

Jake laughed. 'The things you learnt from us. Ball of chalk.'

'Gotta say,' said Nicky. 'Begun to get annoyed with all the secrecy, but now I feel damn sorry for him. This be for life you reckon?'

'Maybe, maybe not. OCGs tend to move on to the next shipment, to the next pot of gold. Hopefully he'll be able to involve you more in his life given time, but as you can imagine he's got to be wary of everyone.' Inga looked at Jake. 'You could easy drop him in it for ten grand.'

'What do we do with the rest of the team?'

'They as curious as you Jake?'

'Not nearly as much, just bits and pieces,' he responded. 'Any chance somebody can have a word with him. We'll need a credible reason for him being away when he come back. They'll want to know.'

'How about a course?' Nicky suggested.

'Good idea,' said Inga. 'Something obscure I'll find and pass onto him. Good.'

'Still good down here?' Nicky asked of her ex-boss as she sat back, cup in hand savouring a biscuit

'Long way from what I learnt at uni about cops and robbers. Oliver and his super recognizer skills and in an hour,' she glanced at her watch. 'I've a chat with an independent sexual violence advisor.'

32

'Here we are again,' was bearded DI Oliver Bristow sat as he sometimes did propping himself against a spare desk, coffee mug alongside, tablet to hand. Back in Lincoln from his special duties. 'Got to say,' he opened with. 'When I first arrived here Inga Larsson took the time and trouble to explain all the ins and outs of the job. She told me this place is kept busy. Fortunately with it not being some ghastly urban sprawl some cities are infested by, there are never daily stabbings on street corners some poor sods have to cope with.' He hesitated and scanned the room. 'No?' he chuckled. 'What's all this then?' he asked pointing at the boards.

'Be fair boss,' was his second in command DS Jake Goodwin, who on his return asked Bristow about the Course dealing with large scale multi-agency investigations, in front of the team. 'To some extent she is right. We'll never be able to sit back all day and play Scrabble. Have a round of golf on Wednesdays or meet up in the pub Friday afternoon. But,' he went on, then hesitated. 'This is way away from our norm. I've been here a good while and I've never experienced cases as serious as these almost one after another.'

'Thanks Jake,' said Bristow. 'Back to it. An Andrew Ross and Operation Simmental this time. Postmortem tells me this was never a nice sight, not that any of them are. Got to say Marcus Meller was absolutely right.'

Surreptitiously Nicky Scoley was looking up this Simmental. One eye on Bristow spouting, one on her screen. Never heard of the word before and Wikipedia told her why. Yes they are cattle but dual purpose Swiss cattle.

'He did say at the PM he reckoned this was probably text book stuff,' said Jake who had attended in Bristow's absence. 'Ross'd been tidied up of course as they do, but that gaping wound in his neck nearly reminded me of my lunch.'

'Realize we're looking for a connection if there is one,' was Bristow back. 'If I remember rightly the PM for Brendon Quinton had no mention of a professional job and Simm of course just froze to death. Nothing new or dramatic so far, until maybe when the tox results are back. Just as Meller explained to you I think Jake. Precision cut through the artery and he'd bled out in no time. Grasping at his neck to stop the flow knowing death was rushing up to him at a fast rate of knots.'

'Gardener,' says Nicky Scoley when Oliver looked at her and lifted his china mug. 'Lived alone…'

'Nicky,' was Oliver back licking his thin lips. 'Sorry, but can I just say at this juncture. All these we've had recently all seemingly unconnected, but you're quite right two lived alone in Lincoln or close by which has to make Simm the odd one out,' and returned to his black coffee. Was this a new look Oliver Bristow, more lucid, more genial? Had Larsson had a word?

'Except,' Jake slipped in. 'We now have two people linked in some way to the environment,' and stuck a hand up. 'I know, I know. Its a very loose link but it is there. Did they spend their spare time caring for frogspawn and then beating the living daylights out of their partners? And crucially. Were they known to each other and they're researching the ecological impact of some development proposals? Rare insect stops a hundred homes for the homeless nonsense.'

'Yes boss,' sighed Jamie.

'You don't know the question,' Bristow smiled a chide.

'Go to the council check any links. Did the environment people use Ross to cut their lawns?'

'Except Ross's a private contractor not like salaried Quinton.'

'Still worth a check.'

'There's more on social media this time,' made the DI glance at Alisha momentarily. 'With Simm,' he carried on. 'The news rush to some extent was very quiet. We presumed that to be because as the boss man says he lived alone, lived out at the coast and as well as looking like Worsel Gummidge he had that quirky shop. Went to watch Grimsby mid-week when they were at home. Met a couple of guys for the odd pint or two, but nothing much apart from that. Dour individual by all accounts who had no proper connection with anybody. Things reacted a bit faster with Quinton and this new one Ross.'

'Could be because Quinton was therefore part of a team, when he didn't show up for his shift would be missed straight away. With Ross he'd have bookings and folk'd query where he was' Alisha hesitated in case some wanted to ask questions.

'Boss,' was tentative Michelle. 'Maybe just two are linked?'

'Quinton and Ross you mean?'

'Weak environment link, close to the city. Simm has no link.'

'That we know of,' he grimaced. 'Two stabbings in double quick time in their hallways and living alone. And Simm?' Oliver shot back. 'What about him?'

'No knife, not near the front door, no drugs, no cash, no phone except one under the table and he's over in Mablethorpe. Hardly the crime capital even of Lincolnshire.'

'You forgot the passport. Which route d'you think?' Oliver Bristow asked.

'Drugs.'

'Why?'

'Cases very similar in a lot of aspects and we've tracked down Quinton's amphetamines. Drugs link or a bit of a turf war is a good motive.'

'Thank goodness,' Oliver sighed. 'Thought for a moment you were going down the homophobia route. Just because we have guys living alone.'

'Not at all, but we could check that out as well if you want.'

'You think we should put the idea in Shona's mind and she brings in the drugs dog just in case. Look for links between Ross and Quinton?'

'And Simm as a sideline.'

'Why?' Oliver queried.

'Insurance policy.'

'Where's the connection?' he asked of the whole room and spread his arms. 'Because I don't see a link.'

'Cover our backs guv,' Sandy joined in.

'Oh, you're in on this too.'

'Take away blood'n DNA,' Jake offered up before Sandy could respond. 'Concentrate on everything else. Track down a burner phone, cash and if we're really lucky bags of coke in the loft. Until tox tell us it's the same knife what pucker link we got? Both male, both living alone? That could run into millions,' was inevitably sarcasm from the senior Detective Sergeant.

'How about Simm? You really serious about adding him to the list as well?'

'Why not?'

'Why not?' was louder from Oliver Bristow. 'Because we've handed the keys back to Jodie Simm that's why. We were never looking for drugs among all that garbage. Also might I remind you, no drug paraphernalia and toxicology never mentioned a word.'

'Give her some twaddle about Proceeds of Crime Act to hide our real concern,' said Nicky as things were heading towards getting out of hand.

'Proceeds of Crime have been delving into the money he'd got stashed away,' frustrated Bristow suggested. 'Quinton had that secret bank account in Ireland. What about Simm? He got offshore accounts for buying crap?'

'What if they were in this together and they upset somebody?' Jamie fueled the fire. 'Trampled all over their turf? Where did he go on holiday?'

'We know where Quinton went on holiday. Off to these gaming things.'

DI Oliver Bristow faced the most serious and complex time of his working life. He knew the Simm case was going nowhere fast, even if they'd uncovered what Quinton was up to. He stood there arms folded looking at his team.

Those chats with Inga Larsson told him he had a team he needed to make the most of and according to her the senior two had his back. Parking that issue for future consideration, scanning the room he mentally went through his checklist of the team's basic tasks.

'I'll speak to Shona about a dog,' he agreed, once he was done. 'If she's not already got one. No,' he said in an immediate change of mind. 'Tell you what Jake. You speak to Shona, but first I've got to arrange the prospect of a search with that Jodie Simm woman, before they sell the bloody shop.'

They had logged less than fifty calls from the public since the Ross murder had hit the streets. Even Simm had managed a great deal more. Sometimes the call totals in such cases would be over two hundred. Missing children would see them go through the roof of course. Resulting in great difficulty sorting the genuine from the cranks.

What Alisha had discovered on her social media search about Ross she knew would be of interest to Jake Goodwin. He and Sally used social media but not extensively. Both messaged friends on their phones but not over much so she knew he could at times be critical of those who almost live by them.

Alisha pointed out the comments from customers, the hearts, smiling emojis, graphics applauding and innumerable people clicking on *Like*.

'All this good reaction, yet someone was upset enough to stab him,' said Jake as he read. 'Reminds me of something about a Petunia in an onion patch, but this is the other way round.'

'My dad had a bloke rotovate the scratty flower borders when we moved house,' she told Jake. 'Seemed to us like just an average gardener. Truth was his hobby was growing flowers and a gold medalist at Chelsea.'

33

Hello again. I've just been thinking. Government of whatever hue have a habit of introducing new laws which are never quite right. A Domestic Abuse Register is just one case in point. This is where convicted abusers are required to inform the police of any new partners in order for them, to be notified of their track record.

Couple of flaws in all that. The word convicted, even the Home Office admits is the tip of the iceberg. And, what about all those where the woman decides not to press charges or never goes anywhere near the police station, because she thinks they're a misogynistic waste of space?

The people I was dealing with or acting secretly on their behalf would not be covered by such a ruling.

Cyberflashing is one they concentrated on. For those unaware of how some men behave, this nasty business amounts to sending unsolicited sexual messages, frequently pictures or in many cases ghastly selfies.

That's something I can never get my head round. Read somewhere people can take as many as 800 selfies a year. I was in one once, but've never seen the point. After all taking photos of oneself is a form of narcissism, I want no part of.

Cynthia Hart I see a few times a year asked me at the end of one session if I'd pamper her daughter as a birthday treat. Unnecessarily she then explained how Millie had recently escaped from a relationship with this guy who'd been done for drugs.

I had no plans to go anywhere near the subject but it was pretty little Millie who almost immediately explained why her mother had paid for two sessions.

Almost as if she had a need to get it all off her chest with a stranger, she described this Darren in glowing terms with talk of him initially being affectionate, attentive, funny and well up for a good time. The sort so she claimed, remembered the anniversary of their first meeting with a bouquet of roses.

Really happy birthday treats when she said she'd been spoiled rotten. Two birthdays it was until as if somebody tripped a switch and it was all change.

Apparently they went through the screaming and shouting phase with episodes at times almost daily. This of course true to form was followed by tears and apologies, said it would never happen again, until of course it did.

Then a sudden unplanned pregnancy produced a change back to sweetness and light, to how they once were with tenderness and love. Once more, until.

Millie when talking to me was convinced it was the way she looked when well into her term, after the morning sickness she'd suffered from badly. He demanded sex on Sunday mornings but her priority at that time had been kneeling, heaving into the toilet bowl.

Then it was her obsession with the baby, the clothes, cot and decorating a bedroom. Jealous of how life may become when his desires would be pushed to the back of the queue turned into rage. Rage that turned violent and too many punches resulted in a miscarriage.

Always remember roses are red, violence not violets are blue.

A child lost purely by uncontrollable rage from low life forever snorting and dealing in cocaine.

She'd been a sensible one having moved back home to her parents for rest and recuperation and he'd been given weak punishment, a restraining order for two years.

I'm telling you this because Millie was absolutely gushing when out of the blue she phoned to tell me what she'd heard on the news. This Darren had knifed a woman in a bar in town. As a result of his arrest the Police had raided the flat where he now lived to discover drugs and all the paraphernalia involved in dealing.

I had begun to develop plans to slip in number four after I'd learnt of how ghastly Millie's life had become.

To be honest I'd worked and planned hard to gain the experience before dealing with Andy Ross, and to a great degree that and other issues had reduced my enthusiasm. With this Darren suddenly locked up and likely to be for a good while, I decided things should remain as they are and to end my career as a serial killer with three boxes ticked.

That is unless something really nasty turns up which I can easily deal with quickly. In a world where the manager of a Burger joint sexually harassed a staff member in the store room, anything is possible.

I do get to hear all sorts of course. Not all about women suffering at the hands of brutes.

Names have of course been changed to protect the vulnerable, but one young woman I'll call Melanie talked to me over a few weeks about the daily degradation. Moving her away from her friends, some she'd had since childhood were the worst aspects, apart from the brutal thuggery. Told me one harrowing morning as I attempted to treat her, of how she was this monster's plaything. Like a piece of Lego he could do whatever he wanted with.

Fortunately some of what I listen to is nothing more than pointless nosiness and idle chatter. Women full of jealousy often about the daftest of things they've got themselves into a state about.

One fairly new client just a week ago jumped from talk about her granddaughter to talk about the murder of Brendon Quinton. Just the time for me to become a half-hearted listener. Make no comment and show a modicum of interest. With difficulty.

It was good to realize she was doing nothing of danger to me other than repeating what drivel she'd read on social media or been told.

My sigh of relief was obvious when she moved onto chattering about her rheumatism, but in the confines of my treatment room I was safe.

One woman who walks her ten year old to school for some reason is always chuntering about the School Run. About how the narrow road close by is utterly chaotic and dangerous with parents insisting they drop their brats as close to the classroom as possible.

My guess is, all her friends put their children's lives in danger by insisting they get the car out and block the streets. Means she has nobody to grumble to.

Obviously I keep dropping into the local *Lincoln Leader* website and check the radio to see if my exploits get any mention.

Sort of thing you don't notice normally, or at least I don't. How in this day and age the media move on to the next disaster, major crime or political wrangling at speed. Always remember when that Boris Johnson finally resigned and they just cancelled programmes on the telly, extended the news, even broke into Wimbledon to thoroughly annoy me. All at a time when we had the Ukraine war, a Covid upsurge I seem to recall, but am open to being corrected. Murders and rape and all that sort of stuff. Then what did they do? Bored us to death about who might take over the Downing Street mess.

Another case of ignoring what makes our world go round to give us all another dose of politics in looking for the next to follow the narcissist failure.

The coffee shop attack of course has been long forgotten by the media. Be a good wait now for it to come to court.

Got to be more than him just wanting to get rid of competition. If that's the latest trend we'll have senior staff at Tesco being issued with a Colt 45 to deal with the manager of a new upstart supermarket in their part of town. Thought amusing ideas at one time how in some society's it could easily have been a landlord chasing unpaid rent or the council after more Council Tax. But no its that young man. Even an amusing idea was put to me by one client, suggesting it was probably the barista asking a customer if they wanted an extra shot.

I know we get a lot about mental health these days, but this has to be the problem in this case surely.

Been meaning to go out to see if the coffee place is still open, but I see their website's still up and running so guess whoever owned the place got somebody fresh in.

We are a nation of curiosity and as a result a sales boost for Shires Coffee would not be a big surprise since the shooting. After all there are some folk who visit places used on programmes on the telly. People even so I'm told, go on a bus trip around Edinburgh stopping off at all the major places mentioned in Ian Rankin's Rebus novels.

34

Easy Monday morning call for Michelle Cooper was to visit Mrs Daphne Gumbrell who had told Sandy about the couple on the top floor facing Ross's door being away at a wedding.

Aware Mrs Gumbrell was the sort who would know the moment they returned, she set out to see what the latest news was.

It was very much a case of one of those "Come in pet, have a seat, I've just put the kettle on." situations. Aware this could well be the one person with an inkling of information, Michelle played along with her.

It was a very tidy if slightly old fashioned ground floor flat with her front door right close to the main door to the building. Two-bedrooms with a small kitchen but a lounge from front to back. One end was home to a dining table and chairs and to her left when she entered Cooper discovered it to be pleasantly comfortable with a television, coffee table on a big rug and bookcase filled with cozy books.

Fully wallpapered and all the paint a nice cream. Not a job she imagined Dumbrell herself had managed. There was a view of the road and the car park outside at the front with four cars including her own. To the rear was an area of grass and the next block of three with a cut through.

Mrs Gumbrell who asked to be called Daphne busied herself in the kitchen making tea. When she returned to the lounge she was not pushing a hostess trolley as some she'd come across. Two mugs on a tray rather than the expected cups and saucers, plus a plate of Bourbon biscuits.

Sat down opposite Cooper, Dumbrell appeared respectable and smelling of an eu de cologne to remind Michelle of Matthew's aftershave which is probably a darn sight cheaper. From where she sat this Daphne had a good view out onto the road. Before she supped the detective introduced herself properly and explained what it was she had called about.

'Just managed to catch hold of her this morning as I said,' was what Daphne already explained at the front door. 'Just caught sight of her off out on her way to work. Told her Police need to talk to her, like that policeman asked me to if I saw her.'

'Did she appear surprised by what you told her?' Cooper asked.

'Most definitely. Put on my best Miss Marple mood and said she had no idea Mr Ross was dead.' A moment's hesitation as Cooper waited. 'This what you do all day?'

'Whole variety of things to be honest. What makes the job so interesting. How about the husband?'

'Asked me all about what'd gone on,' said chubby cheeked Daphne eagerly ignoring the question. 'Told her what I knew about Mr Ross being found dead by the postman. Poor man.' She stopped to grin to herself and just glanced out of the window. Cooper decided that's what she did to keep an eye open. Not well liked by neighbours up to all sorts, but always proved beneficial in such an inquiry. 'He was well shaken up. Poor man. Being doing this round on and off for years.'

'The husband?' Michelle Cooper had to remind.

'Oh yes, of course,' Daphne chuckled to herself. 'He's long gone by then. Hear the front door sometimes as I'm getting up. No idea what he does, sorry,' told Cooper maybe she was not the complete busybody Jake had suggested.

'Do you have their name?' Cooper checked then sipped the tea.

'No idea, sorry,' Daphne responded immediately. 'Could be the just first or second time I'd spoken to either of them. Only been in a few months. Live up top you see, not like Rhona next door and the Lawlers round the corner. There's a big man lives upstairs,' she offered as she pointed to the ceiling. 'Be at 36 I think. Never met him but gotta say doesn't look very nice at all.'

Job when she got back Michelle told herself if nobody'd done it already, was to get all the names off the Council. But she wondered if that was the way Daphne thought? He's a well built man so he must be on the short list. 'D'you know his name?'

'No, sorry. Big man bit of a bruiser if you catch my meaning.' A brutal but probably fair description was still a surprise coming from the old dear.

'Have you heard anything more since Saturday morning?' Cooper wanted to know.

Daphne shook her head and just got on with her tea and DC Cooper did the same. 'Reckon folk are keeping their head down. Think they musta come back late on. No sign of their car when I locked up for the night. Good television Sunday evenings with *Countryfile* to start so get myself all settled, especially this time of year.' Cooper had to assume without names she was still talking about the neighbour she'd spoken to first thing.

'What do you know about Andrew Ross?'

'Polite, to be honest, lass. Says morning and evening but like the others living up top I've no need to speak. Must do some sort of physical job, goes out early with all that flourescent clothing business on. Somebody reckons he drives something,' she shrugged slightly, Cooper knew was not his job but used a vehicle daily. 'Don't think anybody's really sure,' she said as she got to her feet. 'Oh it's gone of course. Just going to say that red Kia car's his.' As she flopped down came the first recognition. 'Nice man, planted roses out front for us, makes a nice show come summer. Who'll look after them now?'

'Only need pruning now,' Cooper responded. 'The car. We've had it removed for our forensic boys to have a look at,' seemed to surprise her. Living in the world of Miss Marple there'd not be much forensics and DNA. 'What about people generally hanging about?' Connor asked.

'Get some sometimes, wandering about like they're looking for someone.'

'Nobody in particular you think? What about the same person you might have spotted quite recently on a regular basis?'

‘Same folk most days walking back and forth to the shops and Doctors and that,’ Daphne offered. ‘Get kids on bikes sometimes and those scooter things. Somebody’s going to get seriously hurt, you mark my words,’ she said and pointed at DC Cooper. After that outburst Daphne was back to her tea, she drunk the majority of and put her Jane Eyre mug on the coffee table.

‘Realize its difficult from your perspective, with not knowing which flat people are heading for, but is there anything more you can tell me about Mr Ross?’

Neat and tidy Daphne sat up and looked out of her front window again as if seeking inspiration. ‘Tidied up the front garden last year sometime. All a bit of a mess but he planted some lovely roses. Had to be quality with them blooming all summer long. Tidy price they tell me,’ was a repeat of what she’d already said.

‘These days most people get parcels delivered, what about Ross? Have you ever been asked to take in parcels for him?’

‘Must be a year ago maybe more, got one of them people ask if I could take something in. Said no, sorry. Can’t take responsibility for stuff. Start that, where will it end?’

‘This for Mr Ross?’

‘Not sure now. Don’t think so. Foreign name. Er…’ accompanies a gritting of teeth grimace. ‘Coulda been couple one floor up. Foreign you know.’

Cooper drunk down the last of the good mug of tea, packed away her note book and got to her feet.

‘Thank you Daphne,’ she said down to Gumbrell and handed over a card ‘Don’t get up, I can see myself out,’ and Cooper moved to the door. ‘If by chance you spot or think of anything interesting be sure to let us know. Bye.’

Back in her car Michelle pulled out her phone to check for messages and then flipped to the local *Lincoln Leader* website for news.

At Central, Michelle was not surprised to learn how results from the door-to-door so far amounted to next to nothing.

She related what little she had discovered and was immediately tasked with looking at the names Rufus Barrie had obtained from the Council, in greater depth.

From the list provided Michelle then began a search and immediately one individual came into view. Fernan Pehrrson had form.

The old dear had mentioned somebody being foreign, was this the one?

Drunk and Disorderly twice, did time for Actual Bodily Harm when involved in a fracas at the station on the way to Rotherham for a Lincoln City match three years back and a general anti-Police attitude. Daphne had described him as not very nice. *A bit of a bruiser*, quote unquote. Fernan Pehrrson a Cuban lived at number 36, second of the three on the first floor. PNC told her he had been brought to this country at the age of eight by his Cuban parents. Occupation was listed simply as 'Driver'.

Pensive Michelle sat there thinking about what dear old Daphne had got round her neck. Her 'wrong un' turned out to be hefty most certainly, but Oscar Matinese living with his wife Sinako was from South Africa originally, with no criminal record. The 'foreigner' as it turned out was the Cuban Pehrrson with a record on PNC and HOLMES2 [Home Office Large Major Enquiry System]. Daphne bless her soul, thought Ross was a driver when it was the Cuban.

Pensive Michelle sat and wondered why Daphne had not known or realised Ross was a gardener, when he'd planted roses in two triangles outside the block?

The list had also given her the names of the couple away for the wedding. Oweyn and Kayleigh Bevins she guessed immediately were likely to be Welsh. Had dear Daphne Gumbrell been told she'd likely as not remember. Hints of her forgetfullness were there.

As it turned out a William Farr next door to the Bevins's was the only one apart from Pehrrson with any sign of criminal record. That for speeding twice.

When she reported her findings to Jake Goodwin with the DI out of the office it answered one of his own questions.

'Could be why door-to-door came up with nothing, no strangers, no cars. He was in the block all the time or saw the traffic lads heading his way and was down the stairs, out the back door and away.' He spun round in his chair. 'Sandy. Number 36, what's the score with that one?'

'Nae good boss. Nae reply all day back then.'

'Have we spoken to him since?' Sandy shook his head to. 'Wait a minute,' he said and glanced at Jamie Hedley as he said it. Jake then brought up PNC and hunted down Fernan Pehrrson. 'Driver,' he said then he looked back at Sandy. 'Which d'you fancy? This evening or first thing, bear in mind he's a handy one to cope with.'

'Morning,' the Scot replied.

'And you Jamie?'

'Same gaffer.'

'Order a car will you,' he told Sandy. 'Early as you like and I'll get a van on standby.'

'What about these Bevins's?' Jake asked up to Michelle.

'I'll do them this evening. Only a case of discovering what they know and finding out about the wedding. Daphne Gumbrell said she'll phone me when she sees her come home from work.'

Not as much of a busybody as Jake had initially thought, Daphne Gumbrell was true to her word and phoned Michelle when she saw Kayleigh Bevins arrive home from work just before half four. Quick text to partner Matthew to say she'd be late as she'd pre-warned him.

Kayleigh Bevins opened her front door dressed in a track suit as if she was about to go out for a jog. Introductions over with the flat layout familiar to Dumbrell's, Cooper followed Bevins through to a stark red and black lounge. Furniture all black including a dining table and chairs at the right hand end and all the walls painted a deep red with matching patterned curtains. Too stark for Michelle or Matthew's mother who chooses furnishings for the properties they transform before renting out.

'Old lady downstairs mentioned it all this morning,' said Bevins the moment they were seated. 'Bit of a shock, got to say that. Away for a few days and miss all the fun,' she sniggered. 'Typical.'

'Good wedding?' Cooper asked rather than comment.

'Excellent. Old college mate of mine. Second marriage of course as seems to be the going rate these days.'

'Sorry to have to ask this Kayleigh, but their names and venue please.'

'Why d'you need to know that?'

'We need to establish everybody's alibi's for the time period of the attack. Just went to a wedding is not enough as I'm sure you'll appreciate. It's a process of excluding you from any list of suspects.'

For a moment or two Michelle Cooper thought the woman was about to stupidly refuse. 'Jenny and Alex Dearing in Newmarket,' she eventually gushed out. 'Reception at the...Bedford Lodge Hotel and we stayed over in the Premier Inn…'

'Thank you,' stopped the woman being sarcastic.

'Andy Ross. What can you tell me about him?'

'Very little,' Kayleigh replied. 'Think saying Hi is about as much as we've got out of him. Oweyn discovered he's a gardener when he spotted an advert in one of those free magazine things they stuff through the door.'

'And Oweyn, what does he do?'

'Works for Siemens.'

There was little point in asking anything more about his employment. If need be Siemens would provide information on somebody by the name of Oweyn. But she doubted that would prove necessary but she had the wedding to check just in case. 'And you?'

'Asda administrator.'

'Ross any thoughts?'

'Nothing really. Just a neighbour we don't have anything to do with,' she sighed and blew out a breath. 'Don't get involved if I'm honest. Only speak to old Daphne to be honest. Think she's lonely but it's only a quick chat mostly as I get home. Got our own bunch of friends we socialise with.'

‘Thank you,’ Cooper said as she got to her feet. ‘Need anything else we know where you are,’ she added as she walked into the hall with Kayleigh traipsing after her. ‘If you hear anything about what went on we’d appreciate a call,’ and handed over her card.

Back at Central she actually looked them up on line and called the Newmarket Hotel to receive confirmation of the wedding reception. The evening event went on until a bit past midnight a good 100 miles from Lincoln.

Time to head off home and a quiet evening in.

35

DI Oliver Bristow had been briefed on his return from Salford by Inga Larsson over the need to let his Detective Sergeants in on certain aspects of his former life.

Morning briefing for once he handed over to Jake Goodwin he was able to watch and listen to and Nicky Scoley in order to reconsider his options.

Might be a way to brush away the boredom. Move his life carefully and slowly away from endless hours stuck down near Grantham or out at the holiday home. Always an element of risk, but then life is always a risk as is crossing the road. Maybe going for meals for starters, inviting them home, but softly softly to not cause any great concerns.

He knew it was not his imagination, as his few days away had confirmed his own thoughts on the matter. Since the height of that Covid epidemic people had become less tolerant of each other, much ruder and as many of his uniformed colleagues knew to their cost, less respectful of the Police and more prone to violence.

A very odd arrangement has developed over what, twenty odd years. Where increasingly the public have absolutely no respect for law and order, yet when they're the ones in trouble the first thing they do is dial 999.

The Simm woman he knew from talking to her previously would not be an easy task. In for a penny in for a pound, time to call her.

'Yeh,' was one of those telephone attitudes to annoy Bristow.

'Mrs Simm? Mrs Jodie Simm?' he asked.

'Who wants to know?'

'Detective Inspector Oliver Bristow.'

'Oh its you. Mighta guessed.'

‘We’d like to gain access to Harry’s shop for another search.’

‘Why?’ was instant. ‘What for?’

‘Some matters have come to our notice and we need to double check. Are you planning to sell?’

‘What’s it to you?’ there was the anti police attitude already.

‘Better we carry out our work now rather than disturb an estate agent or new shopkeepers.’

‘What yer after?’

‘Nothing in particular,’ he lied. ‘Just need to cover some of our forensic modules,’ above her intelligence level he made up. ‘We’ll not be there long,’ he told her. ‘So what’s the situation? Is it on the market?’

‘Clearing it out, and that.’

‘That’s no problem. Now when’s best for you?’ Thoughts of getting rid of all that junk rambled across his brain.

‘Dunno.’

‘Tomorrow maybe?’ he suggested in hope.

‘What if I say no.’

‘That’s very simple. We get a search warrant. One way or another Mrs Simm our Senior Forensic Manager and her team will be carrying out a search of the property.’

‘Typical coppers eh. Always bloody threats,’ Bristow ignored. ‘Have to be afternoon.’

‘Would it be best if we picked the keys up from you at the salon?’ There was no reply. ‘What d’you think?’

‘Any time then,’ sounded as if she’d given up on her belligerent attitude.

‘Tomorrow morning. What shall we say. About ten suit?’

‘Yeh,’ she sighed. ‘Okay.’

‘Thank you Jodie,’ he said with little feeling.

‘Place is in a bit of a state with getting rid of stuff and that.’

‘No problem.’

Oliver’s mind returned him to the enigma overshadowing everything he did. Knew had to succeed in this role or face the possible consequences. The mantle of a Detective Inspector trying to solve major crimes going nowhere at break neck speed.

Attempts to badger him into changing his life completely had so far failed. The thought of handing in his notice, heading to join his mother, to be put to work labouring on her bloody vineyard filled him with horror. Along with the thought of living in some ghastly French village with no pub or coffee house, frequented by tourists renting nasty scruffy stone gites half the year.

He had to solve this triple murder mess or they'd come calling again, and find himself back living a life in some hell hole watching, listening and spotting once more. To him that was a real no no, no life. Helping out here and there maybe he'd struggle to avoid, but he couldn't stand the thought of looking over his shoulder for the rest of his life.

Having been raging an internal battle alongside all his worries over complications his new role had produced with nobody to turn to. The new situation on reflection offered him the possibility of a relationship with steady as a rock trusted Jake Goodwin. Time to hone his cooking skills and look at inviting Jake and his Sally round.

His biggest worry was his mother selling the family home to in the end force him to fend more for himself or join her. Be coerced into marrying some skinny young French girl named Delphine or Noelle and produce blonde giggly little girls.

Next morning Shona sent two of her search team along with Chuff the Cocker Spaniel and his handler to go through the shop out at Mablethorpe. Chances are Kev will make the most of the opportunity and give Chuff a run about in the sea and play ball on the beach. Especially if he comes up trumps.

Forensic team's Mickey Willis reported back with the bad news. The shop was never spick and span but there were no drugs or cash or burner phones the team or Chuff were able to locate. They'd even examined down the back of the boiler just in case.

Mickey was also able to report back how the shop didn't look any dissimilar to how they'd left it previously. Oliver Bristow decided was an interesting observation.

Oliver sat in his black chair hands on head as he watched members of his team hard at work in the main chasing up this that and the other about this Andy Ross.

Things were often difficult enough when they had one murder. Now the total had reached three and those trying to link all three together using drug warfare as ammunition would now be disappointed with the search of Curious.

Thinking about him, sat there fingers steepled Oliver knew serial killers are almost entirely men and their victims are categorized as 'soft' targets. Women in the main. Whoever had killed three men had to be experienced and well trained to leave so little. Simm's phone with virtually bugger all on it but business messages and that sugar sachet. You don't do that if you just lose your temper but to his mind this had not been a spur of the moment thing. Carefully planned, meticulous even which took his thoughts neatly back to a serial madman. If that were the case what on earth was the connection?

Had Simm done his creative work for either of the other two. Unlikely, as most of what he produced such as Celestial Moon and Stars to plonk in your garden or abstract figures you could stick on top of a gate post hardly come into play in an urban flat or bungalow out at Waddo. Nobody had mentioned spying a Simm created objet d'art in the flat. It was always possible Quinton knew Ross yet unlikely, as their only connection was a link to the Council. One a member of environmental staff the other having worked for the refuse operators in the past. Could refuse collection using the assortment of bins be classified as environmental work and involve them both, Oliver had considered sat home alone the previous evening. Anyway, Jamie had come back with a nil point on that one.

Nobody he had spoken to could see how they would meet, other than through the normal bin man relationship. Even so, according to Sandy and Jake there was a bin area out the back for Ross, and Simm used the ones in his yard. Not like chatting to the bin men when they stop outside. Doubtful, with where his bins were located if he even knew they'd been emptied, let alone having a cheery chat.

Alisha was busy all the time keeping up with the people sending get well messages for Gwen Abbott. Certainly more active than the small dribble for Simm and already more than for Quinton. Be the one the public have come into contact with who've been given good service, not like odd-bod Simm.

One woman she contacted was indignant that Andrew Ross had died before he'd sorted her rockery out for her. For the most part they were simply customers of his, some fairly new, some had dealt with him before.

Nobody it appeared had developed any sort of relationship with him away from the work he'd done for them.

The only link to any known relatives had been curt responses in answer to her inquiries from one or two his Facebook likes had put Alisha onto. Best she'd managed were a number saying "Not spoke to him in ages"…"Not seen 'im,"..."Too long ago," as if they were being linked to his death and wanted out.

One woman however suggested she knew bits and pieces about his past relationships and Michelle was dispatched to have a chat.

Once she was settled in the woman's kitchen she heard the reasoning behind not coming forward to requests put out for information.

'My husband knew one of his ex's who he battered black and blue, mentally that is. His attitude is good bloody riddance and why you and I can speak now, with him at work.'

'Can you provide any further details?'

'When it was all in the news he said he knew that…'

'Ross.'

'Yes Ross at one time. Be years ago before me and Tommy got together.'

'The woman?'

'Mentioned it to him this morning so I've got it right. Somebody called Janis Reay,' she spelled out for Michelle who made a note.

'Mental cruelty you say?'

'Yeh,' she responded then took time to think. 'According to Tommy she was humiliated in public all the time, and he felt she was being forced to circulate through his threats. Says it was as if he needed her there to abuse. Few rows with their friends about it and he always suggested it was just a bit of fun between them and she knew he didn't mean it.'

'Did she seek help do you know?'

'Sorry. Before my time.'

'Anything else? Anybody else we can talk to, you know of?'

'Not sure. Tommy did say once, if Ross was out on his own with the lads down the pub he was often morose as if he was missing an opportunity to humiliate her. No chance to argue, to lie about or abuse.'

'What about physical?'

'No idea. Not mentioned or could be Tommy doesn't know. Think monsters like him keep it all hidden as much as they can.' She stopped to think again and patient Michelle waited. 'Some time back, think somebody said she wasn't the first to suffer mental and emotional abuse from him.'

Back at Lincoln Central before reporting to Jake she went onto the Police National Computer system to check out a Janis Reay. Only two others popped up but neither would be of the age. One was in her late teens for Drunk and Disorderly and another for fraud offences back in 2004.

36

Months later

The Lincoln County Police Major Incident Team had by then been trying to fathom a number of other major cases. It had become clear after the Coffee Shop shooting and with Dominic Archer-Lees remanded in custody after two court appearances it was an isolated incident. Now the whole county awaited his trial.

The identity of a killer of three had never been within their grasp. No clue whatsoever to who or why. A case two of the team returned to on a fairly regular basis.

Victims were all male. One drugged and frozen, with the other two stabbed to death and throat cut just inside their own front doors.

Time to return to a social media search by Alisha O'Neill but this time much deeper. Aided by a couple of the Tech Crime Team she was able to sit there at the back of the room ploughing through the protagonists.

Just following each one's subsequent on line activity was time consuming and boring in the most part. To then check back and forth on each of their friends seemed never ending. The garbage some people put on such sites was amazing to view, but even so the young DC after a while found it difficult to concentrate. Hopes for a mention of Ross by Simm's friend of a friend he'd not messaged for two months was tedium at its best.

The media had decided as they do after the third, there just had to be a serial killer about in the quiet backwater that is Lincolnshire.

Except number three the coffee shop shooting when investigated and resolved, had turned out to be totally unconnected to the other two at that time. Then number four dropped into their lap and serial was introduced into the synopsis but not for breakfast.

At one point the rumour was DCI Inga Larsson former boss of the MIT would be requested by big boss Craig Darke to offer her advice and experience. This fortunately for Oliver Bristow never happened when her time was better spent dealing at that time with a vicious rape by a stalker.

Instead Bristow had divided some of the team into three pairs, each one concentrating on a particular incident. Yet all the time remaining as active members of the team overall.

DC Michelle Cooper with her cold case experience had been designated to re-investigate the Andrew Ross murder in particular. Cooper had been involved in handling cold cases in the past and these were close to it. The first had been when she returned to work following a period of sick leave, due to a serious assault. Since then she'd taken on another one from five years previous and now although not as yet cold cases Operations Galloway, Holstein, and Simmental were still regarded as warm and certainly unresolved. Murders two and three in particular had now been unofficially joined together with next to nothing linking them.

Michelle had been given the task once more of hunting down who might have been responsible using little more than a meagre drip- feed of what little information they had to go on, and her cold case experience.

Having read every word of the three murder books she decided to go back to the DNA discovered on a sugar sachet under the coffee table in Simm's home. With that being pretty much all they had as evidence.

From that starting point she'd thoroughly investigated the link to a Miriam Rebecca Lewis who had committed suicide in London after being arrested for illegal use of a Pepper Spray. Even to the extent of looking at the Inquest and court papers on the case.

Spent time checking Pepper Spray which confirmed for her it is designed to cause harm and as a result it is therefore regarded as illegal.

According to friends and witnesses at the Inquest, information had been gathered to suggest Miriam Lewis had suffered untold months of domestic abuse in Lincolnshire. In the end after spending time in a Refuge she had upped sticks and headed for

London to stay with a friend and after a while found herself a new job and was planning a fresh life away from the torment.

According to the people she was living with in London, Miriam knew her abuser was quite often still travelling down to London and stalking her. Despite living two hundred miles away he was still on the alert when somebody somewhere carelessly let slip her Instagram details to become an anonymous caller to add to his campaign.

Illegal Pepper Spray bought off the internet she used only once, walking home alone. Verified by forensic analysis of the instrument.

Unfortunately for Lewis she was spotted by a witness on the other side of the road. Police called and she was subsequently charged with the offence. Eventually fined and the Met did nothing more than take a brief statement and release her controlling bully they saw as the victim.

Three days after leaving Court with a criminal record she threw herself under an Underground train at Blackfriars station.

Reports on the unpleasant committing suicide episode complete with photographs of her mangled body, Michelle also had to go through. The Lewis woman had the good sense to put distance between herself and Ross by moving to south London from Lincoln on the lookout for a new life. According to friends she chose London for two reasons. It is where you could literally disappear within the morass of millions and was where she had friends.

Refuge name and Lincoln had been her starting point and telephone calls to local Refuges had resulted in Michelle accompanied by DS Nicky Scoley visiting each one over a couple of weeks. That particular day was the turn of a navy blue door to a big old Victorian house in the city, uphill not that far from the cathedral.

Invited in by a big bustling woman for the pre-arranged appointment, the pair of detectives were shown into a small room and offered seats together on a scruffy two-seater sofa in need of attention.

They went through the usual introductions before Nicky brought the talk round to their reasons for being there.

'The purpose of us being here today as Michelle explained, ' said DS Scoley. 'Concerns a string of murderers who have so far eluded us. We're going back around seven or eight years ago when a woman living in South London. Thornton Heath to be precise, committed suicide. The fallout from that is, we now discover her originating from Lincoln and according to friends and family she spent time in a refuge.'

'We're not the only one,' Dalton stressed.

'Appreciate that,' said Scoley. 'Rather than issue a round robin email we're taking one at a time.' Truth was Michelle Cooper had already done two others.

'Do you have a name?'

'Miriam Rebecca Lewis,' Scoley read from her tablet.

'Doesn't ring a bell with me,' Roxanne Dalton admitted with an air of disinterest. 'But I've only been here eighteen months or so.'

'Do you have a database or anything you could check for us?' DC Cooper joined in.

A sigh the woman tried hard to disguise, showed her true reaction. 'What am I checking for?'

'What we have is DNA we've managed to lift from an item found in one of the victim's homes. Trouble is,' Scoley carried on. 'It's what we call familial DNA. This amounts to discovering genetic information indicating a relative of a person we are seeking to identify.'

'And you'd like me to see if this…Miriam Lewis this dead woman,' salt and pepper haired Dalton wrote down on the top of a magazine on the table. 'Is possibly on our records? Let me get this right,' she pondered as she sat up and leaned back, head down hand to her forehead. 'You've got DNA…'

'At a murder scene,' said Scoley as a reminder. 'We can't identify on our database except to an incident in London years ago. We've not been able to trace family and we're hoping her being here or at another local refuge for a period might be a clue.'

'The DNA is a match you got from Lincoln,' Dalton says slowly. 'Is genetically linked to some woman who killed herself in London. That what you're saying?'

‘That’s about it in a nutshell,’ said Scoley without being pedantic by saying it was actually in Mablethorpe.

‘Would you like a coffee?’ Dalton checked surprisingly as she got to her feet.

‘Yes please,’ was chorused.

‘I’ll get somebody to organize while I check for this...Lewis woman for you.’

Scoley waited for the Dalton woman to leave and close the door behind her. ‘What must it be like to be stuck in a place like this?’ she contemplated out loud. ‘Pleasant enough, but its not home is it and guess because of what’s happened to them they’re not free to just nip out to the shops.’

‘Not quite as cushy as it appears,’ said Michelle as she scanned the room. ‘Remember some of the residents are fleeing for their lives. Domestic and family violence is the reason they run away to take refuge in somewhere like this. Bit like a motel I’ve been told with some just staying a day or two, with others with children becoming more residential.’

‘Chances are back in the day all this was somebody’s home.’

‘How the other half live.’

A matronly looking stout woman entered with a request about whether they preferred their coffee black or white and at the same time slid a bowl of sugar and sweetener sachets onto the table. She then left after they both requested white. Scoley and Cooper looked at each other. Same make of sugar sachets as the one discovered in Simm’s house.

‘You know what we think about coincidences,’ Cooper chuckled.

‘You don’t think…?’

‘Someone from here?’ she gasped. ‘Really?’was a heavily grimaced query.

‘Hundreds o’places have them,’ she pulled a face. ‘Can’t imagine...but…’ Scoley shrugged as she picked one up carefully by the edge and dropped it in her wallet. ‘Stranger things have happened.’

‘It’s only familial remember.’

Three coffees were delivered and out of politeness the pair waited for the return of Roxanne Dalton. When a minute or two was extended they agree to taste the coffee and eventually were sat with mugs half empty by the time Dalton returned to hers.

'Not the best coffee in the world but we have our regular donors to thank in a place like this. Rise of food banks unfortunately means we lose out sometimes.'

Despite that, before she said anything of real interest Dalton drank some of her cool coffee. 'Trouble with this place. Cold coffee becomes the norm.' She took another good swig before picking up a sheet of paper she's placed on the table. 'Miriam Rebecca Lewis,' she announces. 'Here for getting on for two months back in early 2010. Records show she was referred to us by your people as to some extent you were concerned for her safety. She refused to bring charges and your people saw it being for her protection.'

'Protection from who?'

Dalton sucked in a breath through her white teeth. 'Not privy to all that, I'm afraid.'

'What do you mean?' Scoley slipped in.

'Only our Manager has access.'

'Access to what?' Cooper joined her DS.

'Information linked to….what shall we say, perpetrators, abusers.'

'Like who?'

'No guarantee of course, but whoever was behind the violence meted out.'

'Why don't you have access?' Scoley asked firmly. 'Others we've been to have.'

'I'm only the duty manager,' she trotted out with. 'Remember, we're open 24/7 and I'm sorry but it wouldn't be right for staff on the night shift to be spending their time indulging in searches for goodness knows who. Some of it could be like they have with classified information. A great deal of course is only hearsay and what women tell us when under severe stress. May not be absolutely pucker so we dare not allow access to any of the part time or casual staff or women staying here.'

'And the manager?'

'Day off. Visiting her sick mother down in Lowestoft,' appeared to Nicky Scoley to be a trifle too convenient.

‘Can we make an appointment to come and see her? Looks as though with luck we just might have the same Miriam Lewis as you.’

It took the Refuge Manager a good week to get back to the detectives and it was Dalton who met the pair at the door again before showing Scoley and Cooper to the same stark room they’d been in before. Within minutes a tall, lanky Sandra Ashcroft the Manager, walked in dressed in denim dungarees, blue blouse and bright white trainers.

Arrival ritual the same and then it was the fetch and carry procedure by the tubby one with coffee again but this Ashcroft drank water from a glass. Or at least that’s what it looked like with there being no smell.

‘Now ladies. How may I help?’

DS Nicola Scoley was first up. ‘As part of a wider murder investigation we’re looking into the history of a Miriam Rebecca Lewis. Resident here for a period so we understand, back around 2010, who then moved down to London and sadly ended her life by committing suicide.’

‘So Roxanne was telling me.’ Ashcroft said giving no sense of being surprised by the information. ‘Look,’ she said pointing at Scoley with a too long red fingernail. ‘I’m sorry we had to ask you to return. Unfortunately more than once a violent partner has turned up at the door claiming to be a plain clothes policeman looking after one of our women’s case.’

‘But we’re women.’

‘And?’ confused the detectives. ‘I know of one young woman whose mother beat her badly on a daily basis from her early teens. She’s been in and out of refuges for quite a few years. Now d’you understand?’

Scoley nodded, aware they’d been checked out.

‘Not always men of course. Yes in the vast majority of cases, but we can never be too careful. I’ll be honest with you we are not as progressive as some facilities. There are refuges in other cities who have opened their doors to male transgender victims of abuse. Even been told about a transgender paedophile living alongside highly vulnerable women and their children.’

'Difficult to manage then,' Scoley suggested as she sucked in a breath.

'Indeed. We're always short of space and lack the staffing to deal with what could so easily be awkward situations. Anyway,' she sighed. 'I've looked back in our records and discovered brief mention of an Andrew Ross,' the pair prick their ears up to. 'We have to be so careful in the world of domestic abuse I'm afraid,' the duo hardly hear so staggered are they by the name. 'Men use so many different ways to inveigle their way into our community in order to gain access to women they have already abused on the pretext of forgiveness. As a result we have always tended towards keeping names at the very least, of people we need to be wary of. Miriam's case was one in which all we recorded was a name as somebody likely to want to cause harm or at least come out with all the apologies on earth and plead for a fresh start.'

Ashcroft stopped to sip her water before she continued. 'In some cases of course we have much more detail especially if the matter has been to court. In others they don't even get help from a Sexual Offence Liaison Officer. Photographs even have proved useful on a number of occasions. Trouble is our women tend to leave home in a hurry and items such as photographs are quite often left behind, as I'm sure you can imagine.'

'I don't suppose...?'

'No sorry,' stopped Cooper. 'Just a name and address.'

'What about family members, relations?' Cooper asked.

'Visitors have to sign in. The system is we insist on knowing who is calling in advance. Even solicitors handling cases. Never a case of somebody claiming to be an aunt knocking on the door and being admitted.' She stopped again to sip water while the intrigued detectives have yet to start on the coffee. 'Then it turns out to be the perpetrator's mother.'

'I don't suppose you have the Visitors Book for...' a shake of her head stops chestnut-haired Cooper.

'Why would we, for all that time? Got the past couple of years, but doubt that's any use'

'What about the staff here now?'

'How on earth would that help with somebody who died all that time ago?'

'I'll be honest with you Sandra,' said Scoley leaning forward. 'To some extent we're clutching at straws. Bear in mind the case we are dealing with is current. The unexplained death we are dealing with is recent. Just a few months ago, not 2010. We're not looking at the death of Miriam Lewis, we know all about that. Our case involves a local man. Not as the abuser, but abused, in fact murdered.'

'Can't imagine what use that would be.'

'Just if there's a link somehow, 'Scoley explained. 'In cases such as this there can be a whole volume of names come past us. Our IT people can upload your staff names just in case there is somehow even with the smallest of links. No matter how tenuous.'

'We have to cover all bases,' said Cooper joining in. 'And to be honest we are struggling with this one. If we could have a list of everybody working here, then as the case progresses we have it at hand when names pop up. Or at least the system does. Bit like our databases where names pop up out of the blue sometimes.'

The sigh and shaking head was ignored as Ashcroft reluctantly got to her feet leaving the pair to start on the coffee.

Once drunk and it was then a question of waiting for the Manager to come up with the list. Eventually she walked back in and handed over a print out of the names.'

'And you have full details on all of these should we need more?'

'Of course.'

'These all full time?' Cooper checked as Scoley scanned down the list hoping to spot somebody.

'Goodness me no,' Ashcroft retorted.

The DC waited. 'And?'

'Sorry?'

'Are you saying these are full *and* part time?'

'Three full timers. Me of course along with our two Duty Managers, Roxanne and Amelia. The remainder are part time volunteers, some of course have been through the trauma themselves in the past. Just one name I've not included. Jules.'

'What does he do?'

'She,' Ashcroft corrects. 'Julia Dawkins, but everybody knows her as Jules. One of our regular volunteers. Aromatherapist and pediatrician got her own practice but offers her services free of charge to our women once a week.' Ashcroft sighed and looks at the floor. 'Tragic case,' she said as her head came up slowly. 'Don't know her life history of course, but you tend to pick up on bits and pierces. Her parents tragically were both killed just south of Stamford on the A1 a year or two ago by a drunk texting driver.'

'Oh I'm so sorry,' said Scoley as Cooper sucked in her breath and pulled a face.

'Fortunately your people decided in that case to go down the death by careless driving route while under the influence. The result was five years and a bit I think it was, at Her Majesty's pleasure. Good hefty fine over a thousand pounds, driving ban starting when he's released and the added bonus of an extended driving test.'

'And the reason for not including her on this list?' said Scoley holding it up.

'Somebody like Jules, an aromatherapist and pediatrician makes the women feel pampered and good about themselves. She'll be sorely missed.' Ashcroft stopped and grimaced slightly to herself. 'Jules is currently in a local hospice. Terminal cancer I'm afraid. We all visit of course but having no family apart from her dear wife Ruthie makes it difficult. We had Ruthie here a year or two back having been physically abused and raped. How the pair met. Jules did so well to keep going as long as she did. Continued to put our women first by providing her services free when she wasn't really up to it. Bless her.'

'I'm so sorry to hear that.'

'Her gift to the women. Did work with food banks as well, she was such a generous lady of the sort the world is desperate for.'

'Sounds like she'll be a big loss,' said Scoley as she slowly got to her feet. 'With a bit of luck going through your list might start a few bells ringing,' she said holding it up. 'Appreciate your help. Really we do. Thank you.'

ACKNOWLEDGEMENTS

Shall we start with 'Yellerbelly's'? Talk was of farm workers bending down in the field thus acquiring a brown back from the sun, with their stomach pale almost yellow in comparison.

As with so many tales from wandering minstrels there were other's who claimed to know the truth. Waistcoat colour from the Lincolnshire Regiment was one. Women keeping a secret purse for their gold coins or a special pouch for them meant in good times they had a yellow belly is another. The flipside is, nobody is absolutely sure.

Starting at the beginning in Mablethorpe I have local people in general to thank for their co-operation during my research. Including friends on Facebook's Mablethorpe and Sutton – Talk of the Towns site who confirmed all the bad weather.

Jim Carruthers – a celebrated fund raiser for the local Air Ambulance – has to be thanked in particular for his guidance and knowledge of the town.

As does Eva Coates the Hall Manager of St Mary's Church Hall I was able to use with her help, as a location for my temporary Incident Centre. Thank you.

Tale of another Yellerbelly Murder coming your way soon.

PREVIEW

Being forcibly turned over was absolute torture with handcuffs biting hard into her wrists and the nagging discomfort to her back becoming far far worse. Utterly scared and desperate Molly Perkins shut her eyes, in an attempt to avoid looking at the nasty smirk filled with pleasure across the bastard's face.

She'd just woken up again from whatever he'd given her but nothing had changed, except for him standing gloating over her and she's wet herself again. Breath slowly through your nose she'd read somewhere as a way to reduce the pace of that thudding beat of her heart.

'Please, please I did what yer wanted,' she tried again. 'We can do it again, do its loadsa times, promise. Do it up 'ere if yer want. Be your slave, dress up, do anything,' she offered in desperation there in the room in the loft. Why in God's name she asked herself had she climbed that bloody ladder?

If this was some sex game it certainly lacked any kind of enjoyment, this was not fun, never exciting. She'd heard about violence in sex, with whips and leather and all that. Was this it? This what he was really after? The fat slob's big turn on?

That nasty bossy Irish Siobhan she'd shared a cell with for a good five months, was forever dragging on about what she'd got up to with blokes. Was the skinny smelly drugged up shit bag lying, when she said it was always great? Was the tattooed bitch talking shit about the pain and discomfort?

Molly's confused mind struggled to comprehend the awful turn of events. He'd seemed so nice, and kind with his offer of help and guidance. Exactly what she was in need of. His home was really great and so comfy. That big telly on the wall was brilliant, be good watching *Love Island* on that. The food though, not so good; no chips and cheese or burgers. Oh how she craved Maccy Ds as she'd done day after day in that stinky cell.

'I'll do anything, please. Do what you want, do it again anytime. You teach me, please' she implored up to see him shaking his head.

'Do it again?' he snorted down. 'You really are a stupid bitch, d'you know that?'

'We can. Of course we can,' she gasped. 'Nobody knows. Be our secret, be better, last all day. Please.'

'There's two things in life you can't do twice, remember. Lose your virginity and die. You were crap at the first and for your sake hope you make a better job of what's next,' he chuckled menacingly.

'No, no! Oh shit no!' She screamed and was sick all down her shirt. It felt horrible, it smelt and no hankie to help. 'You can't,' she struggled to say through a mouthful she tried unsuccessfully to spit out.

'And the alternative?' he asked down calmly. 'Let you go, allow you to walk out of here on a sunny day like today. Head straight for the cop shop and start gobbing off. No bloody chance.'

'I wore the gloves, I let you…'

'You stupid cow! 'he shouted and moved away out of sight. Molly wriggled onto her side to ease the pain and give her back a break. 'You really think the gloves were some sort of bloody stupid game eh?' He laughed.

When Molly looked up, the big man was stood there beside her grinning down. The silver and white needle gripped in his hand she knew was for injecting like they'd used for Covid.

'Oh no,' she gasped. 'Please, what have I done wrong? I'll be better next time, promise.'

'Punching a paramedic doing her job. That not wrong then? In your eyes probably not. What about those stupid marches blocking the streets and upsetting decent people out doing their shopping? Let you go and you're stupid enough to join some toss pot march about menopause or something else equally ridiculous. Tell you what. How about I let you go and you can bugger off and join all those old hags doing Ban The Bomb. Kindly inviting the bloody Russians to crawl all over us. Good idea?' he laughed out loud. 'Not.'

'Please. I'm sorry. I really am, I did wrong I know that, paid my price, done my time. Please just wanna go home to me mum,' gasped a sobbing Molly Perkins.

'Just shut the fuck up will you!' Let's get this done with. I've got better things to be doing than piss arsing about with you.'

Molly had to watch, but desperate to close her watery eyes all at the same time and hopelessly praying for it to end. To be free and in less pain. Get out in the fresh air and a hug from mum.

'What's that?' she pleaded as she started shaking and a chill ran through her. 'What's that for?' she gasped frozen in terror at the sight, as the hypodermic needle was raised and he made a point of making liquid spout out the top. 'I won't tell anyone, promise. Please don't hurt me, please, please I beg you.'

Her out of control body and mind issued more warm urine to add to her discomfort as all she could think about was the mess she was making and mum would be cross.

'For your own sake keep bloody still,' he said as he knelt down beside her. Peering down at the petrified eyes he'd so enjoyed admiring the look of his body. 'You move and the last thing you'll remember will be a bloody awful prick,' he thought amusing, she barely heard through her sobbing uncontrollably and shaking.

'I'm sorry, please, I'll do anything. Please, please no...I beg you!'

SAID THE SPIDER
COMING SOON

Milton Keynes UK
Ingram Content Group UK Ltd.
UKHW020735271123
433342UK00009B/71

9 781916 981249